CORI LYNN

This book is dedicated to
my loving parents Larry and Shellie,
for your never-ending support
and showing me what it means to put family first.

CHAPTER 1

L aura gripped the steering wheel for what seemed like the
tenth time. Looking at the antique shop in front of her, a
recognizable feeling overwhelmed her. The shop had been
her escape to find new projects to keep her busy. How long would
it be before she could leave her home without familiar memories
haunting her at every turn? The only thing that could numb the
pain was pouring her energy into work, at least for now.

An elderly couple waved to her as they passed in front of her vehicle. She lifted a few fingers and forced a half-smile acknowledg-
ing them. They held hands as they strolled by enjoying the afternoon. Laura turned to grab her purse and paused. She pushed away
the unexpected rush of loneliness, grabbed her phone and swiftly
made her way inside the shop. All she needed was a diversion and
she could ignore the twisted emotions trying to take over.

Laura turned from the leather antique luggage set to see Stanley
Tate, the lanky shop owner walking down the aisle toward her.

"Hi, Stanley."

"I need to hire you to come work for me." The elderly man
smiled. "After all, you're one of my favorite clients.

"You know I can't resist seeing the merchandise before anyone
else." Laura assumed a false sense of lightheartedness to cover her
true feelings. "I need another project. Anything new come in?"

"Didn't you say you were looking for a traveler's trunk?" He stood there a moment before waggling his finger above his balding head, "I know just the thing!" He turned quickly for a man his age and headed back the way he'd come.

Laura eagerly followed, dodging items in her path to the back of the store. Stanley was far from organized, but he did have the best things in town. Squeezing through narrow passages and tripping over light fixtures seemed a small price to pay.

"I've always wanted a steamer trunk." She maneuvered through a maze of objects. Stanley pushed against the back door revealing a potential hoarding situation. She paused in the doorway.

"What kind of condition are we talking about here?" Laura lifted a brow in concern.

"Take a look for yourself." Stanley put his hands out like a game-show host presenting a prize. He was clearly unfazed by the clutter closing in on them.

Laura walked over to a flat top trunk with a large bronze lock anchored to the front. The metal had lost its original shine, and the fabric would need to be replaced. She knew immediately she'd be taking it home and wondered what stories it had to tell as she reverently touched the metallic corners. It would take some work, but with a little elbow grease she could bring it close to original condition again.

"Have you checked inside?" She looked up.

"Not yet." Stanley tried to lift the lid and frowned when it didn't budge.

Laura covered a smile as she watched the small-framed man continue to wrestle with the heavy chest. Not able to watch any longer, she came to his rescue.

"The hinges are broken, but I can use the keyhole as leverage." Laura slid her finger into the opening and lifted upward. The lid creaked loudly in resistance. She propped the trunk's bulky top gently against the back wall. The smell of aged wood and metals assailed her senses. She peered inside. Her shoulder-length chest-nut locks fell forward as she brushed a strand of hair behind her ear. She discovered a missing hinge and the other damaged. She gazed upon the brittle fabric lining, hesitating to touch it, fearing it would crumble under the pressure.

"How much do you want for it?" Laura stood, masking her excitement.

"Seeing as you're my best customer, I'll let it go for $200."

"I'll take it!" Laura looked back down at the trunk, wiping her hands against her jeans. "This is going to keep me busy for a while."

"You say that now, but I'll believe it when I see it." Stanley chided. Laura narrowed a playful gaze in his direction. "I'm not complaining," he teased. "You're keeping me in business."

Laura pushed the trunk a little farther into her SUV and closed the hatchback. Her phone rang as she walked around to the driver's side, the name flashing gave her pause. She tossed her purse into the passenger's side and reluctantly answered.

"What is it this time?" She said playfully.

"Why do you think every time I call, it's because I have a problem?"

"Because every time you call, you do."

"That's beside the point."

"So, what can I do for you, April?"

"Listen bestie, tonight the girls and I are going dancing. You in?"

Laura looked in the rearview mirror at the trunk in the back. She knew she should spend a night out with her friends, but she didn't feel like socializing, much less entertaining whatever idiot would inevitably ask her to dance.

"Hello?"

"April, I'm beat. It's been a long week and I think I'm going to take it easy tonight."

"Let me guess, you're at the antique shop."

"Why would you—" Laura couldn't think of a quick excuse.

"I knew it! Laura, you need to stop hiding away and get back out into the world."

Laura traced her finger along the steering wheel, waiting for the pep talk.

"How much longer are you going to play the introvert card? You spend all your time restoring old furniture, and for what?"

"I appreciate your concern, but I'm happy doing what I love."

"Ugh. I haven't seen you in weeks. Your friends miss you. You can't let a broken heart keep you locked away forever."

Laura sighed and quietly looked down at the ring she absently rotated on her finger. Her thoughts were lost in her memories while April kept talking.

"Laura?"

"Why don't I call you later, okay?"

"Tell me what you picked up this time."

"I finally got my traveler's trunk. It's in rough shape, but nothing I can't handle."

"Well, if you go out tonight, I can stop by and look at it."

"Nice try."

"It was worth a shot—my best friend is acting like a hermit."

"It's not that bad."

"You can't hide out forever. I won't let you."

"I'm sure you won't. In the meantime, I'm going to give my attention to other things." Laura had become accustomed to her friend's tenacity.

"Yeah, things that can't breathe."

"Call you later?"

"One of these days I'm going to come over there and drag you out by the hair if I have to."

"Bye, April." Before her friend could say a word, Laura ended the call, shaking her head at April's audacious spirit. She slowly backed her SUV out of the parking lot and drove home, excited to start a new project.

Her two-story blue-and-white bungalow felt like a welcome site as Laura pulled into the driveway. She loved the quaint little porch sporting two white wicker chairs and a small table in-between. Off to one side was a swing with seating for two, covered by a large cushion. A small garden ran along the wood fencing near the bottom, separated by a set of stairs leading to the front door. The flowers were bright and cheery, and the lawn freshly trimmed. The roof had a few cracked tiles, but otherwise, it was perfect. It reminded her of a house one might see pictured on a greeting card.

She opened the hatchback, revealing her antique treasure and took a deep breath. It was extremely heavy and would be awkward to get into the house.

"I should have thought this through."

With two people it had been easy. However, though strong enough, the trunk's missing handles made it a problem. She stood with her hands on her hips turning the trunk, so the handle side faced her and assessed the drop from her car to the sidewalk.

"Need some help?"

Laura nearly fell over in surprise. A man about her age stood on the sidewalk with a golden retriever. He wore blue jeans and a steel-gray T-shirt that fit in all the right places. He moved closer; his blond hair tousled by the breeze like he'd just stepped out of a magazine.

He lifted an eyebrow still waiting for her to answer.

"Help? Oh, yes, if you think your friend won't mind." She nodded to the dog watching their interaction.

"He'd appreciate the break." He smiled.

"And what's your name?" Laura knelt down by the dog, scratching him behind the ears. The dog's soft fur felt comforting but when she pulled her hand back covered in loose fur, it reminded her she wasn't ready for the responsibility of pet ownership.

"This is Rufus." He wrapped the dog's leash around the mailbox;

his large leather wristwatch accentuating his sun-kissed tan. Based on his physique, the trunk wasn't going to be a problem for him.

"It's missing a handle on one side." Laura focused on the trunk hoping to cover her nerves, but the smell of his cologne was an alluring reminder of his proximity.

The man walked up and a second later grabbed both sides of the trunk, pulling it from the SUV like he'd done it a million times. "Where do you want it?" His voice strained slightly under the trunk's weight.

She had not thought that far ahead. "If you could bring it inside, that would be great." Quickly she walked around him and head toward the front porch. "Are you sure I can't get one side?"

"I'm okay as long as we aren't walking around the block." He followed her cautiously, checking for each porch each step as he ascended.

Laura beat him to the front door and made quick work of the lock. She swung the door open, and he brought the trunk inside. "Right here will be fine."

As he set down his load in the hallway, the wooden floors producing a slight creak.

"I'm not sure how I would have done this alone." Laura began opening her purse pulling out a few dollars she'd found inside.

"No need." His shirt now sported a few spots of dirt that hadn't been there before.

"It seems my trunk has damaged your shirt." Her brow wrinkled. "Are you sure I can't pay you?"

"It's an old shirt, nothing to worry about." He wiped at the spots, but they stubbornly stayed put.

"Well, then, uh...thank you."

"Caleb." He rubbed his hand on the front of his pants and reached to shake hers.

"Laura." She took his hand, and he gave her a slight smile.

He paused as if he wanted to say something, but instead turned and walked down the driveway until he stopped at the SUV, pointing to her trunk. "Did you want this closed?"

"Sure."

He dropped the hatchback in its place. From the front yard, Laura called out one more time, "Thank you!"

He grabbed the dog leash off the mailbox and waved before disappearing behind the bushes that separated her yard from the neighbor's. Was it possible Caleb lived in the neighborhood? She wiped the idea from her mind and turned back toward her house. Once inside she leaned against the wall. Letting out a sigh, her hair lifted slightly as she eyed the monstrosity before her. How would she get the trunk into the back room?

CHAPTER 2

The dolly was out of control as the trunk rocked forward, landing with a thud on the floor in the workroom. Somehow, she'd managed to maneuver it down the corridor. The room was filled with sturdy wooden shelves along one side and a large island in the middle. Pegboard lined an entire wall, making good use of the space for her many tools. There was a bench running the length of the opposing side, situated underneath a window, which perfectly framed the afternoon sun.

Even though it was a cool day, she had worked up a sweat. She noticed movement out of the corner of her eye. An orange-and-white tabby cat walked into the middle of a sunbeam shining on the floor. He stretched out his front paws and raised his hind legs as if he had just woken up from an afternoon nap.

"How did you get in here?" She looked around the room and saw the open window. "Ahh," she murmured. "I thought we had a deal—you stay outside, and I occasionally feed you?" Rolling her eyes, Laura knelt next to the cat as he rubbed his head against her denim jeans. She sighed and began to pet him wondering which of her neighbors he belonged to.

"Should I give you a name?" She pondered the idea before sneezing. She had a minor allergy to cats but had always been a bit of a pushover when it came to animals.

"Dusty it is." She stood and walked over to the trunk. In one swift

9

leap, Dusty turned a few circles before making himself comfortable on top of the bench. Clearly, he planned to enjoy what was left of the afternoon sun.

Laura propped open the lid of the old chest and laid it carefully against the metal table behind it. The broken hinges would be a challenge to replace but she would deal with them later. She began to pull again at the fabric in the corners along the back. It was like peeling a stubborn hard-boiled egg. She kept chipping away at it until the wood shone through.

"This should be fun." She positioned herself on a small stool and began to work along the edges. Slipping a trowel between the exposed wood and the brittle fabric, she slowly pushed downward, making sure she didn't damage the siding.

She had nearly finished the back of the trunk when her doorbell rang. Dusty looked up from sunning himself. Laura couldn't tell if he was irritated by the interruption or just displaying a natural cantankerous frown.

"Don't give me that look." She put down her tools and stood up. "You don't even live here." Wiping the dust from her jeans, she made her way to the front door. She cautiously peered through the peephole wondering who could be stopping by unexpectedly. A flurry of activity through the vintage glass told her exactly who had shown up unannounced. "I'm not going." Laura waited, her hand on the doorknob.

"Open the door, Laura." April began pacing on the porch, her boots making a sharp clack with every step.

"I've made up my mind." Laura hesitated briefly, then gave in and opened the door.

April pushed past her like a tornado. "You are *not* going to believe the day I've had."

Laura smiled as her overly dramatic friend unwrapped her scarf. She shut the door and slowly turned to face April, preparing for the conversation to follow.

April was stylishly dressed. Her designer jeans tucked into her leather boots, showing off her shapely legs. A light brown bomber jacket draped a fitted white cotton blouse. She began snooping around the hallway, her hoop earrings swinging with every move. She looked over at Laura standing in front of her, arms crossed. "Why aren't you ready?"

"Ready?"

"To go dancing." April stared at her, tilting her head confused. She looked down at Laura's rumpled pink T-shirt, paint-speckled jeans and giant blue fuzzy slippers. "Please tell me you're not wearing that." She wrinkled her nose as she touched Laura's hair. "And I think we can do better than a ponytail, don't you?"

"I told you," Laura shooed her hand away. "I'm staying home." She began walking back to her workroom, April storming down the hall after her. Laura resumed her position on the stool in front of the chest and began chipping away at the fabric—ignoring April.

"Come on," April whined, stomping her feet like a two-year-old throwing a temper tantrum. She leaned against the doorframe, crossing her arms. "Laura, it's been a year since the accident. I think it's time to move on."

Laura paused mid-scrape and lowered her head. How could April sit there and lecture her when she'd never experienced a loss of this magnitude?

"I know you're still hurting. Far deeper than most, but you can't hide forever." April walked over to her and put a hand on her shoulder. "I worry about you. We all do."

"I'll think about it, but that's the best I can do right now." Laura turned away from her, hoping her friend wouldn't see the tears threatening her resolve.

"I don't want to push you, but you're not giving me much choice." April stood and played with some of the tools on the wooden table near her. She flippantly tossed them on the wood bench, her interest quickly lost. "When you're ready to date again—"

"Who said anything about dating?" Laura's voice creaked. An image of Caleb flashed through her mind. She quickly pushed the idea away. If April even got a *hint*, she'd met someone, she wouldn't let it go until she'd tracked the man down and grilled him on every detail of his life.

Considering she knew nothing about him herself, it was safe to say April wouldn't find out anything about him either. *It's not like I'm going to see him again anyway.*

"Because it's like they say, it's better to have loved and lost, than never to have loved at all."

April's exasperated tone brought Laura back to the conversation.

"Are you even listening to me?"

Laura shook her head missing half of April's speech on love and hoping she hadn't read into the look on her face. "Can I get back to my trunk here?"

"Fine." April rolled her eyes. "I hope you two will be very happy together."

"At the moment, it's a bit of a mess."

"It's actually a nice piece." April leaned in to take a closer look. "You'll make a pretty penny off it once you're done."

"*If* I even put it up for sale. This would look great in my living room."

"I wondered where it's traveled and what stories it has to tell?"

"Every piece has a story."

Dusty meowed from his spot under the window, walking toward the edge of the workbench. He gave the girls an irritable look and jumped to the floor.

"When did you get a cat?" April's eyes grew wide.

"I didn't."

"Then how do you explain that?" She pointed her finger in Dusty's direction.

"I think he's a stray. He managed to get in through my window when I was out earlier."

"Well, thank God! Being single and alone is ridiculous enough. You don't need to add a cat to the mix." April leaned away from Dusty. "And a stray of all things...how could you even let him inside? And with your allergies?"

Laura stood and grabbed April by the hand, cutting off her rant. She pulled her along toward the front door.

April continued. "You're still young; you have a lot of life to live. Don't resort to becoming a cat lady. I won't let you."

"Why are we friends again?" Laura stopped short.

"Because you love my honesty, and I make you a better person." April fluttered her eyes.

"You forgot one thing." Laura tapped her foot impatiently. "Your charming humility." Laura placed a hand on the doorknob and swung it open with her opposite hand making a sweeping gesture in front of her. "I believe you have some dancing to do?"

"You sure you don't want to change your mind?" April grabbed Laura by the shoulders, assessing her outfit. "I can do magic with your, umm... outfit." April grinned.

"You're persistent, if nothing else."

"I hate it when you use big words." April stepped onto the porch. "Don't stay in that head of yours for too long. I'm afraid I'll never get my best friend back if you do."

Stepping forward, Laura gave her a playful push towards the yard. "I promise. Now get out of here and go have some fun."

"I'm going to call you tomorrow to tell you how much you missed out." She threw her scarf over her shoulder as she sauntered down the porch steps.

"I wouldn't expect anything less." Laura laughed and closed the door behind her.

She leaned back against it, the solid wood firm against her shoulders; a sudden emptiness filled her home. Should she have given in and gone with April? She couldn't wrap her mind around the idea of socializing, but April had a point. It had become too easy to stay at home and if she didn't do something soon, the empty world could become a prison. As if on cue, Dusty came down the hall and sat in front of her, aggressively whipping his tail from side to side.

"What?" She threw her hands in the air as she strode over to the cat and picked him up. "Not you, too." She walked him to the front door and put him down on the outside doormat. "I'm not about to be reprimanded by a cat. Now go back to wherever you live." She shooed her hand in his direction, hoping to encourage him off the porch.

Laura closed the door. A small part of her wanted to let Dusty back in. *I AM turning into a cat lady.* The quiet brought a familiar sense of loneliness. She slid to the floor, bringing her knees to her chest and folding her arms across them. A vase full of once red roses sat underneath the hallway mirror. They were withered and nearly black in color.

They'd been sitting there for nearly a year, but she couldn't find the strength to throw them away. Instead, they sat as a reminder of that awful night. Tears sprang up again. She pushed away the thoughts like she'd done a million times before and wiped her eyes looking down the hall towards her workroom. The project sitting inside would surely distract her but would have to wait until tomorrow.

Heading to the kitchen, Laura looked for a spoon and pulled her favorite ice cream from the freezer. Walking toward the living room, she caught her reflection in the hall mirror. Disheveled and tired, she couldn't help but chuckle.

"No wonder April was having fits. If I let that cat back in, I'm the ideal stereotype." Laura frowned. "Great. Now, I'm talking to myself."

The next morning, Laura rose before sunrise to go for a run. When she returned, the horizon was bright pink like the embers of a burning fire. She grabbed the newspaper from her driveway, pulled out a key from her sports jacket and took the stairs two at a time, hoping to grab a quick shower before breakfast.

The warm water soothed her muscles, but she didn't linger. She had become quite adept at staying busy. Relaxing in the shower gave her too much time to think, and the memories were too hard to ignore. She quickly changed into her casual clothes knowing she would be a mess by the end of the day. Heading straight for the kitchen, she grabbed a yogurt and some granola for breakfast. Her hair still wet from the shower, she sat down to read the headlines in the paper. Not much caught her interest. Mostly town gossip and posted events, none of which concerned her. The clock on the wall rang seven times; time to get to work.

Dropping her bowl in the sink, she pulled her hair back in a ponytail and walked down the hall to her workroom. As she rounded the corner, she noticed the morning light filling the room casting a new perspective on the vintage chest. Dust particles filled the air as they floated around in the sun's glow. Laura resumed her seat from the previous day. How would she bring this chest back to life?

"What's your story?" She caressed the worn edges of the ancient box. Not getting any answers, she continued where she left off, removing the fabric one chip at a time. The interior lining on the sides of the chest flaked away faster than the back and soon she had a pile of brittle chips all over the base. Laura grabbed a brush to sweep it out, then tossed the debris in the trash.

Laura dropped the dustpan back in to sweep some more when it clattered against the wood, creating a slight echo. Laura leaned in, noticing the bottom of the trunk was uneven. The middle looked to be a bit higher than the edges.

"Well, that's odd." She used the edge of the trowel to scrape around the lower sides of the trunk. The fabric came up in one piece, revealing a raised wooden panel beneath. She carefully popped it open and discovered what could only be a false bottom. Laura looked around the room as if she'd just uncovered a secret she wasn't supposed to find.

"I wonder how long you've managed to keep this little treasure hidden?" She whispered before ducking to investigate further. The false bottom only seemed to be a few inches deep, but there was definitely something inside.

She reeled at the possibilities, including the idea there could be dead critters hanging out down there, too. Not wanting to touch anything that may have crawled inside and died, she put a glove on before she began to poke around. Feeling a bit more confident, she snatched a flashlight off the shelf and slipped her hand into the dark space. Laura felt something soft and pliable, like leather, and then she brought the item into the light.

The brown, heavily aged leather-bound book looked like it could fall apart at any moment. She carefully wiped a bit of dust from the front cover, revealing the letters A.S. embossed in the lower right-hand corner. A leather string wrapped around it several times, keeping it securely closed, but Laura could see loose papers sticking out from within the pages.

She brought the book to the workbench to get a better look. Cautiously opening it, she looked inside the cover. The name AVA SUTTON was scrolled in perfect cursive. A chill swept through her. So, the trunk did have a story to tell.

Laura pulled over her stool and sat down slowly, her hand shook slightly as she turned the page. She couldn't resist; she began reading the first entry dated NOVEMBER 6th, 1941.

Chapter 3

Dear Diary,

Today is my nineteenth birthday. Mother and Father gave me a new journal, and I'm excited to have a safe place to share my thoughts. We are going to have a party on Saturday night, and I'm awfully excited. I love the view from my second-story window. Today, I saw the neighbor boys playing a game of stickball on the street below. They are so cheerful, not a care in the world.

Father has been concerned about the war developing in Europe. I pray it doesn't reach the United States. This country is an ocean away, so everyone still feels safe. It is unlikely we will become a part of the fight. I pray that is the case, as I fear it would destroy our quaint little town if we did.

Tonight, Dean is taking me out for my birthday. He wanted to take me into the city, but he has to work early in the morning. I was a bit disappointed, but I put on a brave face, as he seemed more upset than I. He told me he'd make it up to me at the party Saturday night. I'm a bit nervous, not knowing exactly what his plans are, but I can't wait to see what he has up his sleeve to surprise me.

I wonder if he will ever grow up, but then I think of his boyish ways and it makes me laugh. It's hard to believe it has been a year since our first date. I could tell he was nervous when he asked me. He tried to

17

portray confidence, but I knew better. I'm not sure why I said yes, but now I can't imagine being with anyone else.

Ava Sutton's bedroom was a perfect reflection of who she was—from the delicate white curtains framing the large bay window to the writer's desk tucked in the corner. An old steamer trunk sat near the far wall next to her. It was one of her favorite places to sit and overlook the neighborhood below. If only she could see the whole world from that spot.

Ava closed her journal and walked over to the traveler's trunk. She lifted the lid with ease as the strong bronze hinges creaked under its weight. Removing a blanket from inside, she stuck her finger in a small hole at the base of the trunk. A wooden plank about ten inches wide popped up, revealing a false bottom. Slipping the journal into the space, she returned the wooden board and placed the blanket on top of it. She closed the lid and locked the big bronze latch on the front of the trunk.

"Do you think, after all these years, I don't know where you hide your journal?"

Ava jumped, surprised by the sudden company. Tessa strolled in and plopped down on the end of her sister's bed.

"It's for that reason I keep it there." She held up the key. "You know where I hide it, so I am forced to lock it away." Ava tucked the key inside her sweater pocket, tapping the outside lightly.

Tessa's self-assured smile turned to a frown. "It's not like you have anything good in there anyway."

"How would you know?" Ava playfully pushed her sister's shoulder as she walked over to her writing desk.

Tessa frowned again, then her eyes lit up. "Are you writing about Dean?"

Ava ignored her as she put away things on her desk, but her smile betrayed her.

"I knew it!"

"I'm not telling you *anything*." Ava strutted toward her closet.

"At least tell me what you plan to wear. I can't have my sister go out in something terrible."

"Since when are you an expert in fashion?" If Ava was honest, her younger sister did have a better sense of style.

"You know I have better taste than you." Tessa jumped off the bed and joined her at the closet doors, quickly scanning the contents. She thumbed through shirts and pulled out a white blouse with black stitching along the collar, a plaid black-and-white swing dress, and a pastel-blue sweater. "Done."

"That was quick. Don't you want to think it over a bit more?"

"Trust me, Ava. You'll look great in this." Tessa pushed her toward the mirror and they both looked back at Ava's reflection. Tessa held the light-blue sweater up in front of her. "This is the perfect color to bring out your eyes."

Ava studied herself in the mirror. Tessa was right. Her crystal-blue eyes were framed by long lashes and sparkled against the blue tones in the sweater.

Tessa stared back at her, waiting, her blue eyes the exact image of her sister's. Tessa moved the sweater in front of herself, turning to one side and then the other. "This sweater doesn't look half bad on me either. I should borrow it."

"Okay, you win. I'll wear it." Ava grabbed the hanger away from Tessa before she could walk off with yet another piece of her clothing.

"You'll thank me later." Tessa waved her hand in the air.

Ava smiled, watching her retreat. Looking back at her own reflection, she noticed her lips and frowned over their lack of color. She grabbed a nearby tube of lipstick and slowly applied her favorite bright red color. The cooler weather had given her pale cheeks a pink hue. She scrunched her nose and turned back to the rest of the clothes Tessa had tossed on the bed. She took a deep breath. She had better hurry. There was only one hour to get ready if she planned to make it to dinner on time.

Ava walked inside the diner and stopped near the entrance to look around the familiar scene, her heart beating excitedly. The diner, as always, was bright and cheery with only a few framed pictures on the walls; most of them were of high school football teams that had won championships in the past few years.

Her blonde hair was partially pinned back and held in place by a large white ribbon. The lower half hung loose around her shoulders in waves. She looked around the diner for Dean. The restaurant glowed inside from the reflection of the outdoor neon sign.

"I hope you were looking for me." He flashed one of his mischievous grins.

Ava jumped. Dean had snuck up behind her. "Really, Dean. It's a wonder I keep you around." Ava playfully hit him in the arm.

Laughing, he placed an arm around her shoulders as they made their way to a booth in the back of the diner. He slid in on one side while Ava slipped across from him on the other.

"Are you giving me the silent treatment?" Dean raised an eyebrow.

"You startled me. This is your penance." She raised her chin.

"Fair enough," he laughed, the sound filling the small diner. He opened his menu but winked at her over the top of it. "Do you remember the first time I saw you here? It was right after Kingston High beat Mason Prep in the championship game. The whole football team was celebrating their star quarterback."

"I don't know if I'd have called you a *star*," Ava teased, gazing at her menu.

"Of course, you would! It's why you fell for me in the first place."

"Was this before or after you spilled a chocolate milkshake on me?" She narrowed an accusatory look in his direction.

"That was an accident."

"I've never been so embarrassed in my life. I'm not sure why I ever forgave you."

"I'm glad you did." Dean reached across the table and touched her hand. At that moment, Charlotte showed up to take their order. Ava watched as he chatted casually with the restaurant owner. There was a slight bit of stubble on his chin, which accentuated his strong jawline; his brown eyes were warm and endearing. He wore tan slacks, complemented by a button-down vest, but it was his white dress shirt casually rolled up to his elbows that made his style so compelling. Ava loved that he could be relaxed, poised, and charming all at the same time. She'd been staring at him when he looked up and caught her. Her face warmed and she quickly shifted her eyes to the menu.

"My girl seems a bit distracted." Dean grinned.

Ava chose to ignore him and instead set her menu down. "Honestly, I don't even know why I bother looking. I get the same thing every time."

"The usual?" Charlotte smiled, and Ava nodded. "Burgers and fries it is." She took their menus and left.

Dean held the door as Ava walked out into the night air. The evening was cool and brisk as she struggled to put on her sweater. Dean offered her an extra hand before draping his own coat around her shoulders. He entwined his hand in hers as they head towards downtown Main Street.

It had sprinkled during dinner, and the street reflected the lights from the storefronts. The two walked in comfortable silence for quite a while before Ava spoke.

"This is my favorite time of year." She pulled his jacket closer to her. "Are you sure you're not cold?"

"I'm made of steel." Dean posed with his hands on his hips. He looked so ridiculous she couldn't help but laugh.

"What's so funny?" Dean held his hand over his heart dramatically before taking her hand again as they continued toward the edge of town. "Even if I was cold, I'd never ask for my coat back, leaving my girl to freeze. Mother raised me better."

"How is your mom?"

"Asks about you all the time."

"She does not." Ava swatted at him playfully.

"She wants to know when her son is going to find a wife and settle down."

"And?"

"I think mother, has good sense."

Ava smiled. "You do enjoy toying with me."

"I suppose I could do worse."

"Dean!" Ava shoved him away.

He tumbled dramatically toward the center of the street. Seizing her opportunity, Ava sprinted in the direction of her home, but Dean ran after her, making quick time. She'd barely made it past the gate when he grabbed her by the waist and spun her around to face him. She set her hands on his chest while he tugged on the collar of his jacket, pulling her closer to him. "You're trapped, Miss Sutton." Ava's heart raced double time. His proximity made her legs go weak. Was he going to kiss her in the middle of the yard?

"I'm not sure I could live my life without you." His voice was deep as he stroked her cheek. Wrapping his arm around her waist, he lowered his head toward her.

"Ava! It's time to come in now." The deep baritone voice of her father cut through the night air like a knife. Dean released her and took a step back.

Benjamin Sutton stood in the doorway of his home. His large frame, illuminated by the lights inside, made his silhouette intimidating. Ava slowly removed Dean's jacket and reluctantly handed it back to him.

"Next time," he whispered, and she felt her face warm. Ava stood on her tiptoes to give him a quick peck on the cheek before running to the porch where her father was waiting. She hoped the cool air would mask the blush in her cheeks.

Dean put on his coat and nodded to Ava's father.

Her father pulled the pipe from his mouth and nodded in return before guiding her inside. Ava watched Dean's retreating form from the living room window. Her father took a seat in his reading chair. Turning to face him, she stood there waiting for the speech she knew was coming.

"Are you getting serious about that boy?"

"We've been dating for a while now, I thought you approved of Dean." She walked across the room and sat on the couch.

"Of course, but you're still young, Ava." Her father smoked his pipe and watched her.

"Plenty of girls younger than me are getting married these days."

"Married?" Benjamin sputtered, choking on the smoke from his pipe. "Who said anything about marriage?"

"Honestly, Daddy!"

"You'll have plenty of time for marriage." He picked up the newspaper next to him.

Ava's head snapped in his direction as she knew he wasn't reading a word of the paper anymore. Ignoring the front-page headline about the war, she got up and pulled the middle of the newspaper down, meeting him face to face. "He knows very well he wouldn't be able to step foot in this house if he didn't run it by you first."

Just then, Ava's mother walked into the room. She carried a vase filled with fresh flowers, which she placed on the table near the window. Her pink floral dress was accented by white lace around the neckline and a slimming white belt to show off her waistline.

"Which one of you plans to fill me in?" She eyed her daughter curiously as she sat on the couch.

"Hannah, your daughter informed me she's getting married."

"Ava, you're much too young."

"I never said those words exactly, but if you must know, Dean has hinted at the idea." Her parents weren't taking her seriously and found herself feeling defensive.

"Oh, honey, men say things they don't mean all the time." Benjamin coughed over his wife's comment, and she ignored him. "What makes you think Dean has marriage on his mind?"

"He told me he wants to spend the rest of his life with me."

Benjamin dipped his paper and removed his pipe, ready to speak up. Ava noticed her mother give him a look only a married couple could exchange, and he went back to his reading. Her mother turned toward her, speaking softly. "I think you should take your time. Has he said he loves you?"

"Who said, 'I love you?'" Tessa made her way into the living room, her white blouse perfectly pressed and tucked into her wide forest-green trousers. She hurried around the coffee table, taking a seat on the other side of Ava. "Are we talking about Dean?" Tessa's face lit and she clapped her hands together waiting for details.

"Tessa, hush, let your sister speak." Their mother remained focused on Ava.

"Not in so many words." Ava smiled wistfully. "Had Daddy not interrupted us, who knows what he would have said?"

Her father made a gruff sound. "Based on what I saw, the boy wasn't *saying* anything." He spoke around his pipe in a serious tone.

"Daddy!" Ava squealed, a warmth creeping up her neck. Her father continued puffing on his pipe, pretending to read his paper, but he didn't fool her. Ava knew he'd heard every word. Her mother's look told her now wasn't the time to push the subject.

Tessa broke the awkward silence. "Ava? Let's go upstairs. I'll show you the fashion magazines I was telling you about." The girls got up and Ava leaned down to kiss her father on the cheek. "Goodnight, Daddy."

Benjamin shook his head and the girls giggled as they took the stairs two at a time.

That night, Ava sat at her writing desk and opened her journal. Tessa had spent the last hour going through magazines and talking about her ideas for the perfect wedding, but the thought of planning a wedding made her insides turn. She loved Dean, but was she ready for marriage? Ava absently touched the necklace hanging at her collar before she began to write down her thoughts from the evening.

Dean took my hand tonight as he walked me home from the diner. It was warm and strong, and I knew at that moment I'd always feel safe with him.

He told me he wants to live the rest of his life with me, and he nearly kissed me goodbye. We've exchanged displays of affection before, but somehow, tonight seemed different. I was partially terrified and partially excited. I saw something more in his eyes. I don't know if this is love. I've never been in love before, but I can't imagine my life without him. If that means love, then maybe I am.

CHAPTER 4

An incessant meowing broke Laura's concentration and she placed the journal to the side. It had been so enthralling; she hadn't realized the time. She rubbed the back of her neck, knowing better than to sit on the stool in a hunched position. She walked over to the window where Dusty sat outside eyeing her curiously.

"Whatever will I do with you?" She slid open the window and Dusty made his way in. He snuggled down, getting comfortable in the same place he'd laid the day before. Laura shook her head and picked up the journal, placing it under the light with a magnifying glass.

Turning the book over, she could see the vintage-style leather had begun to wear on the sides but that the engraved initials on the front were impeccably done. She could see why Ava's parents had given it to her as a birthday gift. In those days, debossing was most likely a luxury. The diary had seen its fair share of use. The pages were brittle, and the ink had begun to fade in places, but Laura was still able to make out most of it.

Ava's perfect cursive writing reminded her of her grandmother's. If only her grandmother was alive. Laura pictured them reading together, sharing the history she now held in her hands—and maybe feeling a bit guilty about reading the intimate details of someone else's life.

Based on the date of the first entry, the words had been penned before World War II. She scrolled through a few pages. The book was filled with daily entries. What a gift to get a glimpse of the past; a time when the country had been a very different place.

"I'll never make it through a night of reading perched on top of this stool." Dusty followed her as she wandered from the back room to the kitchen for a quick snack, and then to the living room. She grabbed a blanket off the back of the couch, plopped into the corner seat getting comfortable and opened the journal, excited to continue.

"This journal is far more interesting than my life right now." Dusty responded with a *meow*. "Great, I'm talking to a cat." She rolled her eyes. "You tell April about this little chat and we're done." Dusty licked his paw ignoring her as if her words meant nothing at all.

CHAPTER 5

NOVEMBER 8, 1941

Dear Diary,

Tonight is my party. I can hardly wait! Mother has been in the kitchen cooking up a storm and Father has been running errands to get everything we need. Everyone I know is coming. Tessa thinks it will make for the perfect audience if Dean proposes but I don't think he's spoken to Father yet, so I find it doubtful.

Each day brings more talk around town that the United States will soon be pressured to enter the war and there is an uneasy feeling in the air. The tensions between the Soviet Union and Germany are high, but I take hope in the fact we are an ocean away and nowhere near the fight. I've decided I'm not going to let it ruin my birthday. Now, if only I can keep Father and his business partners from discussing it. Unfortunately, that would take a miracle.

I wonder what Dean's surprise is. I've never been one to handle direct attention well, so I'm a bit nervous to be in the spotlight. If only I were more like Tessa; this is where she likes to shine. I pray it's nothing embarrassing.

I sn't my dress lovely?"

Ava looked up from her writing as Tessa barged in. Under her breath she whispered to herself. "Speak of the devil."

"Are you writing about me?" Tessa eyed the diary.

"Possibly," Ava closed the journal, leaving the pen inside to hold her place.

"Nothing bad I hope." Tessa lifted an eyebrow as if daring Ava to share. Her powder-blue dress was squared at the shoulders and pulled in at the waist. The bottom flared out making her sister look older.

"Tess, your dress is exquisite." Ava knew her sister was easily distracted by fashion and secretly hoped the change of subject would divert her focus from the journal.

"I should dress it up a bit, maybe a hair ribbon or a bracelet?" Tessa walked over to Ava's mirror and did a twirl.

"I have just the thing!" Ava jumped up and went to her jewelry box. She withdrew a beautiful pearl necklace.

"That's the necklace you got from Mom and Dad for graduation." Tessa's face lit up as Ava stood behind her and placed the set of pearls around her neck. Her dark curls fell down around her shoulders, framing her heart-shaped lips. She was only a year younger, but Ava had missed the day her sister grew up. She wasn't a little girl anymore. Her porcelain skin set off the sapphire color of her eyes, matching the dress perfectly.

"All the boys will be asking you to dance tonight." Ava smiled as she looked at her sister in the mirror. Tessa's eyes dropped. She turned to face Ava, suddenly quiet. "Tess? What's wrong?"

"It's nothing."

"It's something." Ava took her arm, pulling her to the foot of the bed where they both took a seat. "Tell me what's wrong."

"Is Grayson coming?" Tessa wrung her hands; a hesitant smile crossing her face.

"Of course, why wouldn't he?" Ava eyed her suspiciously. She'd rarely seen Tessa lack self-confidence. Grayson had been a family friend for years. He was responsible for introducing her to Dean and at one point almost went into business with their father. Why was Tessa suddenly shy?

"Tess," Ava questioned carefully. "Do you like Grayson?" The silence confirmed her suspicions. Ava smiled.

"Please don't tell."

"Your secret's safe with me." Ava wrapped her arms around her sister, pulling her close. "Grayson is a sweet guy. A bit quiet, but now that I think about it, you talk so much, you'd balance him out."

"Ava!" Tessa pulled away as Ava laughed. "It's not funny."

"My baby sister has a crush on an older man."

"He's not *that* much older." Tessa rolled her eyes.

"He's known you since you were in overalls."

"Considering you're only a year older, I guess that would go for you, *too*."

"I've always been mature for my age, so it's not the same." Ava flipped her hair and held her head high. Her playful attitude changed as she noticed Tessa still had a rather serious expression.

"I don't know what to do."

"I am the last person who should be giving relationship advice. Half the time I don't even know what Dean is thinking." Ava smiled coyly. "He told me he has a surprise for tonight."

"He is going to propose!" Tessa perked up.

"He knows better than to do so without asking Daddy first." Ava touched the hem of her skirt; her heart thumped so loud she swore Tessa could hear it. "Besides, I'm not sure it's the best timing."

"Are you having second thoughts?"

"I don't know. Mother might be right, maybe I need to wait."

"If the man intends to marry you, you best sort out your feelings."

"I suppose you're right." Ava leaned her head against Tessa's shoulder.

"Don't wait too long. I might steal him away." Tessa laughed.

"What about Grayson? He'll be so heartbroken when he learns he can't have you." Ava stood challenging Tessa. "Maybe I *should* tell him after all." Ava took one quick sidestep before running toward the bathroom with Tessa hot on her heels.

"Ava, don't you dare!"

Ava applied the last bit of lipstick as she heard attendees arriving downstairs. She better hurry, or mother would come looking for her. With one last look in the mirror, she decided she was satisfied with her efforts. She'd pulled her blonde locks back with pins on one side that allowed for full, wavy curls to form at the top of her head and down her back. She'd gotten a new dress for the occasion and with Tessa's assistance, her makeup was flawlessly applied. There were voices in the living room, and she rushed to the staircase to see who had already arrived.

She walked down the stairs like a princess arriving at a ball. As she neared the bottom, she froze, and time stood still. Dean held a dozen red roses. Dressed in a tan suit and polished brown loafers, his eyes twinkled when they met hers over the top of the bouquet.

"For the birthday girl."

"Is this my surprise?" Ava took the flowers, taking in their sweet scent.

"Maybe."

She took the arm he offered, eyeing him suspiciously as they walked towards the backyard. Some of the other guests had already begun mingling, partaking in the drinks and appetizers. Her mother rushed from place to place, making last-minute adjustments as her father poured drinks for his colleagues. She could hardly believe the transformation of their yard.

Her mother had decorated all the tabletops with pastel pink-and-white table linens. The center table held a two-tier birthday cake decorated in the same colors. Rows of white lights hung over the patio and the makeshift dance floor her father had pulled together using large wooden boards. Music from the radio played softly in the background and people mingled enjoying the last of the season's agreeable weather. Ava was grateful the party could be held outdoors. She turned and caught Dean staring and her cheeks warmed.

"I don't know why I'm so happy. It's not even my party."

"It's beautiful." They made their way to the cake and Ava could see the words HAPPY BIRTHDAY AVA scrolled on the top.

"Your mother outdid herself." Dean took the flowers from her and set them on a table nearby, then intertwined his fingers with hers. As if her mother had known she was being discussed, she appeared before them.

"Oh, hello Dean. What lovely flowers. If you don't mind, I'll put these in water." Her mother picked up the flowers smelling the one on top.

"The cake turned out beautifully Mother, and the backyard looks lovely! I don't know how you did it." Ava hugged her tightly.

"I'm glad you like it. Anything for my girls." Ava's mother became distracted when she noticed Tessa wrestling with a set of balloons in the corner. "Excuse me, it looks as though one of them is in need of assistance as we speak." She smiled and left to rescue Tessa.

"Is that Theresa?" Dean paused, working to focus with the dim light.

Ava covered his mouth with her hand. "Don't you dare let her hear you. She hates being called by her given name." Dean tried to speak, but her hand muffled his voice. Ava laughed, releasing him. "Take my word for it. She *refuses* to let anyone say it aloud."

"Okay, okay. I'll be careful not to say it around her." Dean rubbed his jaw looking back at Tessa. "She looks like she'll be giving her older sister some competition tonight." Dean jumped when Ava punched him in the arm. "What?"

"You *have* a girlfriend."

"Oh, I'm aware." He looked at her suddenly, taking on a more serious tone.

"Already getting punched and it's only the beginning of the

evening?" A tall young man, holding a birthday gift, stood behind them. He wore a steel-gray suit vest with a crisp white shirt underneath that had been rolled up to the elbows. His dark hair was perfectly set in place, minus a small curl that fell stubbornly over his forehead. His eyes were kind but haunting, as if holding onto a secret. A slow smile spread across his face, highlighting the cleft in his chin.

"Happy Birthday, Ava."

"Grayson," Ava brought her hands together as she approached him, and he enveloped her in a hug. "I'm so glad you could make it." Grayson's frame was slim but sturdy as an oak tree. He released her and reached out to shake Dean's hand.

"Hey, Superman." Dean slapped him on the back.

Grayson shook his head. "Are you ever going to drop the nickname?"

"If you really want to shake it, you might comb your hair." Dean shrugged.

"His hair is fine." Even though Grayson was nearly a foot taller than her, Ava reached up, attempting to smooth the piece of hair to one side. She huffed dramatically as it immediately fell back into place.

"You see my dilemma?" Grayson smiled. "It's been like this as long as I can remember."

"I guess Superman's not all bad, as far as nicknames go." Ava shrugged and both men laughed.

Grayson held up the gift he'd been holding. "Is there a place for these?"

"You didn't have to get me anything."

"I can take it back." Grayson lifted the present slightly out of her reach.

"No need," Ava plucked the gift away from him but nearly toppled over. Once in her grasp, she eyed the silver-and-black box curiously. Grayson's family had been well-off due to his father's success in the banking business. Ave couldn't help but wonder what was inside. Even though she had known him for years, Grayson had always been a bit of a mystery. She went to place the gift on the table, working to contain her interest until it was time to open presents.

She looked back at the boys now talking to Tessa. Their expressions indicated that they were seeing her differently; the way Ava had done earlier that night. She smiled; her sister had to be enjoying the attention.

The dance floor saw its fair share of use and some of Ava's friends sang along to the tunes on the radio. Ava opened her gifts later that evening and Grayson's turned out to be a record player. Dean's gift was nowhere in sight. Maybe the flowers had been it. She tried not to be disappointed. Not long afterward, the group gathered around as Hannah passed out slices of cake. Ava's father teased her when she didn't blow out all the candles.

"Whatever you wished for won't come true." He came up next to her, putting his arm around her.

"I have all I need right here." She looked around at her family and friends, a slight tear glistening in her eye, and Benjamin wrapped his daughter in one of his bear hugs.

After cake and presents, most of Ava's friends called it a night. Grayson and Tessa helped her parent's clear tables and clean up. It wasn't long before Grayson began chasing Tessa playfully, threatening her with the extra frosting that had gotten on his hand. Ava watched as her sister managed to evade him behind a table. Their laughter faded when Tessa ran giggling into the house, Grayson following her lead.

Dean approached Ava. The song "Harbor Lights" began to play on the radio and Dean held out his hand. She took it and he wrapped his free hand around her waist as she placed hers on his shoulder. He slowly swayed back and forth, occasionally spinning her away from him and pulling her back again.

They danced in silence as Ava wrapped her arms around his neck, their faces inches apart. She laid her head on his shoulder and the world around them faded. The song ended before she was ready, leaving them standing still in the middle of the dance floor.

"There is one last gift." Dean pulled a piece of paper from his pocket. "I'm not known for being a serious guy," he slowly unfolded the piece of paper, "but I told you I had a surprise."

Ava's heart echoed in her chest, not knowing what Dean would say next.

"It's nothing compared to the record player Grayson got you or the expensive ring your parents gave you."

"That isn't what matters to me." Ava put her hand on his cheek.

"This is a list of the 19 things I love about you." His voice cracked on his last words. He looked around nervously before he began.

Ava caught her breath. Did he say "love"? She worked to regain focus as he began reading.

"I love the way you laugh at my jokes, even when they aren't funny. I love how you bite your lip when you're nervous. I love that you are stunningly beautiful and still chose me. I love how innocent you are and how it makes me want to protect you. I love your heart and that you never speak ill of anyone. I love your deep appreciation for family and how you put others first. I love when you make eye contact with me in a room full of people and you seem to know what I'm thinking. I love when you reprimand me while trying not to smile. I love when we argue—or rather, when we make up. I love how passionate you are about music, drawing, and all things creative. I love how perfectly you fit in my arms and how my heart skips a beat the minute you enter the room. I love that I can imagine you as my wife and what it would be like living the rest of my life with you."

Dean folded the paper and stuck it in his coat pocket. He took her hands in his. "I don't have much, but if I have you, that's all I need. I understand if you don't feel—"

"Dean," she whispered, putting a finger to his mouth. Ava felt tears welling up.

He scanned her face, his eyes falling to her mouth. He pulled her near and when she didn't pull back, he kissed her softly. Wrapping his hands around her lower back, he drew her closer. He tucked a blonde curl behind her ear as they began to sway to the next song. "I've waited all night to do that."

His whispered intentions made Ava question the depth of her own feelings. She had anticipated this moment but hadn't thought about how it would feel. It felt right but were they moving too fast? Her parent's words echoed in her mind and she pushed them away.

"It's a good thing that's not what I wished for when I failed to blow out all the candles on my cake." She felt Dean's laughter resonate between them.

"I wouldn't let a few candles hold me back."

"I'll keep that in mind for my next birthday." She held his hand as they made their way back to the house.

"I should hope I won't have to wait that long to kiss you again." His whispered words sent tingles down her spin but all she did was squeeze his hand in reply. Laughter echoed from the living room as they stepped inside. They came around the corner to find Grayson and Tessa playing with Ava's new record player.

"You have to set the needle down just right or it's not going to work." Grayson leaned over and began to adjust the spike. Tessa slapped his hand away playfully. "I can do it if you let me alone for a minute."

"The two of them are acting like children." Ava nudged Dean. She'd always admired her sister's ability to be flirtatious as it had not been one of her strengths.

"Glad you could finally join us." Grayson gave Dean a knowing look and Dean beamed from ear to ear. Ava caught her breath at the realization he'd been in on it. She wanted to run and hide from embarrassment but instead pointed to the record player.

"Don't break my gift before I try it out."

Tessa carefully placed the needle on the record and music filled the room. "See? It's not that difficult, now that you've all stopped pestering me." They laughed at her sense of accomplishment.

The group spent a few minutes enjoying the music and taking turns swapping in new records when the boys finally called it a night. As soon as Ava shut the front door, she turned to find Tessa standing inches away from her, grinning. She clutched her hands in excitement and squealed.

"Tell me everything."

CHAPTER 6

L aura jumped when the phone next to her rang. Closing the journal, she set it aside and reached for her cell. "Hey, Mom."

"Hey sweetheart, what are you up to?"

"Just a new project."

"Oh really? What did you get this time?"

Laura looked at the journal sitting next to her and began tracing the design etched on the front. "I picked up an old steamer trunk."

"Really?"

"Yes, actually I found a—"

"Listen honey, I called because I'm going to be in your area and wanted to stop by and drop off a cabinet I picked up. Could you fit it in?"

"Can it wait a few days?" Laura stood up and began to pace.

"Oh, sure that's fine."

"That would really help as I'm on a tight schedule."

"Don't work too hard. You always stay up too late; I have no idea how you do it."

"Bills don't pay themselves."

"Okay, someone is grumpy today."

"I'm sorry Mom; you happened to catch me in the middle of something." Laura looked up to see Dusty sitting on her window-sill wanting to come inside. Laura walked toward the window and moved her hands around, hoping to shoo him away.

"Okay, I'll let you go. I'll arrange a time later this week to drop off the cabinet."

"Sounds like a plan." She looked down at the trunk hinges. She'd have to take a trip to the hardware store. "I'll chat with you later Mom."

"Bye, honey."

Laura hunched down, making eye contact with the cat speaking through the glass. "Sorry buddy, not this time."

Grabbing her purse, she caught a quick glimpse of her reflection in the hallway mirror. She frowned at the stained jeans and baggy T-shirt. "No use putting on a dress to go to the hardware store." She grabbed her keys and hopped in her car.

In less than ten minutes Laura strolled the aisles of the nuts-and-bolts section for replacement pieces. She needed strips of leather, so she could create a new handle and a new lock since the original was busted. Lastly, she'd need a new hinge to swap out with the broken one to help hold the heavy lid in place.

As she looked down at her pad, she ran her pen across the last item on the list. She hadn't noticed the man standing in the middle of the aisle—and plowed right into him.

Laura tumbled backward in slow motion. Even though she had reached out an arm to brace herself, her head still hit the ground. Laura wasn't sure if what she heard next was the crack of her head against the cement floor or the sound of a thousand nails clinking all around her.

Dazed, she didn't register the hand reaching down toward her. She touched her forehead with her free hand, trying to regain focus. Once she recognized the man in front of her, she instantly wished she was invisible. *If I close my eyes maybe this will all be a bad dream.*

"You okay?" Caleb had a concerned look as he knelt down next to her.

"You sure came out of nowhere." The pounding at the base of her skull overtook her normally polite manner.

"You hit your head pretty hard." Caleb steadied her arm helping her sit up. He wiped off a few nails still clinging to her.

"I'll be fine." She looked around at the mess longing for the aspirin in the bottom of her purse. "It's going to take forever to pick all these up."

"Can you stand?" Caleb extended a hand to her.

"I might be better suited if I start the task from down here." She attempted a smile.

"Good point." He crouched near her, clearing off an open space so he could sit and began cleaning up with her. Laura stopped his hand by covering it with her own then quickly withdrew.

"It's my fault; you don't have to—"

"This happened to be the exact box of nails I wanted to purchase." He shrugged. "I guess I don't have a choice now." His mouth curved into a smile as he continued to fill the box between them.

Laura studied him, unsure how he could be so accommodating.

"There are a few over there." He nodded toward the shelving on the opposite side. His eyes twinkled. Laura looked away, working to collect the remaining nails.

Before long the box was full, and they'd managed to put everything back in order. Caleb stood, towering over her as he assessed the situation. "I think we got most of them."

"I hope so." Laura held the box up to him. With his free hand, he gripped her wrist, raising her to her feet unexpectedly. Surprised, Laura worked to steady herself.

"I appreciate your help."

"It seems I have a habit of helping you." He flashed a grin and Laura's face warmed. She avoided his stare and attempted a half-smile.

"I don't typically find myself in awkward situations." She began to sift through her purse, to avoid feeling self-conscious.

"So, only when *I'm* nearby?"

"I haven't seen you around." Laura continued to avoid eye contact. "Are you new to the area?"

"Only recently. I'll be here for a few weeks. I've been helping my parents with some projects around their house."

"A few weeks?" Laura pulled out her keys. She needed to escape, and they gave her a small sense of security that the conversation would soon be over.

"Is that a problem?"

"Oh, not at all!" Laura touched his arm instinctively trying to re-assure him but swiftly removed her hand. Why was she continuing to invade his personal space? The longer she stood there, the more awkward things were becoming. Looking behind him, she pointed. "I think I see... um, what I came for."

She brushed by him in the aisle, inhaling the faint scent of his aftershave. Of course, he smelled like a model on the day she looked like a train wreck. She turned back in his direction and gave a slight wave as she made her way to the register. He smiled in return. She wondered how many times that grin had gotten him out of trouble. She could feel him watching her as she waited to check out and she prayed another customer would get in line behind her.

Slipping into the front seat of her car and out of sight, she let out a sigh of relief. Her head throbbed as she checked her disheveled appearance in the rear-view mirror. Why hadn't she changed before she left? But worse, why did she suddenly care? Laura shook the thought away and tossed the items onto the passenger seat.

By the time she returned home her headache had subsided. She planned to get back to work when she noticed the journal lying on the counter. Looking down at the bags in her hand, she checked the clock. It was only noon so it couldn't hurt to read another couple of entries before she immersed herself into the restoration again. In no hurry to finish the project, she could use the downtime after the embarrassing episode at the store.

Chapter 7

Dear Diary,

It's been a few weeks since my birthday party, and yet, every moment is etched in my mind as if it had happened yesterday. I still haven't come down from the clouds after the romantic evening Dean and I shared. When we are apart, I am thinking about the next time I will see him again. I guess this is what it feels like to be in love.

Tessa says it's pathetic how saccharine we are, and she hopes one day her love life will make me just as sick as I've made her. Maybe I've lost my senses, but I see everything with new eyes. I'm afraid the feeling will fade as quickly as it came, but for now, I am enjoying every minute.

Ava opened the door of her family's Chevy wearing a new pair of sunglasses and looking like a movie star hitting the red carpet for a premiere. Her father had washed the car the day before and the metallic teal sparkled in the sunlight. The chrome siding glistened as she stepped onto the church parking lot in her low-heel pumps. Her white dress had yellow daisies on it and her hair was tied back in a ponytail held in place by a matching yellow scarf. Ava scanned the grassy picnic area outside the church.

She shut the car door, catching a glimpse of her reflection in the window. She had been particularly impressed with her outfit. Tessa had pulled off a miracle on her hair which seemed to have a mind of its own. It wasn't long before her moment of silent admiration was interrupted.

"Ava, can you carry the peach cobbler?" Her mother held the dish out from behind the trunk of the car.

Tessa nudged her in the back. "So much for daydreaming about Dean."

Ava's dark glasses shielded the glare she aimed toward Tessa as she followed her to the back of the car. Their mom had already loaded up their father with food, sending him on his way. She passed out items to each of the girls and they began walking toward the picnic tables a few yards away.

"There you are." Dean came up behind Ava, plucking the cobbler away from her with one hand.

"If you ruin that dessert, Mother is going to have a fit."

"Relax, I'm in perfect control." As he spoke, he stepped on a rock and lost his balance.

Grayson came out of nowhere snatching the cobbler from Dean as he fell towards the grassy field landing with a *thud*. Ava squealed and quickly retrieved the dish away from Grayson.

"What is it they say? Pride comes before the fall?" Grayson stood over Dean laughing.

Dean got up and rubbed at the grass stain on his pant leg. Ava bit her lower lip trying not to smile. Her concern shifted to her mother's potential reaction to their childish ways rather than the welfare of her boyfriend's trousers.

The three of them continued toward the gathering crowd each taking turns reprimanding Dean for his carelessness. Ava joined her mother and Tessa, dropping the cobbler at the end of the dessert table. All sorts of baked goods and side dishes were displayed. The annual church picnic had been around since she was a child, and she knew most of the families in attendance.

The day felt brisk, and Ava soaked in the warmth of the sun hitting her arms. She strolled along, watching Dean help the younger children test out the potato sacks for the race that would take place later. A few of the older children clung like monkeys to the big oak tree a few feet away.

"I remember climbing the same tree when we were that age." Grayson cut into Ava's thoughts as he walked up alongside her.

"Oh, Grayson you startled me." She watched the children turn their play into a game of tag.

"I always had to coax you to join the fun."

"I was a bit of a bore, wasn't I?" Ava lifted an eyebrow smiling.

"You never wanted to get your clothes dirty."

"I still don't." She turned towards him, crossing her arms.

"We could change that. Why don't you be my partner in the three-legged race today?" He held up a ribbon twirling it in the air.

"And ruin my dress? Hardly." She laughed brushing past him.

"Some things never change."

"Why don't you ask Tessa?" Ava called over her shoulder, challenging Grayson to follow.

"My winning title could be at stake." He matched her stride with his long legs, easily keeping pace with her shorter ones.

"Then why on earth would you ask *me*?"

"We used to be a pretty good team. If I recall, we won some of those titles together."

Ava eyed him with a slight tilt of her head. What was he up to? She had no desire to participate, but Grayson looked so helpless, and she found herself feeling sorry for him.

"Are you going to make me beg?" He pouted like a puppy waiting for her reply.

"I don't have the right shoes."

"Go barefoot."

"I'll do it under one condition. If you ruin my dress, you're buying me a new one." Ava sighed walking back toward the group of churchgoers who'd begun to gather for prayer. She turned to face him awaiting his answer.

"If your dress gets ruined, I'll buy a new one."

"Deal."

She instantly regretted caving in. She had a sinking feeling it wouldn't end well but there wasn't time to back out now. Her mother was motioning them toward the group because the pastor intended to say a blessing over the food.

Ava opened the baby-blue fridge in the tiny church kitchen. She scoured the shelves for the dish of pasta her mother had sent her to fetch. Moving a few things around, she found the bowl and removed it, simultaneously shutting the fridge door with her foot. She walked down the hallway when she heard Dean's voice from the other side of the door. His comment stopped her in her tracks.

"Marriage is the next step."

"Have you spoken to Benjamin?"

Ava's breath quickened. Did he say *marriage?* She carefully leaned toward the cracked doorway waiting for his reply to Grayson.

"I didn't get the feeling he was pleased with the idea."

"I can't imagine any father is ever ready to have that conversation with his daughter's suitor."

Ava peered through the crack in the door but could only see a slice of Dean. He ran his hand through his sandy-blond hair, pausing on the back of his neck. She imagined having any conversation with her father would be intimidating, much less asking for his daughter's hand.

"What should I do?"

"You're asking me?" Grayson sounded hesitant.

"Why not? You know Ava and her family better than I do."

"Honestly Dean, if you want to marry her, you need to talk to Benjamin. You should have a plan before you do. Can you financially take care of her? Where are you going to live? Things like that."

"I'm not like you, Superman. I don't think I've ever had a plan in my life."

"You'd better figure it out. He's not going to just hand her over." Grayson punched Dean's shoulder in jest while Ava froze, waiting for his reply.

"Who are we eavesdropping on?" Tessa whispered, causing Ava to jump.

Ava turned to see a sly grin on Tessa's face and quickly grabbed her arm while holding tight to the dish with her free hand. "You have the worst timing." Ava whispered back as she pulled her sister outside toward the food tables.

"Are you going to tell me?" Tessa persisted, still keeping her tone low.

"I don't think this is really the time or the—"

"It's about time," Hannah interrupted. "What took you so long? I had to send Tessa to find you."

Tessa spoke first. "It's a good thing you did, Mother."

"Why is that?" Ava's mother looked back and forth between the girls.

"Ava found herself in an awkward situation." Tessa's teasing smile faded when Ava shot her a warning look. She worded the remainder of her comment carefully. "She was having trouble balancing the dish by herself."

Ava released the breath she'd been holding. She didn't care to explain to her mother that she'd been eavesdropping. Tessa lifted an eyebrow toward her with a slight smirk on her face that told Ava she fully intended to get the juicy details later.

Luckily their mother had been distracted by the remaining food on the table and was only half-listening. She wiped her hands together; glancing up in time to catch the suspicious looks being passed between the two girls.

"The two of you are up to something but at the moment I'm too busy to discuss it now." She gave them one last look and left to join the ladies serving desserts.

"Are you trying to give me a heart attack?" Ava asked once their mother was out of earshot.

"Oh Ava, don't be dramatic."

"That's rich coming from you."

Tessa had a retort ready to fire back when one of the church elders stood from his table to announce they were going to begin the games. She promptly closed her mouth as both girls listened in. They would start with the three-legged race. He held up various colored scarfs, which the teams were to use. Ava noticed Dean and Grayson heading their way.

"Which of you ladies will be my partner in crime?" Dean looked from Ava to Tessa who laughed at his question.

"I'll do it." She grabbed one of the scarfs from Dean and waved it in Ava's direction silently challenging her sister. "Ava hates competing in the picnic games."

"Actually," Ava straightened. "I'm going to race, and I have a partner."

"I bribed her, and she said yes." Grayson covered a smile with his fist.

"*Convinced* is a better word for it." Ava waved her hand.

"My girl is racing with another guy. It's a good thing I'm not the jealous type." Dean placed his arm around Ava's shoulders as the race moderator passed by encouraging them to line up. "Tessa, what do you say? Let's show these two how it's done."

"Ava's out of practice; this will be the easiest race of the day." Tessa motioned Dean to follow her to the starting line.

Ava shook her head. Why had she agreed? Her sister was nothing if not competitive.

The four of them prepared to race as church members headed down the field carrying the finish line—a roll of toilet paper. The teams began tying their legs together. Grayson bent down to tie the first blue scarf around his and Ava's ankles. He went to tie the second one a bit higher up when she swiped it from him.

"I'll do this one."

"Based on your height, you may want to tie it around my knee." He grinned.

"I'm glad you find this amusing." She focused on the scarf. "I don't know why I let you talk me into this." She pulled tightly on the knot.

"Isn't there a tiny part of you that wants to join the fun?"

She paused, looking upward. The sun caused her to squint, and he held a hand up to shield her eyes from the light. "I have fun, just in different ways."

He waited for her to finish the knot and they wobbled toward the starting line where Dean and Tessa looked as though they were already discussing their strategy. They took their place at one end of the line when two teenage guys stepped up beside them. Dean and Tessa were a few teams down getting into position. Grayson placed his arm around Ava's shoulder and she around his waist. They crouched down, waiting for the whistle.

"Your kind of "fun" must be eavesdropping on a private conversation?"

Ava opened her mouth to respond but noticed Grayson continued to stare straight ahead. She tensed; his comment had hit its target. The announcer was saying something, but Ava wasn't listening. Grayson must have seen her in the church. He knew she'd overheard him talking to Dean. "It's not what you think."

"I saw you and your sister make a quick exit, giggling over your little snooping adventure." The corner of his mouth lifted slyly but before she could reply Dean yelled down the line at them.

"Take note of my face, from here on out you're only going to see the back of my head."

Ava could see him wiping his hand through his hair attempting to grandstand, so she hunkered down ready to start the race.

"I think it's cute you assumed you got away with it." Grayson spoke in hushed tones as he leaned in closer to Ava's ear. She could feel the warmth of his breath on her neck, and it sent a chill through her. Why was he chiding her right before the race was about to start?

"You're implying I was doing something wrong." She kept her voice low enough for only him to hear.

"Weren't you?"

"I was in the kitchen. You two were talking so loudly I couldn't help but overhear. It was hardly my fault." She nudged him in the side to create some much-needed personal space between them.

The announcer shot the mock pistol. Ava stiffened. The teams took off running. Ava saw Grayson attempt to take the first step forward as the realization hit her, they were being left behind.

Quickly coming to her senses, they nearly caught up to the group when the teenagers next to them tumbled directly into their path. Ava tried to correct her steps but fell out-of-sync with Grayson. The ground quickly came toward her, and Grayson drew her close wrapping his arms around her. His reaction time equaled his strength as he pulled her toward his chest and turned so his back took the pounding for both of them.

Ava slowly opened her eyes, the grass mere inches from her nose. She worked to catch her breath and felt Grayson's arm still around her waist. She attempted to shift away to avoid looking improper, but her dress had gotten caught underneath him.

"Well, that couldn't have gone any worse." Grayson held his hand to his forehead still on his back.

"A little help here?" Ava tugged on the hem of her dress as Grayson lifted his body weight so she could get free. "I knew this was a bad idea." The grass stains were clearly evident as she agitatedly began untying the scarfs. In the distance, Dean and Tessa could be heard rejoicing.

"We're never going to hear the end of this."

"At least you don't live with one." Once free of one another, Ava held up the edge of her dress pointing to the grass stains. "I told you."

"What?" He lifted his hands innocently.

"At least I still won."

"How do you figure?" Grayson stood to his feet offering a hand to help her up.

"Because Grayson Rockwell, you promised me a new dress." Ava dusted herself off taking the hand he offered.

"A deal's a deal." Grayson chuckled hoisting her up as if she weighed nothing at all. The two of them looked toward Dean and Tessa who were being carried around on the shoulders of other racers. Grayson sighed. "I guess we better get this over with."

The sun began to set, and Ava yawned while putting the last of the empty food containers in the family car. Dean helped her father break down the last of the chairs and tuck them away in the church shed. The bright-pink hues of the sunset closed the end of the day. The games had lasted into the afternoon and everyone had a wonderful time. Tessa and Dean each got a small trophy for winning the race and most of the attendees spent the afternoon indulging in desserts.

Ava walked around the car and smiled at Tessa asleep in the backseat. The scene made her envious. The exhaustion from the day made her want nothing more than to lie down and fall asleep. A light breeze kicked up, signaling the start of cooler weather. It had been a beautiful day. The newspaper spoke of cooler temperatures around the corner. Today's perfect weather would be some of the last they'd see for a while.

Ava watched as the rest of the group began to disband. Grayson had left shortly after the race to prepare for work the next day. The church parking lot quickly cleared out as parents carried sleeping children to their cars.

Although tired, Ava debated whether to walk home with Dean or leave with her parents. Their time alone was rare, and she didn't wish to pass up the opportunity.

"Are you ready to go?" Dean and her parents walked up to the car.

"I may fall asleep on my feet."

"If you're too tired—"

"You'll just have to keep me entertained." Ava grabbed onto his arm.

"See you later sweetheart." Her mother and father slipped into the car taking the hint that their daughter had found another way home. They drove off leaving Dean and Ava standing in silence. The sun had set when they began their stroll. The streetlights began turning on one by one. Dean seemed unusually quiet as they walked hand in hand. The breeze picked up and she shivered.

"Are you cold?"

"I'll be okay." She edged closer to him.

"I should leave my jacket at home more often." He took the excuse to wrap his arm around her shoulders.

"Is that going on the mantle at home?" Ava pointed to the small trophy he held.

"It sure is." He held it up, turning it slightly.

"I never should have agreed to do the race." Ava pointed to the grass stains. "The only thing I got was grass stains."

"I got a few stains myself," he stuck out his leg.

"For being clumsy." She laughed.

"We make quite a pair."

"I'm a mess."

"A cute mess," he kissed her on the temple. They continued to stroll past the shops that lined Main Street. The neighborhood always seemed calm on Sunday nights. They reached the edge of town near the old gas station, which doubled as a mechanic shop. The blinking fluorescent sign caught Ava's attention. It was supposed to say HAL'S, but half the sign didn't light up.

"Has Hal seen his sign lately?"

Dean looked up at the HA and laughed. "He's too lazy to fix it."

"Maybe he hopes his younger, more dashing, employee will fix it." She nudged him.

"Dashing? I don't know anyone who fits that description."

"Do you like working there?"

"Hal's great, but the job's not for me. I think I prefer the idea of working for myself."

"Why does that not surprise me?"

"I'm trying to save money."

"Oh really?"

"There is something I want to buy but it's expensive."

"What?" Ava's heart began racing. She eyed him warily and he turned to look at her.

"A new watch." He stopped short and held up his bare wrist. He'd baited her, and it worked. A sly smile crossed his lips as he continued walking.

"Dean Samuel Wheeler!" She caught up, grabbing his arm. "You're a tease. You had me believing you were planning to buy a ring!"

"I don't know, *Ava Grace Sutton*, what if I am?"

Ava squealed and threw her arms around his neck. She nearly threw him off balance with her exuberant response, but he kept his balance, holding her tight.

"It's going to take some time."

"I'll wait."

"Come on. I have an idea." He took her by the hand and pulled her into a sprint toward the dimly lit mechanic shop.

"Where are we going?"

"Trust me." He pulled her to the right of the building and the side door to the shop. Releasing her hand, he walked up to an old tree stump a few feet away. He dug into the ground and removed a key. Casually making his way to the door and unlocking it, he walked a few feet inside before grabbing a string hanging from the ceiling and turning on the light. The little shop had tools hanging on the walls and a work bench beneath them.

"Dean, I don't think we should be in here."

"We'll only be a second." He held his hand out to her and she accepted. He led her to a chair and she hesitantly sat down. Ava watched as he searched through a few boxes and finally removed a spool of what looked like thread. He walked over to the bench and grabbed some wire cutters from the wall. He clipped a small piece of the delicate wire and began to shape it in front of her, carefully filing down the edges to remove anything sharp. He held it up.

"It's nothing close to what you deserve, and it'll probably turn your finger green, but it's a placeholder, until I can get you a real one." He watched her as she held her hand out so he could put it on. He gently slid the ring on her finger.

"The other girls are going to be jealous." She giggled and caught him staring at her the same way he had the night he kissed her. Her heart began to race. Something inside her told her it wasn't a good idea to be alone any longer. "My parents are going to send out a search team if I'm not back soon." She held her hand out and he took it.

He shut off the light and locked the shop behind them. He approached Ava, standing there in the moonlight, with a pensive look on his face.

"What's wrong?"

"Nothing, let's get you home." He forced a smile and took her hand. They walked the rest of the way home in silence.

CHAPTER 8

Dear Diary,

This morning our family attended church like any other Sunday. Afterward, I exchanged pleasantries with my friends while Mother spoke to the pastor's wife about arranging a ladies' tea and Father planned his golf outing for the following weekend. Then we heard the news on the radio. Deep in my heart, I know this day will forever change my life. The United States may have just entered World War II.

Ava's father drove down Main Street when suddenly the townsfolk nearby began to exit their cars and run into the local hardware store. People frantically motioned one another inside. Her father exchanged a glance with her mother. Ava stared at Tessa who shrugged.

Her father wordlessly pulled into an open parking spot near the hardware store and saw that the men inside were huddled around a radio. Benjamin slowly turned the dial up on the car. A man on the other side spoke in solemn tones.

Today, Sunday December 7th, 1941, Japan attacked Pearl Harbor. The number of servicemen that have been lost is unknown at this time. We

*know very little other than the attack was unprovoked, and many lives
have been lost. We are awaiting official word from Washington and
will be bringing you updates as we know more.*

Ava's mother sat back against the car seat with her eyes closed as
her father stroked the back of her hand softly with his thumb.

"Where is Pearl Harbor?" Tessa leaned forward in her seat.

"I think it's by Hawaii, Tess." Ava shifted forward, noting the
concern on her parent's faces.

"Are we at war Daddy?" Tessa's voice sounded as shaky as Ava
felt.

"I don't know honey."

"Will you be asked to serve?" Their mother opened her eyes,
looking toward her husband.

"Let's not jump to conclusions." He stared at the hardware store
and the men huddled around the radio. Her mother covered her
mouth with her hand and began to cry. Ava sat frozen, rarely seeing
her mother display emotion. Before long, her own stomach began to turn, and she wrapped her arms around herself. Dean and
Grayson could go to war. She couldn't stand the thought. A tear
burned its way down her cheek.

A small hand touched her shoulder and she saw Tessa's eyes were
filled with tears. Ava reached up and covered her sister's hand with
her own. Her father and mother held each other close until he re-
versed out of the parking space and drove them home. Ava watched
as the trees outside blurred into one. The streets were empty. The
town deserted. The ride home was silent.

Ava made her way to the living room. Her parents and sister were
already seated around the radio—their eyes affixed, waiting to hear
any new information. Her father had received numerous calls from
business associates speculating on the United States involvement

in the war. If the country went to war, everything would change.

As if on cue, Eleanor Roosevelt's radio program, *Over Our Coffee Cups*, filtered through the airwaves. Ava slowly sat down on the couch as the First Lady's voice filled the room. She shared that Congress was, at that very moment, discussing what should be done. She quickly went on to address the women of the country, speaking to the fact that their husbands and sons would be called upon to fight. She said her own sons were already on the battle lines and encouraged the young people of the nation to do whatever would be asked of them during this time of hardship. She concluded by calling upon the American citizens to have faith, and stated she, in turn, had faith in our citizens to do the right thing. Her voice sounded soothing and strong. The speech was brief, and Ava wished she would continue since it had a way of calming her anxiety.

When the speech ended, her mother turned down the dial and walked past her father, touching his shoulder briefly. She moved into the kitchen without a word.

Ava sat helpless. She looked to her father staring at the radio with a level of consternation she'd never seen before. Tessa wrung her hands in her lap, her typically cheerful personality absent.

"Father?" Ava spoke softly; the room felt so quiet, her voice echoed. Her father stood and walked over to them, joining them on the couch. He placed an arm around each of the girls and held them tightly. Ava laid her head against his chest, listening to the sound of his steady breathing. For the first time that day, she felt safe. She pushed away thoughts her father might be going to war and focused on the moment.

Her mother came into the room with a tray of hot tea and poured each of them a cup before pouring one for herself. She sat across from her family in her husband's reading chair. They quietly sipped their tea—no one willing to break the silence. If they didn't talk about it, maybe the nightmare wouldn't become a reality.

"We have yet to hear the official word from the President, but tomorrow... the United States will officially join the war." Benjamin cleared his throat. "I can't say I won't be called upon to serve my country. However, it's unlikely I'll be called into action. My body is past its prime. More than likely I'll be stationed at a desk." He paused. "Regardless, our family will be called upon to make sacrifices and forego some of the modern conveniences we've become accustomed to. We will plan to support families whose sacrifice is far greater than ours."

"We can make it work, Father." Ava placed her teacup on the coffee table and grasped his burly fingers with her smaller ones.

"I know you will, sweetheart." He squeezed her hand reassuringly.

"What do we do next?" Tessa's blue eyes glistened, her voice shaky.

"The President will have to address the nation, and based on what he says, we will make a plan as a family." He pulled a cigar out of his front suit pocket and rolled it between his thumb and forefinger. "Right now, I'm going to enjoy this cigar. It may be one of my last for a while."

"Is smoking not permitted during wartime?" Tessa asked. Her father let out a hearty laugh, breaking the tension.

"No pumpkin, but there is a good chance the nation will be rationing, and a man's cigar will no longer be a commodity." Her father clipped the end of his cigar and lit it with a few puffs. "Now, if you'll excuse me, I'm going to appreciate what is left of the evening on the back porch. Mother? Will you join me?" He looked at Hannah who quietly stood and left the room with him. Ava watched her sister who seemed lost in thought.

"What is it, Tess?"

"Does that mean no more new clothes?"

"We recently bought dresses. They should last for a while."

"What will you do for a wedding dress?" Tessa touched her hand, concerned.

"I won't be getting married." During all the commotion, she

hadn't even thought to reach out to Dean. She felt sick to her stomach as she stood walking to the front window of their living room. She looked out into the darkness.

"What? Why not?"

"If we go to war, Dean will enlist."

"You don't know that." Tessa slumped back against the couch clutching a nearby pillow. "He may not have to go."

Ava watched her sister in the reflection, not able to speak her greatest fear aloud. She touched the window softly, the coolness matching the temperature of her own fingertips. Tears began to flow, and she felt her sister's arm wrap around her. Tessa whispered things were going to be alright, but Ava knew better. Even if there wasn't a draft, Dean would surely enlist along with Grayson and many of the other young men in town. The wedding would have to wait.

CHAPTER 9

L aura's stomach growled, bringing her attention back to the present. She'd been so immersed in the journal; lunchtime had slipped by her. The late afternoon sun shone through the windows of her living room as she watched the shadows slowly shifting across the floor. She wanted nothing more than to spend the day reading but the old trunk wasn't going to restore itself.

Knowing her fridge had nothing exciting to offer, she struggled sorting out something to eat. After deciding on a sandwich, she made her way to her work room. She set her plate aside when a sudden curiosity struck her. She pulled out her phone and searched online for the song "Harbor Lights". She'd heard of the song and wondered what version Ava and Dean had danced to, so she chose the original version. The crackling sound of a vinyl record played through her phone speaker bringing her once again back to the 1940's. The song had been done by many popular singers but originally came out a few years prior to World War II. She sat in silence listening to the vocal stylings of Frances Langford and the Hawaiian theme filled the air waves in the room.

She imagined Dean asking Ava to dance on her birthday without a care in the world. There was no way for them to know everything in their world was about to change. As she listened to the lyrics, she could see why it might have become a popular soundtrack during the war.

She looked down at the trunk wondering how many harbors it'd seen in its lifetime. The song came to an end and the moment was abruptly interrupted by an irritating ad for insurance. Laura sighed, taking a bite out of her sandwich. *Welcome back to the present.*

She assessed the project, deciding her next steps as the ad came to an end and auto played another song from the same time period. As the song "I'll Be Seeing You" filled the room, Laura remembered her grandmother mentioning the song had been one of her grandparent's favorite songs. Had they danced together in the same way Ava and Dean had?

It was hard not to wonder what it would be like to live during that time. The music continued to play between ads and Laura let it run. The songs were comforting and brought a relaxing feeling to the space. Laura could see why her grandparents had played it many times when she'd been by to visit.

Her heart sank a bit wishing her grandmother was still around. She'd have loved reading the journal and could have filled her in on the details of what it was like to live during the time. She would no doubt have had plenty in common with Ava. Laura paused over the irony. If anyone had anything in common with Ava, she did. She knew from the letters in the journal the story would take a dramatic turn. Dean was going to go to war and Laura found herself anxious over how this love story would end. Worse than that, could she read through the loss of another as she still struggled with her own?

Pushing the thought aside, Laura sanded the trunk throughout the evening and listened to the music to keep her mind busy. After a few hours, she called it quits. She passed the journal sitting on the table and decided if she planned to get any sleep, she'd better wait to begin the story again the following day.

CHAPTER 10

Dear Diary,
*   The United States is at war with Japan after the bombing of Pearl*
Harbor. The President's speech today made it official. Father reas-
sured us there was a good chance he would not be enlisted. Mother
said if this war is anything like the first, the government will be ra-
tioning food and other household items. Dean called the house last
night, but all he said was he wanted to speak with me in person. I
have never dreaded a conversation more.

Ava sat in the living room overlooking the front porch anxiously awaiting Dean's arrival. She touched the thick curtains hanging next to her. Her stomach ached knowing the
conversation would be a trying one.

In all the chaos, she hadn't thought about how much her life
would change. She nervously turned the wire ring on her finger,
recalling the night Dean gave it to her. Somehow, her love life
couldn't rival the events that transpired the day before. The feeling of loneliness only deepened at the thought of losing Dean. She
closed her eyes, imagining a different day, one where the world

felt peaceful.

A knock on the door interrupted her thoughts. She jumped not realizing how on edge she'd been feeling. She slowly opened the door and Dean stood in front of her. The tears she'd been holding back, began to fill her eyes.

"Ava." Dean barely breathed her name before she walked into his arms. He held her tightly. They stood in the doorway as the breeze harassed the hem of her skirt—both oblivious to anything but each other. Dean guided her to the porch swing. They sat in silence, swaying back and forth. He rested his arm around her shoulders.

"I can't ask you to stay," Ava tilted her head, looking up at him. "But I can't bear the thought of you leaving."

"If I had the choice, I'd choose you," he paused. "Any fella worth their salt is headed down to the recruiting office this week to enlist. I couldn't live with myself if I wasn't fighting alongside them." Dean pulled her close.

"Why?" Ava sniffled. "Why did this happen?"

"I don't know."

"I'm going to write to you every week." Ava sat up and she touched his cheek. The tears stung her eyes as she looked at his helpless expression.

"Promise you'll wait for me." He stroked her hand and Ava nodded. Dean tenderly brushed away her tears.

"When will you leave?"

"I don't know."

"What branch are you signing up for?"

"Navy. Grayson and I made the decision to go into the same branch hoping we could get into the same squadron."

"You'll both be leaving at the same time?" Ava's eyes widened.

"He feels the same, a bunch of the fellas do."

"I can't say the idea of you both going doesn't make me ill." Ava held her stomach bringing the swing to a standstill.

"I'm supposed to put on a brave face but—"

"Dean," she interrupted, suddenly feeling guilty she'd made the situation about her. How had she not realized how difficult this had to be for him? She needed to encourage him, not make him feel worse. She stared him straight in the eye. "Being brave doesn't mean anything if you aren't scared. Courage exists *because* we are afraid. And you are facing that fear head on." She leaned her forehead against his and whispered. "I couldn't be prouder of you."

"I don't know how I'll be able to leave you." Dean kissed her forehead.

Ava nestled against him and he pulled her close. She closed her eyes, memorizing his scent. She wanted to remember every detail and for the rest of the evening, they held each other in silence.

CHAPTER 11

DECEMBER 22, 1941

Dear Diary,

It's nearly Christmas, but very few folks are in a celebratory mood. Mother set up a Christmas tree adorned with lights and decorations. The house would normally smell like baked goods every day, but Father warned Mother to be careful with what we have, so we are waiting till Christmas Day to prepare a few baked goodies. He promised us one last Christmas like we were used to—hoping to boost our spirits. I know he is trying, but the dark cloud of war seems to haunt my thoughts at every turn.

I used to look forward to Christmas Day, but this year I dread it. This may be the last time I see Dean, and I am doing everything within my power not to think about it.

"Ava, can you come down here please?" Her mother yelled up the stairs.

"In a minute." Ava finished the last line of her journal entry and put it away in its hiding space. Would she ever use the old trunk to travel instead of storing old blankets? "Maybe one day..."

"Talking to yourself I see."

Ava spun around. She caught her breath over the unexpected visitor. In the doorway stood Dean. He shifted nervously, his face full of uncertainty. His hair had been cut in the military style and Ava tried to cover her surprise. A song played on the radio downstairs filling the silence between them.

"Dean, what are you doing here?" She swallowed, wringing her hands in front of her.

He soberly walked in. "I got a haircut."

"So, you did." Ava forced a smile, brushing at his shoulders and attempting to center her emotions. Dean grasped her hands. She turned her head away. She knew better than to try and pretend with him. "The fact that you're leaving is becoming a reality."

Dean wrapped her in his arms. She didn't wish to fall apart in front of him. She pulled at his arms attempting to break free. "I must go; Mother was calling me."

"That was on my behalf. I asked her if I could come up this one time. I guess I thought you'd be happy to see me."

"Of course, I'm happy to see you, I—" Ava stared at the floor. Her fear quickly turned to guilt. How could she keep Dean from doing what he felt was right? She searched his face. "Am I selfish for wanting you to stay?"

"If you are, then I'm selfish too. I don't want to go."

"When do you leave?"

"Right after the New Year. We are headed to boot camp."

"Grayson too?"

"Yes."

"What happens after that?"

"I don't know." Dean held her left hand and touched the ring she wore. "But you'll always have a part of me with you." He kissed her forehead. "I promise, we will get through this."

Dean and I spent the evening trying to reassure each other that things would be okay. I don't think either of us left feeling any better. He and Grayson are leaving soon. The thought of it brings tears to my eyes. Dear God, keep them safe.

CHAPTER 12

Laura wiped at the stray tear. Her heart ached for a woman she'd never met. The sobering reality lingered that the freedoms she took for granted, had required the sacrifice of those before her. She noticed worn envelopes tucked away in the back of the journal—letters from Dean. Ava had saved them. Laura closed the journal and placed it on the coffee table, not having the emotional fortitude to continue.

The clock on the wall struck ten. She needed to go to bed, but she wasn't tired. Across the room Dusty had passed out in her chair. If only she could be that carefree? He began to stretch and yawn as the clock finished its last chime. He jumped down and sauntered over to sit in front of her.

"It's late, which means it's time for you to go home." She walked to the workroom and Dusty followed her. Laura tapped the tabletop near the window and the cat jumped up. She opened the window, and he scattered out. It's a curiosity he managed on his own. She wondered where he went at night. As if reading her mind, he gave her a quick meow then disappeared into the darkness.

"April's right. I need a life." Laura closed the window and nearly ran into the trunk in front of her. It was more than a keepsake. The secrets and memories it held from a simpler time had become complicated by war. She touched the worn top and imagined Ava lifting the lid to hide her treasured diary inside. How long had it gone unnoticed and how had the journal been forgotten in the first place?

Laura picked up a sanding block and began to run it slowly along the wood grain. She moved it back and forth, watching the wood's true color appear. She continued to work until the clock struck twelve. Time for bed. Nearly falling asleep where she stood, she wiped at the dust covering her jeans. Putting away her tools she called it quits for the night.

After a quick rinse in the shower, Laura pulled back the covers and slipped into bed, her body sinking into the comfortable mattress. As she reached to turn off the light, she paused, staring at the picture on the bedside table. It had been a year since the photo was taken; the day her life changed forever. Every night reminded her of that fateful day, but she couldn't bring herself to put the picture away. To do so would mean moving on and something inside her wasn't ready to let him go.

Laura kissed the tips of her fingers and pressed them against the glass. She wished Paul was there beside her. Never allowing herself to dwell on his absence, she shut off the light and before long, fell sound asleep.

CHAPTER 13

A knock at the front door startled Laura as she checked her makeup in the hall mirror. She gave her ruby-red dress one last inspection. The V-shape neckline and vintage bodice with quarter-length sleeves was a perfect fit for her frame. She stared at her reflection a moment longer before hearing a second knock.

"Coming!" Once more she turned in the mirror, revealing a low-cut back that highlighted her shapely figure. Pleased with what she saw, she walked down the hall, her matching red heels clicking along the way. She peered through the glass window and opened the door to find a handsome man standing in front of her holding a bouquet of roses. He looked dashing in his crisp button-up shirt and dark gray jacket.

"You look amazing." He stepped inside and kissed her on the cheek. "These are for you."

"You shouldn't have." She took the floral bouquet from him and smelled the rose peeking out the top. "Paul, they're gorgeous."

"I want tonight to be special."

"Any particular reason?" Laura eyed him, lifting an eyebrow playfully.

"I told you it was a secret."

"Well then, let me put these in water so we can get going." She left Paul standing in the foyer as she put the roses in a vase. Walking back, she placed them on the table under the hallway mirror. She grabbed her white trenchcoat from the closet and pulled her house keys from her purse. Paul extended his arm, and she took it with a smile.

The car ride to the restaurant was filled with their usual banter. Laura sat and listened as Paul told her about his workweek. She remembered the day they met. She had been in a hurry to leave the coffee shop and didn't see him walking in. He'd bumped into her as she opened the door, spilling coffee down the front of her dress. She had been horrified. He had made his best effort to help her, even offering to buy her a new coffee. All she had wanted to do was go home and change clothes.

When he attempted to pay for her dry cleaning, she saw the concerned look on his face and gave in. They exchanged numbers and although she had been reluctant at first, sitting next to him now, she knew it was the best decision she'd ever made.

"...and then I told her I wasn't going to say anything about it." Laura found herself back in the present. Her daydream caused her to miss what Paul had said. She nodded and smiled pretending she had followed along.

"Why do I get the feeling you haven't heard a word I've said?" He pulled up to the valet of an upscale restaurant.

"I heard you." Laura lied, hoping he would let it go.

"You have that look on your face." Paul walked around the front of the car and opened her door.

"What look?" She took the hand he offered.

"The one where you bite the inside of your lip because you're concentrating."

"Whatever you say." Laura stuck her tongue out.

"I knew it."

"Knew what?"

He ignored her as they made their way inside. A hostess quietly led them to a romantic table near the back. Laura looked at Paul with a curious grin. A table for two, draped with white linen, was already adorned with water glasses and a bottle of wine. Paul pulled out her chair and waited for Laura to get settled. "What has you so distracted?"

"Huh?" Laura had been so busy taking it all in, she didn't hear his question.

"Babe," Paul teased while taking his own seat. "You ignored everything

I said in the car."

"I wasn't ignoring you." Laura smiled coyly behind her wine glass. "A girl can have her secrets too." She'd let him jump to his own conclusions.

"I can't say I blame you. If I was dating me, it would be hard not to think about anything else."

Laura's mouth dropped open, and Paul laughed, causing a few heads to turn in their direction. "You're making too much noise," she whispered. Her eyes focused on the couples that were now staring.

He leaned across the table whispering back. "What do you say we get out of here?" He held out his hand.

"But we haven't ordered yet?"

"I know."

Confused, Laura took his hand and the two quietly walked out to the back patio, through the side gate. The evening was crisp with a light mist in the air as they walked through the park next to the restaurant.

"Where are we going?"

"You'll see." Paul led them down the sidewalk and through a grove of trees that opened to an old gazebo. As they approached, she noticed it was lit with white lights and there was a table in the middle with a single red rose placed on top of it. Paul ushered her up the gazebo's steps.

"Paul," Laura felt the air escape her. When did he have time to set this up? He walked toward the rose, picked it up, and handed it to her. She inhaled the lovely fragrance before noticing the sparkling diamond ring attached. She could hardly breathe. Could this be happening? She gasped, bringing her hand to her mouth. She turned toward Paul who was down on one knee.

"Laura, would you do me the honor of becoming my wife?" Breathless, Laura nodded, tears brimming in her eyes. Paul stood, removing the ring from the rose. He placed it on her finger and held her hand in his. He looked into her green eyes, and slowly lowered his head to kiss her. She wrapped her arms around his broad shoulders and kissed him back, then the two stood in silence as she took in all the beautiful decorations.

"Paul, when did you have time to do all this?"

"I may have had a little help."

Laura turned when she heard clapping coming from behind her. Looking back toward the stairs, she saw both her and Paul's parents. Paul took her hand and led her down the stairs where they each took turns embracing one another. Laura's mother had tears in her eyes and her dad whispered to her how proud he was of them.

The group enjoyed the moment before heading back to the restaurant where the table-for-two had been turned into a table for six. Paul had thought of everything. This time there was a bottle of champagne waiting. Laura's father popped the cork and made a toast.

"To the newly engaged couple: may your lives be long-lived and filled with many blessings." The group tilted their glasses in agreement. They enjoyed a lovely dinner before finishing the night off with ice cream from The Parlor on Main Street.

The evening had been planned to perfection. Paul was always thinking of others, it's what she loved about him. She stared at him across the table. He looked up from his conversation with her dad and caught her gaze. Laura felt butterflies in her stomach, the same way she had on their first date. This time the feeling was more intense because she was about to start a life with the most wonderful man in the world.

Later that night, the mist had turned to rain and Paul walked Laura to her front door and kissed her goodnight. He waited for her to make her way inside before heading back to his car, his coat covering his head. Laura watched him from her kitchen window, giving him one last wave before he drove off. She still held the engagement rose from earlier and added it to the vase holding the others Paul had given her earlier.

She walked into the hallway counting eleven roses in the vase. She added the final rose to complete the dozen. Kicking off her heels, she enjoyed the soft, cool wood under her aching feet. Sore feet were a small price to pay for the most amazing night of her life.

Making her way upstairs, she considered what would come next. It was too soon to set a date for the wedding—even though both sets of parents spent the evening asking a barrage of questions surrounding it. Paul managed to keep them at bay with his cool and calm presence, assuring them they had plenty of time to sort through the up-and-coming decisions. Laura appreciated how he managed the conversation without a second thought. She got ready for bed and turned out the light, excited for what tomorrow would bring.

Laura slept soundly when her cell phone rang. She sat up groggily, noting the clock read 3:20 AM. Who on earth was calling her at this hour? Her phone registered her future mother-in-law's cell.

"Hello?"

"Laura, this is Pat." Paul's mother sounded worried. "Laura, you need to get to the hospital. Paul's been in an accident."

CHAPTER 14

Laura bolted upright; her body soaked in sweat. She worked to steady her heartbeat and bring herself back to the present. It'd been months since the nightmare. She slowed her breathing gently, reminding herself of her surroundings. "I'm okay. I'm home, I'm safe and I'm fine."

But she wasn't fine. Her cheeks were wet as she'd been crying in her sleep. The real-life nightmare had never been far from her mind. Would she be forced to relive that night forever? She looked at the clock. It wouldn't be daylight for another couple hours. She brushed the blankets to the side, made her way to the bathroom and jumped in the shower.

Exhausted but afraid to fall back asleep, she brushed out her wet hair and walked back to the bedroom. On nights like this she had been thankful she worked for herself. The nightmares would come and go, but she never knew when they would happen or what caused them. The dreams were always vivid leaving her feeling close to Paul but then it always ended in disaster with her receiving the dreaded phone call or sitting at the hospital in the waiting room.

She turned on the light next to her green reading chair. She briefly recalled the day she and April had wrestled it upstairs together. April insisted the chair belonged in the bedroom. Halfway up the steps, she started whining that her ideas always entailed more work than she originally thought.

Laura smiled. April always came up with an idea but never a plan to go with it. She plopped down into the oversized chair. It could have fit two people, but it was the perfect place for one person to snuggle up with a good book. Set near her window, she could see out over the backyard, the picture-perfect spot to relax. As she stared into the darkness, it illuminated her reflection in the moonlight. She leaned her forehead against the glass, the coolness a soothing sensation on her warm skin.

It had been a year since Paul died. She needed to get out in the world again, maybe meet someone new, but could she risk another loss? Her family and friends had moved on long ago and somewhere along the line, they'd decided she should do the same. Hiding behind project-after-project didn't make the feelings go away. Her only choice would be to face them.

Going back to bed would be useless so Laura went downstairs to make some tea. She could get a jumpstart on the trunk and maybe, at the end of the day, read a bit more of the journal. As Laura filled her tea pot, she began to think she had more in common with Ava than she realized. Both were suffering from loss. Ava's had been because Dean had chosen to go, but still, losing the men they loved to unforeseen circumstances connected them. The difficult lesson they seemed to be facing was how you let go of someone you love deeply.

Laura took her tea into the workroom, sipping slowly while she eyed the traveler's trunk. She inspected the work she'd done hours before. The color of the original wood had been a pleasant surprise after all the sanding she'd done.

How had such a precious item been left behind? Covered in fabric, it's quite possible the prior owner didn't know the beautiful wood had been hidden underneath.

Laura jumped at the scratching sound coming from the bay window. In the dim light she saw Dusty sitting outside. He began meowing the moment she made eye contact. Laura propped the window open. She didn't want the cat becoming a permanent fixture, but she wasn't about to let him freeze.

"What in the world are you doing here this time of night?" Dusty stared at her, his lackadaisical attitude telling her he was happy to be inside. "I'm going to have a chat with your owner about leaving you outside." He sauntered around the room, sniffing tools and occasionally stretching his back legs.

"Don't get comfortable," Laura sighed. She'd lost the battle. The cat planned to stay. "You may think you live here but don't get any funny ideas." Laura eyed the cat knowing full well she sounded like a crazy person talking to herself. She shifted her focus as the caffeine began to kick in. The unfinished trunk in front of her wasn't going to finish itself.

The warmth of the sun touched Laura's face and she squinted in the late afternoon. This was the only time of day the sun hit her bed at the perfect angle. Not realizing she had dozed off, she slowly sat up. She'd worked on the trunk all morning making quite a bit of headway. Outside of needing a few more things from the hardware store, she'd made great progress.

Picking up her phone, she noted no missed calls and felt relieved. Some days she wasn't in the mood to talk to anyone and today had been one of them. The sun warmed her room for the moment, but she knew it wouldn't be long before it's soft light would soon leave again. Her blankets were urging her back to sleep but instead she chose to stay awake so she could resume her normal sleep patterns that night.

Heading downstairs, she grabbed a bite to eat and decided to pick up where she left off in the journal. She curled up on the couch as she braced herself. Dean would be leaving for war; she didn't see how any of the next few chapters would be easy to read without shedding a few tears herself.

CHAPTER 15

DECEMBER 25, 1941

Dear Diary,

I went to sleep last night knowing when I woke up, it would be my last real Christmas for a while. Father says if it's anything like the first World War, the government will begin rationing the items we can use, and it appears it may be an extensive list.

Father gave Tessa and I a bike a few years ago and he is in the garage bringing them back into shape. From this point on, we'll be walking, biking, or taking public transportation if we wish to go anywhere. We've been told the car is for emergencies only.

Mother plans to use the butter we have to make a Christmas feast. It's hard to say what will be available, we must plan ahead. She told me when the weather is nice, we'll be starting a garden in the back-yard. I feel blessed to live in a part of the country where we can grow a garden and take advantage of the apple orchards to help supplement our needs.

As for me, I'm still trying to figure out my part in helping with the war effort. Tessa has decided it is her responsibility to entertain any military men who come through town and stop off at the harbor before they ship out. Father felt she could find a more worthy cause, but she insists "what she is doing is necessary for the men's morale."

I hope to enjoy Christmas as much as I am able. It will be one of the last days I will see Dean and Grayson before they ship out. Who knows how long they will be gone? I've been trying to brace myself. I have yet to let my mind wander into the territory of how difficult that day will be. I can't fathom the thought of one of them not coming home again. My prayers will have to be enough as that is all I have to give.

Ava methodically placed a fork at each setting as she walked around the dining table. The smell of turkey wafted in from the kitchen and the aroma of fresh baked bread filled their home. Luckily, her mother had thought to buy a turkey and freeze it for this occasion. Meat could be one more thing that could soon be in short supply. Her mother had already planned to make use of every piece. She hoped to use the turkey juice to cover as many meals as possible. Supply shortages were a given, but one could only guess how drastic the implications would be.

Her father had served in the Great War, so he'd shared with her that their lifestyle would require some sacrifice in the foreseeable future. She looked at the sides on the table in front of her, imagining what it would be like if it were a normal Christmas Day—a day when men weren't leaving their families and children weren't saying goodbye to their father's.

A knock at the front door distracted Ava from her thoughts. The guests had arrived. Hannah told her to invite both the Wheeler's and the Rockwell's, so they could all enjoy the holiday together. She finished setting the last fork on the table as she heard her mother greeting Grayson's family at the door. She turned toward the kitchen and bumped into Grayson.

"In a hurry?" He held her shoulders gently to steady her.

"I'm sorry, I'm feeling a little off today."

"Are you sick?" Grayson's voice held a note of concern.

"No, nothing like that." Ava waved him off.

"I'll chalk it up to general clumsiness."

Rolling her eyes, she passed by him and he followed her to the kitchen. They were both given dishes by her mother and asked to place them on the dining table. They did as they were told while their parents continued to discuss current events in the kitchen.

Ava looked over the delicious display of food set before them. Her stomach growled loudly, and Grayson looked up in surprise. Her face warmed with embarrassment.

"I guess I'm hungry."

He laughed, breaking the tension. "I can't wait to eat either." Grayson walked around the table, joining Ava on the other side. His eyes were distant as if she'd disappeared from the room. Then he spoke softly. "I don't know what they'll be feeding us in the Navy, but I doubt it'll be anything like this."

"I have been trying not to think about it." Ava wrapped her arm in his, leaning her head against his shoulder. "I'm imagining today as if it were any other Christmas Day."

"I've been avoiding it. Everything changed overnight and we can never go back to life as we knew it." They strolled into the living room knowing they had a few minutes before supper.

"I haven't had a chance to talk to you." Grayson stood across from her making a drink from a cart that had been set up in the living room. "How are you feeling?"

"If you want my honest answer, I'm scared to death."

Ava watched as Grayson moved slowly across the living room. He stood sipping his drink in front of the Christmas Tree. The reflection of the white lights flickered across his face, as the radio softly played Christmas tunes behind them.

"I don't know what was harder. Deciding to enlist or telling my parents." He quickly drained his drink, setting the empty glass on a table nearby.

Ava lost her breath, not sure what to say. There were no words to calm his uncertainty. Certain he wasn't sharing his feelings with the fellas, she kept quiet, waiting for him to continue.

"Men our age can't avoid this war, even if they wanted to. The guys are excited and can't wait to get out there." Grayson sat down on the edge of the couch, his arms on his knees. "At least this way, we can choose to go into the same branch."

"Grayson, are you one of those guys? Or would you wish to stay behind?" Ava touched his shoulder reassuringly.

"I want to make a difference, but it's a bit unnerving to put one's life on the line to make that happen. Mother wants me to wait to be drafted due to the fact that my father isn't well."

"Oh, I'm sorry. I didn't know." Ava sat down next to him.

"I hoped that if I signed with Dean, maybe we'd have a chance to be on assignment together. We could watch each other's backs."

"I pray every day for God's protection. I don't know how I'd cope if I lost either of you."

Grayson took one of her hands in his. "Can I ask you something?"

Ava's heart skipped a beat, not able to guess what he might say next. They'd grown up as close friends, but they'd never had a serious conversation like this. He'd become distant after she started dating Dean, respecting the new dynamic of their relationship.

"Would it be okay if I wrote to you? Maybe you could send me a letter or two?"

"Of course!" Ava's uncertainty vanished, and her face lit up.

"I realize you'll be writing Dean and I didn't want to put you out but—"

"Nonsense. You're putting your life on the line for me and my family, the least I can do is write to you."

"Thank you, Ava." He whispered softly.

"Is there something else?"

He looked down wringing his hands and pausing to consider his next words carefully. "With my father's health declining, if anything were to happen to me—"

Ava instinctively wrapped her arms around him, pulling him close. "Grayson don't say such things," she whispered. The tremor in her voice betrayed her own anxious thoughts.

"If anything were to happen to me, would you look after my mother?"

Ava leaned back. The fear he'd been harboring was written on his face. He'd always been strong for everyone around him but now a vulnerable man sat in front of her, a trait she had never seen before. Carefully choosing her next words, she tried to reassure him.

"Nothing, and I mean *nothing*, is going to happen to you." She squeezed his hand in hers. "While you are away, I'll personally see to it your mother and father are taken care of. They are family." She touched his cheek and he leaned into her touch, closing his eyes.

"Ava, where is that boyfriend of yours? I'm starving." Tessa walked in, stopping short. Ava quickly withdrew her hand and Grayson sat up straight, neither making eye contact with Tessa.

"Oh, I'll just check on the—" The doorbell rang, and Tessa changed course, saving them all from an awkward situation. "Finally. I'm starving." Tessa turned around towards the front door.

Ava swallowed hard, knowing the situation wasn't as it seemed. Grayson stood holding his hand out to her. "Shall we?"

Thankful for the change in subject Ava replied, "I don't wish to face the wrath of Tess if we are late."

They both laughed and head to the dining room for one of the best meals they would enjoy for a long time.

CHAPTER 16

Ava stood in front of the Christmas tree, mesmerized by the tiny white lights. As a kid she'd slightly squint her eyes, creating a sea of glistening stars. Tonight, her tears produced the same effect all on their own. With just a small shift in perspective, suddenly everything looked different.

Her mother had help cleaning the kitchen, so she had released her girls to visit with their friends, while she and the other ladies handled the dishes. They had played cards for a bit until the competition became a little intense, so they called a truce instead. When everyone else began visiting in separate rooms, Ava took a private moment to glance at the tree. The realization that Dean and Grayson would soon be shipping off to boot camp lurked right around the corner.

Out of the corner of her eye, she noticed a small present under the tree. Where might it have come from? She knelt and picked it up. The red and green striping glistened under the lights of the tree and a tiny bow adorned the top. A gift tag stuck out displaying her name. Only then, did she recognize the handwriting.

"I couldn't leave without getting you a little something." Dean walked up behind her.

"But Dean, I thought we weren't getting each other anything this year."

"Open it," he smiled outwardly excited to see her reaction.

She removed the ribbon and opened the box. Inside, a pin in the shape of a red V sat on a little white cushion. Ava recognized the symbolism of the gift as her father had spoken of it before. It stood for a sign of resistance by the Allies.

The "Victory Pin" had been used throughout Europe and now that the United States had joined the allies, she'd seen them worn around town.

Dean took the pin out of the box and attached it to the collar of her blouse. "I was hoping you could wear it while I'm gone. Something to remember me by."

"I'd love to."

"Now everyone will know your sweetheart's gone off to war."

"Dean, we live in a small town. I have a feeling everyone knows my sweetheart has already enlisted." She smiled over his reasoning. She would have worn it regardless of his rationalization but knowing how much it meant to him, she'd proudly wear it until his return.

"I know one thing for sure." He grabbed her hand leading her back toward the kitchen.

"And what is that?" Ava held her breath, she never knew what would come out of his mouth next.

"I'm not going anywhere without sampling the desert I saw in the kitchen." Dean rubbed his hands together in anticipation.

Ava laughed. Dean's weakness for holiday treats had never been a secret. "I have no doubt you'll not only clear your plate but attempt to go for a second helping when no one is looking."

As they made their way to the kitchen, her mother served up slices of lemon meringue and banana cream pie. When the men were asked which pie they would like, they responded with "both." The women laughed at their childlike response, but the reality was upon them all, that this would be the last year they'd all be together for a very long time. Dean and Grayson would be shipping off to base training and soon after, they would be sent overseas.

"Oh Ava, where did you get that adorable Victory Pin?" Tessa pointed to Ava's new gift.

"Dean gave it to me." Ava's face warmed as the attention of the room now focused on her.

"I want one," she sighed aloud as if she'd been left out.

"Of course, you do Tess." Dean took a large bite of pie and winked in her direction. He failed to be affected by her request. Their mother handed Tessa her dessert and, never wishing for either of her daughters to be left out, responded. "Honey, I'm sure we can find you one. If not, we will make one of our own."

Tessa seemed satisfied with the response and let the matter drop. Before long Ava's father cleared his throat as he directed everyone's attention to Grayson and Dean. "I don't have boys of my own, but you two are the closest thing to it. Having served myself, I know how you must be feeling right now. Serving your country is a sizable honor but it is also a great sacrifice... and don't you think any of us will ever forget it. As your family and friends, we could not be any prouder and we pray for your safe return home." He lifted his glass, 'to Dean and Grayson.'"

Everyone raised their glasses, but Ava subconsciously touched the pin she now wore. Knowing what it represented and the significance it held, gave her pause. Her emotions were already running high with sentiments brought on by the holiday, but this year had a solemn undertone of a war-torn world. She found herself silently praying for a miracle, that her loved ones would come home soon so they could all be together again the following year.

Later that evening, Ava sat alone on the couch in front of the Christmas tree. Her parents had gone to bed and she'd turned off all the lights, taking a moment to reflect on the day's events. She heard rustling in the kitchen and knew Tessa was in search of a glass of milk. Her sister soon sauntered into the living room.

"I love the way the tree looks in the dark." Tessa sat in their father's reading chair across from her.

"Me too," Ava shared in her sister's excitement. The moment reminded her of when they were little girls in their jammies hoping to stay up long enough to catch Santa in the act. Ava was struck by the sobering fact they were no longer children and that in recent years the Christmas magic had faded. Part of her grieved the past, wishing things didn't have to change.

"What's on your mind?" Tessa broke the silence.

"The holidays don't feel like they used to."

"We aren't kids anymore." Tessa took a sip of her milk. "I don't like it any more than you, but we all have to grow up some time I suppose."

"Is it me or have you been more quiet tonight than usual?"

"I've been doing a bit of thinking myself."

"Oh really? What about?"

"Earlier... when I walked in on you and Grayson." Tessa shifted uncomfortably. "It seemed like I interrupted something more than friendship."

"Tess, it's not what you think." Tessa had taken the situation the wrong way and Ava had forgotten about her crush on Grayson.

"Then what was it?"

"You know my heart belongs to Dean."

"It looked like I'd caught you two playing hooky from school." Tessa set her empty glass on the side table next to her.

"You surprised us."

"Well, it's no wonder. You two were sharing a special moment."

"He asked me to write to him, to keep his hopes up."

"I wish he'd asked me." Tessa's face turned down.

"Oh Tess," Ava's heart dropped, and she tried to back pedal. "You know you can write to him also. I'm sure he'd love the letters."

"I'm not sure that's the point, Ava."

"What do you mean?"

"Are you sure there isn't something more between you and Grayson?"

"It was only a few weeks ago I'd considered marrying Dean. Grayson wouldn't do anything to jeopardize that." Ava got up from the couch and walked over to where her sister sat. She attempted to read her reaction in the dim light. "Besides, he's known me for years and never hinted at anything more than friendship."

"Are you sure about that?"

"I'm sure." She squished herself into the chair next to Tessa and wrapped her arms around her. Tessa squirmed but Ava held on, rocking her sister back and forth dramatically.

"Okay, okay," Tessa pushed against her, but Ava pushed back until she cried mercy. "No need to torture me with your love." Tessa began giggling.

"Hush, you're going to wake mother and then we'll both get it." Ava laughed quietly, releasing her sister. "Tess, I'm sorry I didn't realize how you might have been feeling."

"It's okay. You didn't do it on purpose." Tessa scooted over making enough room for them to comfortably sit side-by-side.

"Forgive me?"

"I'm going to write Dean behind your back; then I'll call it even." Tessa pushed against her sister, getting the desired reaction.

Ava's mouth opened wide. Shocked over her sister's boldness. She began to tickle her and both girls found themselves in a fit of giggles. Staying up late into the night trading secrets and sharing memories, Ava didn't wish to go to sleep. For one night she could pretend that tomorrow would never come, and she'd not be forced to face the world as it had become.

CHAPTER 17

APRIL 13, 1942

Dear Diary,

The last few months have been a blur. Today we send Dean and Grayson to basic training. They will eventually ship out with the Navy overseas. They aren't being told where they will end up, but wherever they go, it won't be safer than home.

I am supposed to leave in an hour to meet them at the train station and my stomach is in knots. Tessa is going with me because she wants to say goodbye too. Mother made some baked goodies for the train ride and Father said to send his goodbyes.

It's only been a week since Christmas and already so many things have changed. I don't know how I'll manage to get through the day. All I know is today will be one I remember for the rest of my life and not with good reason.

Ava stepped onto the train platform. She didn't live far from the station, but her father said they could take the car. She stood in a sea of townspeople. Making a fist with one hand, she pressed it firmly to her side. The cookie tin in her other hand, she nearly dropped it as she couldn't stop shaking.

Tessa stood next to her, quietly scanning the large group of people for a familiar face. Mothers said goodbye to their sons not wanting to let them go. Their fathers remained stoic, but the sadness shone in their eyes. Sweethearts gave farewell kisses, not ashamed of being affectionate in public. These weren't the men Ava had imagined; they were merely boys. How could they be leaving for war? Truly heartbreaking were the families sending off more than one son. Ava saw the look of devastation in their mother's eyes. Her own mother had declined to go to the station and now Ava knew why.

"I see them." Tessa grabbed Ava's arm and pulled her out of the moment and toward the train in front of them. The train came with a daunting presence. Soon it'd be pulling away and taking Dean with it. Tessa ran ahead to greet the guys, running into two giant hugs while Ava hung back unsure.

Suddenly she couldn't breathe. She wanted to run in the opposite direction, but she took a deep breath instead. They stood there holding large white sacks filled with a few belongings. The bags were half their size; it seemed every man nearby had a sack the same color. Their parents were in the middle of saying their goodbyes. Grayson's father pat him on the shoulder while Dean's parents wrapped him in another hug once he'd released Tessa.

Ava approached slowly. Dean dropped his cloth sack. His eyes held hers. She memorized every detail. Who was the man standing before her? He looked different. The military haircut made him look older. He stepped away from his parents and now stood smiling down at her. How could he be so cheerful? Her feet cemented down, she struggled to remain strong. She firmly gripped the metal tin in her hands.

"Please tell me those are your mother's famous cookies." His grin and playful tone didn't hide the concern in his eyes. Dean wrapped his arms around her, pulling her close.

Ava nodded against him, unable to speak. She closed her eyes. At that moment, everyone else faded away. "Please come back to me." Her tearful voice sounded muffled against his shirt.

"I'm counting the minutes." He kissed the top of her head.

"I'll write to you every week." She took a second to collect herself and Dean released her.

"And I'll cherish every word." The train instructor called out that it was five minutes to boarding. Ava made eye contact with Grayson. She hardly recognized him with his new haircut.

"Oh no!"

"What is it?" Dean jumped at her sudden squeal.

"Grayson's curl. It's gone." She put her hand over her mouth as she ran to greet him.

"I'm sure it'll grow back, don't you worry." Grayson smiled, pulling Ava into a brief hug.

"He'll always be Superman to me." Dean stated boldly. "I hope you packed your cape; we're going to need it."

"With your crazy antics, you're bound to need me to watch your back." Grayson slapped Dean on the shoulder.

"We'll see who has to babysit whom." Dean's laughter echoed across the platform. The conductor began walking the platform yelling, "Last call!" Men hung out the windows of the train holding on to their loved ones and waving.

"I guess that's us." Dean picked up his cloth sack and put his hat on. They said their final goodbyes; each of them gave the girls one more hug.

Grayson spoke into Ava's ear when it was her turn. "Don't forget your promise."

"I won't." She handed him the cookie tin she'd been holding. "Take these, or Dean will eat them all before you get any." Grayson laughed as Tessa offered to walk with him to the train entrance.

"I hope you saved one for me." Dean wrapped his arms around Ava from behind. She turned towards him and he smiled down at her. He touched her cheek, and she closed her eyes. Was it possible to memorize his touch? He held her close with one arm around her waist, the other holding his nap sack, and he kissed her.

He didn't let go when the instructor yelled "Last call!" He kissed her forehead, her nose, and her tear-stained cheeks. "Everything is going to be okay."

She nodded as he let his lips rest against her forehead. They walked toward the train and Ava reached into her purse. She pulled out letters she'd written the day prior and handed them to Dean.

"What's this?" Dean flashed a huge grin.

"The next time you get lonely, open one. I didn't want you to have to wait on the mail. Oh, I almost forgot." Ava drew out a small picture of herself, kissed the back of it leaving red lip marks, and handed it to Dean.

"I will keep it with me always." Kissing her one last time, he placed it in the inside pocket of his shirt and leaped onto the first step of the train entry. He held her hand as the train jolted. The whistle pierced the air and the train slowly moved forward. She stayed in step, never breaking eye contact. The platform descended a few feet away forcing her to let go. Her fingers slipped through his.

"I love you, Ava." Dean called out, not concerned that anyone had heard his declaration.

"I love you too." She whispered through her tears. He kept her in sight till he found the same open window that Grayson was already hanging out. They both shoved through the window waving goodbye. Ava watched the train fade from sight and then they were gone.

Ava's tears had been silent as Tessa drove them home. Neither spoke a word. By the time they pulled into the driveway, the emotions of the day had caught up with her. She went straight to her room, needing to be alone.

Pulling out her journal she went to her writer's desk, but she couldn't find the words. A small metal bucket that held pens and pencils sat on her desk. She'd stuck a tiny American Flag inside on the Fourth of July. She pulled out the flag touching the red and white stripes. It suddenly had a new meaning. A symbol of freedom, what Dean and many other men were fighting for.

The wooden stick had words on it: MADE IN JAPAN. Her face warmed and a deep-set anger overtook her. Japan was responsible. They were to blame for changing her life and taking away the ones she loved. She couldn't bring herself to throw away the flag, so she cracked the stick against the writing desk, breaking it in half. She took the bottom half with the words on it and tossed it in the trash. It didn't change the fact it hadn't been made in America, but somehow it made her feel better to throw it away. She carefully returned the top half of the flag to the bucket and grabbed a pen in its place. She knew exactly what she felt now.

My heart is a mix of emotions. I'm angry that the country has had to enter the war. I'm suffering to say goodbye to the man I love, the man I one day hope to marry. Now our plans are on hold and God forbid, may not happen. Why can't the world be in harmony for once? I'm finding it awfully difficult to be hopeful.

In the end, I'll find the strength to do what needs to be done, I'll have no choice. However, at this moment, I have no idea where the resolve will come from. Lord help us all.

CHAPTER 18

Laura cuddled the blanket closer as she sat on the couch, the journal still open in her lap. It had been 80 years since the war, but it felt like she'd been living in 1941 the last few days. Several yellowed pieces of paper stuck between pages near the end of the book. Curious, she unfolded the last letter. It seemed to be a standard sheet of paper that looked like a telegram. At the bottom it said V-MAIL. Laura recalled the military had their own mail system during the war. After shuffling through the pages and checking the dates, the first few letters were in envelopes and then switched to the V-Mail method.

The one she held was from Dean to Ava. She hesitated. She had read their story in chronological order and there were quite a few letters tucked between the pages near the end of the journal. Considering the age of the paper, she had to be careful not to ruin them. She didn't want to damage any part of Ava's history. The memories were precious, and they belonged to someone in her family.

The clock chiming in the hall told her Stanley had already closed up at the antique shop. She would call the next day to see if he had a record of where he got the chest. Walking into the kitchen, she set the journal on the table but opened the letter she still held. Noticing an address on the top, she tried to make it out. The street name sounded familiar. Her heart skipped a beat. It wouldn't be too far-fetched to think Ava and her family could have lived nearby.

Too tempted to hold back now, Laura went through a few more letters. If she could find one in good enough shape, maybe she could put a full address together. The likelihood Ava's family was still at the same address would be slim but in her small town, it wasn't out of the ordinary for folks to stay in the same place for years. A small flicker of hope filled her. If Ava's relatives weren't living there, maybe there would be a clue to help her locate them.

Laura called it a night. She decided to take the following day off and turn her full attention to the journal. She couldn't push away the feeling that she had to find the family. This precious memento needed to be returned.

Chapter 19

Dear Diary,

It's been a month and a half since the boys shipped out and I haven't heard from them. I've sent a few letters and so has Tessa, but the mail is running slower than usual. It's eating me up inside that I don't know where they are or what they are up to.

I am keeping myself busy helping mother with the chores but it's not enough to keep my mind from wandering into dangerous territory. I must find another cause to pour my heart into or I won't be able to stand the constant worry. A distraction is what I need, although I'm not sure how much it'll help.

Ava looked out the kitchen window to the backyard. The drizzling rain had turned the sky a mix of purple and gray. While it wasn't pouring, the damp weather made for a dreary atmosphere to match how she felt inside. She touched the Victory pin on her shirt. Could it be raining in Dean's location?

"Ava, how come you're not ready?" Tessa frowned as she marched into the kitchen. "Daydreaming again, I see."

"Just thinking."

"Same thing." Tessa began to put on a dress jacket sweeping her long curls out over the collar. "You need to get ready or we're going to be late."

"Tess, I'm going to pass tonight."

"But I promised Jimmy you'd be his dance partner." She looked in the mirror as she applied a red lip rouge but eyed her sister in the reflection as she did so.

"Jimmy?" Ava put her hands on her hips. Tessa had set her up... again. "Who's Jimmy?"

"Pete's friend."

"Who's Pete?" Ava threw her hands in the air.

"The marines? You know, the ones meeting us at the dance tonight? I wonder if you ever listen to a word, I say." Tessa primped her hair unfazed. "Well?"

"Well, what?"

"I promised the boys we'd be there when it starts."

"I didn't make the promise."

"If you don't go, who will dance with Jimmy?"

"We both know full well there will be plenty of girls at the dance."

"Are you going to break the heart of a man going to war?" Tessa pressed down on the long jacket seemingly satisfied with her appearance.

"Tess, don't be overly dramatic."

"But I want you to go." Tessa sulked when Ava's no-nonsense stare fell into place. "You don't do anything fun anymore."

"Tonight's not going to work for me, but you go have a good time."

When Tessa realized Ava wasn't going to budge, she sighed loudly enough for anyone in the next room to hear. "I'm going to be late trying to force you to have a good time."

Ava smiled when her sister rushed out the door yelling back not to wait up. She knew if she'd held out long enough, Tessa would move on to her next victim. She had gone to every dance since the war started. She claimed she was doing her part to lift the spirits of the soldiers, but Ava knew she went to get attention from overly adoring men waiting to depart overseas. Ava looked into the same mirror Tessa had just vacated. Staring at her own reflection, she wondered how she could dance with strangers, when her heart belonged to Dean?

The clock chimed in the living room, breaking her concentration. For the first time that day, Ava felt a flutter in her stomach. She grabbed a light coat off the hook, pulled up the hood and rushed out the front door. She held her breath. She did so each day hoping for a letter from Dean or Grayson.

The rain sprinkled on her as she walked to the sidewalk, her heart filled with anticipation. She opened the front of the mailbox and pulled out a stack of letters. Sifting through them, she looked for one with Dean's writing. Becoming more disheartened as she got toward the end of the pile. She had nearly given up when she reached the last letter. The scroll of Dean's handwriting lifted her spirits.

Ava held it close, running back to the shelter of the porch. She could care less about her damp surroundings; she opened the letter and sat down on the porch swing.

My Dearest Ava,

It's only been a few months and I've read all of your letters. In all honesty, I've read them over multiple times. I miss you. Wherever I go, know that I am thinking of you.

Due to military secrecy, I don't yet know where they are shipping me or if I'll even be able to say once I get there. After basics, they put us on a train, then a ship headed to the Pacific. Grayson and I are together so far. Whether that will remain is still to be seen. For now, we have each other and it's been a nice distraction.

I had grand plans of becoming a Navy pilot, but since I don't have experience, they will be training me as a gunner. The plane we will be flying is called "The Avenger." It holds three guys: a pilot, a gunner, and a radioman. Grayson's height was a bit of a challenge and he had *more experience with radios, so they gave him that position.*

Once we reach our destination, we'll be going on test flights. It's been a challenge taking off and landing from the aircraft carrier. It hasn't registered yet, that one of these days our flights will be real.

Based on the rumors floating around the ship, they want men in planes the minute we arrive. Basic training taught us it's imperative to remain focused, after all, our lives depend on it. I wish I had more time to write, but we are being called out for another drill.

Love, Dean

Ava folded the letter, holding it against her. It had been a relief to hear news from Dean. She hadn't received a letter from Grayson. Dean's letter made it seem they were both doing well. Knowing they were together; she breathed a sigh of relief. The breeze picked up, sending a chill through her and she made her way inside. For now, her boys were safe, and she would carry that with her until the next letter arrived.

CHAPTER 20

Dear Diary,

Only one letter from the boys has arrived. I checked with their parents and they have each gotten one as well. I tell myself the mail is slow and there is nothing to worry about, but the worry finds a way regardless.

We have all come to the conclusion that being on a boat is making it more difficult to get to port and ship mail out regularly. I remain hopeful, waiting and knowing they are bound to arrive soon.

We are adjusting to a new normal here at home. Mother has taken to entertaining and feeding soldiers passing through who are waiting to ship out. I look at these strangers and all I see is Dean. We share a commonality that has brought the nation together. It's as if all of America is our hometown and everyone is family. We all hope for a resolution and pray our endurance will lead us to victory over the enemy. I do not wish to be at war, but I'm proud of how the country has responded with unity.

Ava grabbed a few sticks of celery as she began assisting her mother with dinner preparations. Her father came around the corner in coveralls. Seeing him dressed so casually had taken some getting used to.

A few weeks after the war started, her father took on more job responsibilities at the factory. Machine shops across the nation had been transformed into factories to make various items for the war effort and their small town had been no exception. The able-bodied men who were too old to fight, were now working long hours at the plants.

"Father, will you be joining us for dinner tonight?"

"Not tonight, sweetheart. It's my turn for the graveyard shift."
Ava's heart sank. She hadn't seen her dad in weeks. She'd been relieved when he'd been too old to be drafted, but he still wasn't home and working long hours. She worried the work would soon take a toll on his health.

Noticing her disappointment, he pulled his oldest daughter into a hug. He smelled of Old Spice and shaving cream. Even when things seemed to be falling apart around her, they faded away when her dad hugged her. He'd always been there to protect her and always would.

"In that case, we will make sure you are well fed."

"Your mother's cooking hasn't let me down yet." He kissed his wife on the cheek as she stood stirring a pot on the stove. "It's the reason I married her."

"Oh, Benjamin." Her mother shooed him away. Even though her family was dealing with rationing, her mother always found a way to make the most amazing meals.

"Now, where's my other daughter keeping herself?"

"She's down at the harbor inviting a few marines over for supper."

"I can't say I'm fond of Tessa flirting with strangers, but I remember how it felt to have a home-cooked meal when I found myself far from home."

"I hate it when you work the graveyard shift."

"We all must do our part." He wrapped his arms around her mother looking at the counter. "Is that the most recent *LIFE Magazine*?"

"Yes, dear."

"This should keep me entertained on my lunch break." He picked up the magazine, rolled it into a cylinder and put it under his arm. With one last kiss on the cheek, he left for work.

Ava's mother quietly prepared the meal as she sat at the kitchen counter cutting more vegetables for the stew. Her mother had been quieter than usual.

"Mother, how are you feeling?"

"Fine, dear."

"You seem quiet."

Her mother stopped what she was doing to check the rolls in the oven. "I suppose I have a lot on my mind these days."

"You mean with father's new work schedule?"

"That's part of it. I do worry about our men overseas. It concerns me that you girls must go through a difficult time like this. Your father is doing his part, but he's not cut out for manual labor." Her mother stared at the vegetables in front of Ava. "I don't wish to complain, but I still can't help but be anxious."

"Tess and I can handle ourselves." Ava reached across the counter and touched her mother's hand. "We have a good example to follow."

"Thank you, sweetheart." Her mother went back to her task but not before a tear slipped down one cheek. Clearly upset but not ready to talk, Ava continued cutting vegetables until her mother broke the silence. "Have you gotten any mail?"

"Just one letter from each of them." Her mother's attempt to divert the conversation worked but only because Ava played along. Her mother knew if she'd gotten mail, she would have come in shouting excitedly.

"I know it's hard not to hear any news."

"I think about them all the time."

"I'm sure they appreciate your letters." Her mother studied her from across the counter, but it was Ava's turn to avoid eye contact.

"It seems so," Ava laid her chin on the top of her hands. "I can't help but wonder if they are getting anything I send."

"I'm sure they are. It could be months before we hear anything."

"I hate waiting." Ava followed her mother to the dining room and began setting the table for their guests.

"I wonder how many stragglers Tessa is bringing back this time?"

"It's Tess. She's bringing as many as can fit around the table." Ava laughed knowing Tessa was bound to come in with a young man on each arm, both equally vying for her attention.

"I don't know what I'm going to do with that girl, she's bound to have one of them fall head over heels and end up breaking their heart."

"I presume she's gotten over her crush on Grayson." Ava continued to set the place settings but stopped short, hoping her mother had missed it.

"Grayson?" Her mother came to a halt. "Our Grayson?"

Ava covered her mouth, her eyes wide. "I wasn't supposed to tell—"

"Don't worry, sweetheart. Your secret's safe with me." Her mother smiled knowingly. "If she's moved on, I doubt she'll be concerned you mentioned it."

"At one point, she was writing to Grayson on a regular basis but if she's moved on, I may need to pick up the slack in her place." Ava set down plates as she walked around the room.

"She starts off with the best of intentions."

As if on cue, the front door swung open with Tessa and a handful of military men from different branches strolling through the door.

"I'm home!" Tessa came in giggling with a trail of men following behind. Ava made eye contact with her mother who shook her head. Ava's heavy sigh lifted her bangs off her forehead. What were they going to do with that girl?

CHAPTER 21

AUGUST 18, 1942

Dear Diary,

Father went before the ration board today and told them how many people were in our family, our ages and genders. They sure do need a lot of information to give us stamps and cards for groceries. We require a sticker with an alphabetic letter on the car windshield to buy gasoline. Life has changed in so many ways but it's the sacrifice that is needed to support our troops overseas.

Summer is nearly over and I'm still waiting to hear from Dean or Grayson. I've made use of the record player Grayson got me for my birthday. I decided to pick up a few popular records since I'm not patient enough to wait for them on the radio.

One record I've nearly worn out is "Harbor Lights", the song Dean and I danced to the night of my birthday. I imagine the night while listening to the song. I miss him so much and I pray every night that God keeps him safe and brings him home to me.

The afternoon sun shone through the windowpane as Ava sat curled up writing in her journal. She found herself briefly distracted by a group of giggling children dragging a red wagon full of metal down the street. They had been collecting it from the neighbors for the school metal and rubber drive.

The five of them teased one another as they ambled down the street. The oldest of the boys seemed to be giving the younger children direction. He waved his hands around clearly in charge of the entourage. Ava smiled recalling a time where she and Tessa had played outside unaware of the troubles in the world around them. The kids were so innocent and their hearts so willing to help. The ultimate motivation had to be whatever prize would be awarded for first place. Her heart filled with joy to see them tackling the task, nonetheless.

Ava caught something in the distance that gave her pause. She set her pen inside her journal, closing it. The mailman headed her way and her heart soared. She prayed that his bag held a letter from overseas. It had been nearly three months since the first letters had arrived and she knew it would be any day now. Tessa hadn't gotten any new letters either, but when she did, they usually arrived the same time as Ava's.

The mailman went about his duties. Suddenly neighbors left their homes and headed toward their mailboxes, hoping their loved ones had sent word. She waited for him to get closer until she couldn't stand it any longer. She got up trying to keep herself from sprinting. Opening the door, she waited on the porch as the mailman approached.

Walking toward the sidewalk, she was curious how much mail he had bundled up for their address. He saw her approaching and didn't bother putting it inside the box.

"I'd reckon you are waiting for a letter like the others?"

"I am. I have two friends currently fighting overseas."

"From what I hear, the military has a new mail system that will allow letters to arrive a bit faster." The mailman smiled, handing her a pile of letters.

"That would be wonderful." She resisted the urge to sort through them on the spot.

"Well, go on. Don't hold back on my account." He chuckled over her attempt at reserve.

Ava sifted through and found a pile of letters from Dean and Grayson. She clasped them tight, a large smile crossing her face.

"It looks as though you have some reading to do."

"Thank you, thank you so much." Before Ava knew it, she was hugging the mailman and stepped back quickly. His white mustache shook as he laughed. "I'm sorry," her eyes were wide.

"That happens a lot these days. And here we felt our jobs were under-appreciated." He tipped his hat, his silver hair peeking out from beneath his cap. "I do love being around when a loved one gets a letter. Have a good evening, Miss." He sauntered down the street to the people standing outside waiting for his arrival.

Ava rushed inside taking a seat near the window. Finding the oldest letter first, she'd planned to start in order. There were two letters from Dean and three from Grayson. She knew with this type of pile; the mail had been behind. The letters were a few weeks apart but arrived on the same day. She decided to read Dean's first.

My Dearest Ava,

I have now read all your letters a thousand times. Every guy on the ship is homesick, even the ones pretending to put on a brave face. I can't say where I am, but it's somewhere in the South Pacific. They are censoring the letters so I can't say much. Grayson and I are fully trained now, and I can't say either of us isn't a bundle of nerves as we are closer to facing real combat. Some guys have already gone and shared their experiences upon their return. I'm not sure if knowing what to expect only makes the anxiety worse.

I've been getting your letters but very infrequently. It appears they come in bundles each time we go into port. I pray you are getting my letters. I miss you more and more each day.

Love, Dean

Ava quickly opened the next letter. Based on the date of the last letter Dean was okay but it'd been so many months since that date.

My Dearest Ava,

I received your letter concerning things back home. I wish I were there. I know you're waiting for my return as much as I. Knowing one day you and I will be reunited is the reason I continue to put myself in a plane. I've found a place for your picture in my area when I fly my missions. You remind me what I'm fighting for.

The pilot of our plane is Ronald, but the fellas nicknamed him "Tex" because he's from Texas. He's a tough guy, always giving the group a hard time but in good fun. Our lives are in his hands, so he's admired around the ship. He got ahold of your picture and showed all the fellas telling them I had a dame back home that reminded him of Gene Tierney.

At first, I was embarrassed he was showing your picture then angry when he wouldn't return it. He told me we could bet on the next Navy boxing match and if I won, he'd give it back. He also said a few things I'll refrain from saying in this letter. They said if they had a girl like you to fight for, they would do anything to return as soon as possible.

Tex finally gave me your picture back; I think Grayson may have said something. He's the only one who can match Tex in size. Seeing your photo, more than ever, I wish to be home. I'm thinking of you every day and know you are thinking of me too.

Love, Dean

Ava closed her eyes. Dean was being picked on by his shipmates on her account. A few years back he was the big man on the high school campus. But now he found himself in a whole different situation. She opened the first letter from Grayson. Maybe he'd shed light on the part Dean had left out.

Dear Ava,

I hope this letter finds you well. We have completed our training in the plane and will soon be soaring over the battlefront. I've been given the position of radioman in the rear area of the plane. I didn't think about how small everything was going to be or maybe I'm just huge. The bunk beds are stacked three guys high. I'm on the top bunk, which isn't bad. The humid weather is hot, musty and nearly unbearable when you're not topside. It appears we are somewhere in the South Pacific and while the water is beautiful, it's been an adjustment getting our sea legs.

Dean and I are taking time to write every spare moment. I have gotten your letters and they have been a godsend. Mother writes too, but hers are not as entertaining. Please don't tell her I said that.

Yours, Grayson

Ava smiled over Grayson's last words. His mother wouldn't care what he said as long as he remained safe. She made a point not to share that specific letter with his mom. She tucked it away, so she'd remember and moved on to his second two letters.

Dear Ava,

One of my shipmates received a record player from back home. No one knows if it's okay to have on board, but the Admiral hasn't said anything yet. Our leadership is firm and tends to forget we are regular guys turned soldiers overnight. Even though they don't say it out loud, they seem to be sympathetic to certain situations. Occasionally they overlook things because I think they are in the same boat.

They played some of the hits from back home and it made me think of you, Tess, and Dean. I wish to be with you all and yet I know what we are doing here is important. Please keep writing and know how much your letters mean to both of us.

Yours, Grayson

Dear Ava,

It appears everyone on this ship now knows who you are. Dean allowed your picture to be removed from the plane by our pilot, Tex. He saw it sitting out in the open which made Dean an easy target.

The guys like to play practical jokes to balance out the tense situations. Dean is the most recent victim. He practically chased Tex around the boat as he held your picture up, showing it to every chap who would take a look.

We learned straight away to keep our personal lives out of reach, or they could become the following day's entertainment. I felt bad for Dean after a few hours and confronted Tex. He thoroughly enjoyed the torment as Dean's mouth has gotten him into a bit of trouble here and there. I managed to arrange a deal with Tex and got your picture back.

It's now safely in Dean's possession, but I can tell you without a doubt you are the talk of the ship. I can only imagine you blushing right now but please don't. I think you gave these lonely schmucks a reason to keep fighting. They all want to hurry back and find a girl like you. I look forward to your next letter and hope you are well.

Yours, Grayson

Ava's face warmed and not from the heat of the summer. Relieved, Tessa wasn't around to see her face, especially knowing she would carry that information with her for future use. How could Dean have been so careless? She'd been the talk of the ship. Ava held her head in her hands.

Before she could read through the letters a second time, the air-raid siren rang out. Ava caught her breath as the siren wailed in the distance. When had it gotten dark outside? She made haste, quickly closing the blackout curtains next to her. It wasn't long before her family found her in the living room, everyone making sure they were accounted for before turning out the lights. It had become a habit to get inside as quickly as possible, shut off all the lights, and sit in the darkness until they were told they could go back to normal by the air warden. Unlikely they were under attack; Ava couldn't help the panic that lingered every time they had to wait in the darkness.

While they sat in the dark, Ava updated the family on the letters she'd received. Her father laughed when she got to the part about her picture being passed around—whereas her mother seemed shocked over the behavior. Her father reassured them the men were only teasing, but neither Ava nor her mother cared for the idea.

"If only their mothers knew."

Ava could feel her mother's disapproving stare through the darkness. Tessa began to giggle over their mother's comment, knowing the men had probably done worse things. Her father joined in, and eventually the living room erupted in laughter.

CHAPTER 22

OCTOBER 25, 1942

Dear Diary,

We are nearly ten months into the war and it's still not over. I wasn't expecting it to be over anytime soon, but each month feels like an eternity.

Folks in town are already talking about some of their loved ones that will not be returning. The reality is the longer our troops are overseas, the higher the risk they will be injured on one of their missions. Lord, keep them safe today and each day to come.

Ava regretted the decision to ride her bike to pick up groceries instead of taking the car. Luckily, her mother hadn't needed anything that would spoil due to the unexpectedly warm Fall day. She situated the brown bag in her basket and began to peddle down the street. The wind trickled over her sending a cool breeze across her neck the faster she peddled.

Grateful for the relief provided by the shade of the large trees covering the sidewalk, she turned the corner into her neighborhood. She rode along at a quick pace until she approached the corner of Thirtieth Street where she came to a sudden halt. Clasping the handlebars of her bike, she froze.

In the shadow of an old elm tree, she saw a Western Union messenger. Her father had mentioned they may see more of them in the coming months. Struggling to catch her breath, she watched as the boy—no older than fifteen—put the kickstand down on his bike. He pulled a telegram from his pocket, solemnly making his way to the porch. He paused, removing his hat.

Gradually making his way up the steps, he knocked. A moment later, the door opened. A woman stood there, holding a dish towel. Ava watched as it fluttered to the ground in slow motion as the woman's hand covered her mouth. She regretfully accepted the telegram the boy offered.

He dropped his head out of respect as the woman opened the envelope. She fell to her knees with a cry that echoed through the quiet neighborhood. A man came up behind her and knelt next to his wife wrapping her in his arms.

The boy said something to the man, put his hat back on and turned to leave. Ava saw him use the back of his hand to wipe his eyes. He pointed his bike in her direction and began to peddle her way. As he got closer, she could see he was upset and her heart broke. Waving him over, he stopped in front of her, his head low.

"Are you okay?"

"Yes ma'am." The boy nodded looking up at her. His blond hair stuck out from beneath the front of his cap, which seemed a size too big. His blue eyes glistened in the daylight and she noticed a slight dimple in his chin.

"What's your name?"

"Oliver."

"How old are you Oliver?"

"Fourteen."

"Have you delivered many messages?"

The boy swallowed. "This was my first one."

She laid her bike against the elm tree and leaned down to his eye level. "I'd say that's enough for one day." She adjusted his cap and touched him on the shoulder. A hint of a smile broke through over her attention. "Will you be okay getting home on your own?"

"Yes ma'am." His bike teetered as he worked to steady it.

Her hand to her chest, she knew this would not be the only message he would deliver. Looking back toward the porch; Ava noticed the grieving couple had disappeared inside.

CHAPTER 23

DECEMBER 30, 1942

Dear Diary,

I've poured myself into project after project with the hopes of keeping my mind busy. I've been part of a ration drive every month, helped a woman across the street start a Victory Garden, and babysat for the women who have husbands serving overseas. They are working in the factories to feed their families, so it's been tough.

While it's felt good to help others, I find myself constantly anxious over Dean and Grayson's safety. It's been months and I have yet to receive a letter from either of them. I'm trying not to let it bother me, because the last letters came in a bunch. At least it had been promising news to know they were still alive.

The front porch swing swayed as Ava wrote in her journal. The cooler weather was upon them, and the holiday season was coming to an end. It had always been her favorite time of year, but she found it difficult to be in a celebratory mood. She closed her eyes, taking in the quiet, tired from a long day of work. Her morning had been spent helping her mother tend to chores and then most of the afternoon babysitting for a woman down the street. The kids had tuckered her out, so sinking into the porch swing had been a welcome relief.

Lost in thought, she missed the man approaching until he cleared his throat. Ava's eyes shot open. Grayson's father. Her breath quickened. There could only be one reason for him to stop by unexpectedly. The journal and pen slipped off her lap clattering against the wooden planks beneath her feet. Ava focused on Jonathan Rockwell. His facial expression spoke the words he struggled to say aloud.

"Grayson." Her breath came out in a whisper as Jonathan made his way up the steps.

"May I?" He motioned toward the porch swing.

"Please." Ava shifted over to make room, trying to remain calm. Her thoughts raced. All the worst scenarios came to mind as Jonathan tried to find his words. Her nerves were getting the best of her.

"We got a telegram yesterday."

Jonathan hadn't finished his sentence before Ava felt a tear slip down her cheek. Her hand instinctively covered her mouth as she braced for the terrible news.

Jonathan touched her shoulder. "Grayson is hurt but he's alive. His injury has affected his eyesight and hearing making him no longer fit for duty."

She released the breath she hadn't been aware she'd been holding. "How is Mrs. Rockwell holding up?"

"We are trying to remain positive."

"Can I do anything to help?"

Before he could reply, the front door opened. Ava's father walked out; his concern immediately evident.

"Jonathan? What happened?" His large stride allowed him to close the distance in mere seconds.

Her mother joined them but soon after Ava was only half-listening. She touched the hem of her white dress. The same dress she wore the day of the picnic. She'd done her best but some of the grass stains were still evident. She recalled the day she had participated in the three-legged race with Grayson. The glint in his eye as he playfully goaded her into participating. Why had she been so difficult? He'd only wanted her to have fun.

The memory of them sitting by the Christmas tree entered her mind. He had asked her to look out for his folks—his stubborn Superman curl falling just above his deep-set eyes. The same eyes that betrayed his concern even though he'd put on a brave face. Would Grayson be a different person when he returned home? She suddenly felt anxious over seeing him again.

"I'll keep you updated once we know more." Jonathan stood to leave.

"Mr. Rockwell?" Ava stood. "Thank you for letting us know." She pulled him into a quick hug.

"Thank you for praying for my son." Jonathan made his way down the steps.

Ava watched his retreating form until he was no longer visible, and she returned to her spot on the swing. Her father touched her shoulder reassuringly as he went back inside. Her mother joined her on the swing. They sat in silence for a long moment.

"How did you manage it when father was away?"

"I had no choice." Her mother grabbed Ava's hand in her own.

"I thought Grayson...died."

"I know sweetheart." Her mother wrapped her in a hug, kissing her on the temple.

"It must be awful if they are sending him home."

"It's best not to focus on that." Her mother stroked her hair. "When he gets here, we will be strong for him no matter how bad it is."

"I won't stand it if news comes about Dean."

"We will pray it doesn't come to that."

Ava sat straight up. "Dean is alone now."

"He's got a thousand men with him. Grayson may be coming home but Dean wouldn't wish for him to stay if he's in a bad way."

"A selfish part of me wishes he could have stayed with Dean."

"We all felt better knowing they were together."

The creaking sound of the swing filled the night air as they rocked slowly under the porch light. There was nothing more they could do but hope for the best outcome and pray it came true.

CHAPTER 24

L aura slowly closed the journal. Hannah had consoled Ava in the same way her own mother had when Paul died.

The evening he proposed had called for rain in the forecast, but it had only just begun by the time she'd got home. That night she received a call from his mother. Waking up a few hours later, she recalled how quickly she went from a dead sleep to wide awake as she threw on the nearest pair of clothes, grabbed her car keys and left for the hospital.

The frantic sound of rain hit the car window. Laura feared the worst for Paul. The doctors had not yet given word about the seriousness of his condition, so she worked to keep her feelings under control as she drove. She parked in the closest spot and without concern for the rain, grabbed her purse and zipped up her dark jacket as she ran inside the lobby.

She made her way through the sliding doors and a chill swept through her as the cool hospital air hit her wet face. She didn't see Paul's family anywhere, so she checked her cell to see if she'd gotten any messages from his mother Pat. The woman sitting behind the information desk wouldn't provide her any information on Paul unless she was family, so she quickly dialed his mother's number. The phone began to ring as she made her way toward the elevators.

"Laura," Pat's whispered breath came from behind her. "I'm so glad you came."

"How is he?" Laura wrapped the small woman in a hug.

"We haven't heard anything yet. John is in the waiting room. I told him I'd be back as soon as you got here."

The elevator door opened and both women entered when Pat hit the floor five button for intensive care. Blood pounded in her ears, the brevity of the situation engulfing her from head to toe. As they exited, the smell of cleaning products assailed her and she clutched her hands so tight, she could feel her fingernails digging into her palms. The feel and smell reminded her of bad memories. This time wasn't any different. They both walked quietly down the hall till they saw the entry of the waiting room. Paul's dad sat alone in a row of tan faux leather chairs. Staring down at his hands, he looked up when they walked in.

He wrapped his wife in a hug and reached out to hold one of Laura's hands. He said nothing and Laura felt herself screaming inside wanting to know what was going on behind the closed doors at the end of the hall. Instead, she took a seat next to Paul's parents and they waited.

After Pat debriefed her on what she knew, the three sat in silence. The only noise came from a television playing old movies in the corner of the room. Laura took a sip of water from the bottle John had bought her at the vending machine. She instantly regretted it as her chest grew tight with apprehension. She needed some air. Behind the hospital blinds she could see the rain hit the window trickling down in long strands as the droplets collected in one space.

"Mr. and Mrs. Dawson." A man in a white lab coat walked into the room holding a chart. He sat down on the row of chairs across from them. "I'm Dr. Huxley, the physician in charge of your son's care. I'm sorry to say your son suffered extensive injuries from the crash. Our team has done every-thing we can to make him comfortable. Unfortunately, the internal bleeding he suffered before arriving was too drastic. We have him on a breathing machine but it's unlikely he'll survive the night."

Laura felt Pat collapse beside her, and John held her close. The doctor's next words became incoherent, fading into the background. Her concen-tration only focused on his last words. Paul was dying. Laura gripped the armrest next to her as the rest of her body went numb. She wanted to run away but her legs wouldn't let her. She felt a hand on hers. It was Pat's.

"We are going to go see him." She stood with John next to her. "The doctor said you could come with us if you'd like."

Laura nodded, unable to form words. She followed the distraught couple a few feet behind, overwhelmed by her own grief. Two large metal doors on sensors opened to a large ICU area as the three of them stepped inside. The couple found their way to his room and Laura stopped outside the door to give them privacy. She hated entering hospital rooms. There was always a curtain and behind it, a loved one. She watched as Pat covered her mouth and John looked to the side. Pat began weeping and John alongside her.

Laura turned away, leaning her against the wall outside the room. She tried to catch her breath, but it came in short, small bursts instead. This would be how she would remember him. If she didn't go in, she'd only ever remember him as he had been, full of life. She held up her left hand, the ring sparkled ever so slightly in the dimly lit hall. If it had been her in that bed, Paul would be by her side. As difficult as it would be, she had to say goodbye.

She waited for his parents to exit, wishing to let them have their private goodbyes. Pat squeezed her hand as they walked past, and Laura knew her turn had come to slip into the dark room. She could hear the heart monitor beeping and a machine that seemed to be sucking air in and out. As she pulled back on the dreaded curtain near the bed, she saw Paul. His face had cuts and bruises; his head bandaged with a small portion of his dark hair peering out from the top.

Laura swallowed her fear taking a seat on the hard metal chair next to him. She wanted to say something, let him know she was there but the words wouldn't come. She reached for his hand, careful to avoid the IV. The light over the head of his bed shone down on him illuminating the top half of his broken body. She brought his hand to her lips kissing his fingers softly. She sat there, the only sounds filling the room came from the nearby machines. Seeing the distress the accident had caused, the tears broke free, blurring everything else around her.

"Paul, I'm here." Laura held his hand to her tear-stained cheek. "I can't lose you. My heart is breaking." Her whispered words received no reply. She stood and kissed the top of his head lightly. "I love you. Please don't leave me."

Laura arrived home early the following morning. Paul had passed shortly after their time together and Laura's mother had arrived at the hospital to drive her home. Her mother attempted conversation but only got muffled replies, so instead she touched Laura's hand reassuringly. Laura watched the sun rise above the horizon. She spun the engagement ring she wore around her finger; a symbol of what could have been.

She'd gone numb, losing her desire to do anything. Once home, her mother took over, preparing her room, helping her into her pajamas and staying nearby. Laura didn't leave her bed but didn't sleep either. She was living in a dream completely awake. Things seemed to be happening around her, but she took no interest. Other than a few bites of food, to satisfy her mother, she lay still in her room.

As she recalled the worst day of her life, Laura subconsciously spun the ring on her left hand. She could relate to getting dire news about a loved one and the helpless feeling that came along with it. Grayson had been lucky to be alive but the same had yet to be seen for Dean. Laura knew the chances were slim that both men would come home unharmed, but she hoped for Ava's sake that she'd be reunited with them. She'd never wish the fate she'd suffered on anyone.

CHAPTER 25

Dear Diary,

The New Year has come and gone and no news from Dean. Grayson is being transported back to the States, but it will be a while until he fully recovers. We only know bits and pieces, but it sounds like he sustained injuries to his legs and face.

The holidays weren't the same, but we tried to make it special. Mother had saved the ration stamps for months, allowing us to afford a turkey for dinner. The garden stopped producing food during the cooler months, but we pre-cut a number of vegetables and put them in the deep freeze, hoping to last us through Spring. My distraction for today will be helping with the town metal drive.

Ava pulled on the leather strap trying to tighten it across the pile of junk metal sitting in the back of the old Ford pickup. The day was cloudy, but she had worked up a bit of a sweat lugging steel pieces back and forth. She wiped her face with the back of her hand. She fought the leather strap as occasional raindrops hit her on the forehead, adding to her frustration.

Tessa came up next to her wearing a red-and-white bandanna. It held her dark hair in place, her cheeks pink from all the heavy lifting. They each wore blue coveralls and long sleeve shirts, both covered in dirt from head to toe.

"I give up!" Ava huffed, tossing the remainder of the strap over the side of the truck.

"You've been lugging metal around all day and you're going to let a little piece of leather get the best of you?"

"I sure am." Ava stood with her hands on her hips.

"Here, let me try it." Tessa took the strap, wrapped it around her hand giving it a solid yank. It slipped into place, pulling the metal firmly against the truck bed. She lifted an eyebrow toward her frustrated sister.

"Not a word." Ava turned toward the driver's door in a huff. Tessa laughed loudly as she made her way around to the passenger side. She opened her door and hopped in without effort. Ava started the car and they drove to the drop-off spot.

"Ava, there's something you should know—"

"Tessa, I'm hot, sweaty and dirty. I don't need to hear you gloat." Ava gripped the steering wheel tightly.

"I thought you might want to—" Tessa abruptly closed her mouth when Ava shot her a warning look.

The girls arrived at the school parking lot and drove up to the volunteer table where townsfolk were unloading the metal in a giant pile. Tessa unhinged the tailgate, folding her top lip into her lower lip, trying not to laugh. Ava ignored her and approached the ladies at the table to let them know who'd donated the metal.

It wasn't long before a young man, a few years younger than them, offered to help unload the truck. By that time, Ava had returned to help them get a large piece of aluminum out. After they'd set it on the ground, the young man gave her a comical look.

"You, uh… have something—" He motioned to her forehead, a sympathetic smile on his face. He looked to Tessa who motioned for them both to carry the metal away before Ava turned around.

She walked over to the side of the truck and looked in the side mirror. "How long have I had a giant streak of grease on my face?"

She violently rubbed her forehead trying to remove it. No wonder Tessa had tried to warn her. She frowned at her reflection, the oil was not going anywhere without soap and water. She leaned against the side of the truck looking up toward the sky. "This would happen to me."

"Miss?"

Ava groaned not wanting to face another human being. She turned slowly and saw Oliver, the messenger boy. A few feet away, his face registered concern. Her irritation faded when she saw him in his coveralls and blue shirt. He had on a baseball cap that covered his blond hair and he attempted a smile.

"I'm sorry Oliver, I didn't mean to—"

He held out a jar of petroleum jelly but said nothing.

"What's this?" Ava took the container.

"It's what my pop uses." Oliver avoided eye contact and instead stared at his feet.

"Are you sure?" Ava leaned down, lowering her voice so only he could hear. "Shall I keep it this way?" She winked.

Oliver shifted from one foot to the other. "You'd make anything, even grease look good." He grinned before running back to a group of boys his age. As he approached the group, he received a few slaps on the back and some hoots and hollers.

Ava couldn't help but smile. The male species didn't seem to outgrow such behavior.

"Glad to see you're in a better mood." Tessa approached her, wiping her hands together. She cocked her head to one side, examining the can Ava held. "What's that?"

"It's going to help me remove the embarrassing mark on my forehead." Ava tossed her the jar.

"What mark?" Tessa caught the jar with one hand, a smile crossing her face.

"I can't believe you didn't tell me!" Ava slid into the driver's seat.

"I tried, but you told me to zip it." She shrugged.

"You might have tried a little harder." Ava shut the door and turned on the truck. She watched as Tessa ran around to the passenger side. Letting the gas slip a bit, the truck moved a few feet and Ava heard Tessa scream. She laughed loudly as Tessa climbed in beside her. The girls grew quiet when they heard the rumble of thunder above them.

"Okay, you win. Just don't leave me here, I'm way too delicate to walk home in the rain." Tessa fluffed her hair for emphasis.

"Maybe a walk would serve you right."

"It's a grease stain. It'll come off." Tessa pushed her jokingly. "Let's go Sis, I'm famished."

Ava agreed they couldn't get home soon enough as every bone in her body called for a warm bath. It had been a hard day of manual labor, but she was confident their efforts would make a difference.

The girls stepped inside the house both covered in filth. Their mother took one look at them and ordered them upstairs to bathe before dinner. Tessa ran ahead calling dibs on the bathroom and Ava let her, too tired to move.

"Oh Ava, I nearly forgot. A letter from Dean came today." Her mother pointed to a pile of mail on the counter and Ava felt her energy returning. She ran to the pile tossing all the other letters to the side. She slipped open the V-Mail eager for the news and leaned against the counter.

"Ava if you plan to sit down..." that was all she needed to hear before she made her way back outside. Without hesitation she planted herself firmly in one of the chairs a few feet away from the back porch.

> My Dearest Ava,
>
> I'm sorry I haven't had time to write. Things here are difficult, to say the least. Each mission starts with anxiety and ends with relief. I don't know when this letter will reach you, but I'm sure by now

you've heard about Grayson. I have to say that was a difficult day.

We were in the same plane when a destroyer below pelted us. The sound of bullets violently hitting the bottom of our plane will remain etched in my memory forever. It's a terrifying sound. Grayson was hit as he was positioned near the lower side of the plane, and a few bullets penetrated the sides of the plane sending pieces of metal flying all around us.

I yelled to him over the commotion but never received a reply. Once the plane landed, they immediately got him medical attention. I paced our quarters until they let me see him face to face. By the time he left, he was banged up but in decent spirits. I sent him home with some letters knowing he'd make it back sooner than the mail. I don't know what I'll do here without my best friend. Luckily, I've made a few close pals on the ship. Take care of Grayson till I get back.

All My Love, Dean

Ava wiped her cheek. She hadn't realized when she'd started crying. She'd nearly lost Grayson and now Dean would be fighting alone. Bringing her knees to her chest, she wrapped her arms around them. Resting her head on her knees, she wept quietly in the backyard. Before long a light drizzle landed softly on her from above as thunder rolled in the distance.

"Ava?" A deep voice came from behind her. She slowly raised her head. The world around her blurred by her tears. She wiped her eyes. Her breath quickened. She gripped the arms of the chair and slowly turned. She paused trying to make out the man standing in front of her.

"Grayson?" Her voice so quiet; she wasn't sure she'd said his name aloud. Standing a few feet away in tattered jeans and a red T-shirt, he supported his weight with a pair of crutches. His face showed signs of bruising and a patch covered his right eye. His dark hair stuck to his forehead from the rain. She froze, uncertain what to do next.

"Are you going to make me walk all the way over there?" He attempted a smile.

Ava's reserve fell away at the invitation and she ran to him. One of the crutches fell to the ground as he wrapped his free arm around her. She trembled and the rest of her tears broke free, relief pouring out with each one. Dropping his other crutch, he wrapped both arms around her. Her head against his chest, she gripped the front of his shirt. The drizzle turned to rain and thunder rumbled above them. She looked up. Raindrops collected on her eyelashes mixing with her tears.

"Did I miss a new fashion trend?" Grayson tenderly wiped at the grease mark still on her forehead, his voice deeper than she remembered. He scanned her face as if seeing her for the first time.

Ava's emotions heightened by his proximity. As if sensing her apprehension, he released her, taking her hand. The rain began to pour down around them, filling the stillness with the soft sounds of water hitting the shed's tin roof.

"I'm glad you're home."

"Me too."

The rain began to soak them both but neither cared enough to move. Ava found herself so relieved that words were not needed. Only one thing mattered, Grayson was home.

CHAPTER 26

The sun's glare shone directly onto the kitchen table where Laura sat reading Ava's journal. The shadows shifted playfully across the table from the tree branches outside. Laura's stomach growled, breaking her out of her daydream. Lunchtime already? She carefully tucked the last letter between the pages where she'd found it and closed the journal. She hadn't been to the grocery store, so her fridge would be empty as usual.

More intrigued than ever by Ava's story, she had gotten up early that morning to keep reading. What had it been like to grow up in Ava's family? To be separated from the man you loved by war? She touched the cover of the journal, what a different time—a time when people seemed to genuinely care for one another and sacrificed their own life to do the right thing. Before she could dive deeper into her thoughts, the front doorbell rang.

Looking out the window, April's Honda Civic sat parked out front. She didn't remember scheduling a visit, but then it wasn't out of the norm for April to drop by without notice. She opened the door to see her friend smacking a piece of gum; her blonde hair tied back into a ponytail, and a few curls bouncing freely around her face. Silver hoop earrings and a fancy leather watch dressed up her bright pink Lady Crew T-shirt. The matching Converse brought the outfit together.

"You ready to go?"

"Go?" Laura winced. She'd forgotten their plans.

"You know I take brunch seriously." April walked in without invitation. Pointing at Laura's sweatpants she sighed. "You forgot."

Laura attempted a smile. "Maybe?" Her tone begged for forgiveness.

"Laura!" April's voice indicated slight annoyance. "You don't forget *anything*. What's got you so distracted these days?"

"How about I tell you on the way?" Laura plucked her windbreaker off the coat rack.

April put a hand to her chest stopping her. "Not until you change into something a little less, uh homeless?"

"Good point." Laura ran up the stairs.

"You really must get out more!" April bellowed up toward her retreating form.

It had been a while since Laura had spent time out with her friend. It felt good to laugh. She brought April up to speed on the progress of the restoration, Ava and Dean's story, and her frequent visitor: Dusty. The discussion eventually shifted to stories from April's weekend and hilarity ensued. To Laura, April's life seemed chaotic, but April refused to have it any other way.

The two sat at a small table outside a vintage café. The restaurant was located smack dab in the middle of downtown. Charlotte's Cafe had been their go-to place since they'd been in college. They served a weekend brunch too good to resist. Laura tackled the last bite of her Belgian waffle as April sipped on her third cup of coffee.

"I'm going to be in a sugar coma after this." Laura sat back in her chair.

"And I'm going to be on a caffeine high." April crossed her eyes for emphasis.

"Then I count myself lucky we are parting ways." Laura giggled at her friend's actions.

"I could go home and nap, but I have a project due at work on Monday and in true "April" fashion, I have not prepared my presentation."

"Should I be surprised?"

"Procrastination. It's how I work best."

"So, you say."

"Listen, it'll be great. I've perfected the art of waiting till the last minute."

"Lack of confidence is not your weakness."

"I'll take that as a compliment."

"Of course, you would."

The waiter cleared their plates and the girls continued to enjoy each other's company. April leaned to one side eyeing something behind Laura. The look in her eye all too familiar. "Well, what do we have here?"

Laura turned, inadvertently making eye contact with the man headed in their direction. He gave her a casual wave. She quickly turned; her face warm.

"Do you know that guy?" April eyed her suspiciously.

"I ran into him a few days ago... literally."

"He seems to remember you." April went into interrogation mode. "Spill it."

"There's nothing to say," Laura shifted.

"I'll ask him myself."

"Don't you dare!" Laura narrowed a look in her direction. Before April could reply, Caleb had approached their table.

"Hello." His deep voice echoed down toward them.

"Hi." Laura looked up attempting a smile.

"How is that project of yours coming along?"

"I'm nearly half done."

"*Ah-hem.*" April kicked Laura's foot under the table.

Laura sent a subtle kick back. "Caleb, this is my friend April. April, this is Caleb."

"Nice to meet you." He shook her hand.

"I didn't realize Laura had friends I hadn't met yet." April ignored the warning look Laura shot her way. "So, Caleb, how do you two know each other?"

"I helped her with an old trunk. Then we ran into each other at the hardware store."

Laura covered the side of her face with her hand, slumping slowly in her chair. Did he have to bring that up?

"Oh, you did, did you?" April leaned back, crossing her arms. "I see chivalry isn't dead after all."

Rufus started to whine. "I'll let you ladies get back to your meal." Caleb directed a charming smile at Laura. "It was nice to see you again."

"You as well."

"And nice to meet you, April."

"I assure you; the pleasure was all mine." April gave him a subtle wink.

Laura pursed her lips with a slight shake of her head when he walked away. Then unexpectedly he called back to her.

"I look forward to seeing what you do with that travelers' trunk." Caleb's eyes twinkled. She opened her mouth to say something clever, but before she could get a word out, he was out of earshot.

"That was smooth." April leaned forward.

"Oh, please." Laura rolled her eyes as she mocked April's sultry tone. "And 'the pleasure's all mine' was any better?"

"It's better than saying nothing, which you did wonderfully. You need flirting lessons."

"I can flirt."

"Not based on what I just saw."

"It doesn't matter, I have no need for a relationship right now." Laura had hoped to avoid this conversation. There wasn't much to tell but April would proceed to make up her own juicy details if she tried ignoring her. With no way out, she would have to convince her Caleb was an acquaintance and nothing more. She attempted to distract her as she'd succeeded with that tactic in the past.

"Tell me about your work presentation."

"Nice try." April eyed her suspiciously. "Caleb is a much more interesting subject. When did you meet him?"

"The day I bought the trunk."

"Hold up. You've had this guy on your radar for days and you neglected to say anything?"

"There's nothing to tell."

"Based on the way he was looking at you, there's plenty to tell."

"I didn't see anything special about how he was looking at me."

"Seriously Laura, I'm *far better* at assessing romantic situations." April played with the napkin on the table. "So, how did it happen? Did he show up out of the blue?"

"I had just arrived home with the trunk and was trying to figure out how to get it inside. I hadn't been there long when he walked around the corner with his dog."

"Go on."

"He asked if I needed help, I said yes, and he brought the trunk inside."

"What happened next?"

"That's it."

"Did you talk? What did you say? Did you offer him a cold beverage?"

"Good grief." Laura shook her head. "I can't remember every detail. It seemed like a normal encounter. He's a nice guy. Honestly, I never thought I'd see him again."

"But you *did* see him again." April eyed her curiously. "He mentioned the hardware store?"

"Not my best moment."

"Do I even want to know?" April's face contorted. "What did you do?"

"I was looking down at my to-do list and ran into him."

"That doesn't sound so bad." April fanned herself dramatically. "I'd 'run into him' if I had the opportunity."

"No, I 'literally' ran into him. The box of nails I was carrying flew everywhere, and I ended up on the ground. And the worst part? I had to sit there while we picked up each and every one." Laura looked up to see April attempting to hide a smile. "How about a little sympathy here?"

"I'm sorry, but that is too funny." April put a hand to her mouth to cover her laughter, but it didn't help. "At least he helped you clean up the mess."

"Remind me not to come to you for support." Laura's brow furrowed. "I made a terrible impression."

"Oh, you made an impression all right." April chuckled. "But let's look on the bright side, he seems interested in getting to know you better."

"Now you're stretching."

"When it comes to romance, I'm never wrong," April grinned.

"And yet, you're still single." Laura stuck her tongue out.

April swiped her hand across the length of her body. "Not everyone can handle this."

"I'll say," Laura rolled her eyes. "Any man who catches your eye better come with a healthy dose of self-assurance."

"And a healthy bank account wouldn't hurt either." Both girls burst out giggling as they continued to enjoy one another's company for the rest of the morning.

Laura walked in the front door and tossed her keys on the credenza. She stopped when they clinked against the glass vase holding the bouquet of dead roses. She touched one of the petals and it fell to the table. She should do something with them, but she didn't know what. She carefully lifted the vase, leaving a circle of dust in its place. She frowned, realizing the house needed a good cleaning.

Trying to avoid losing any more petals, she carefully walked them into the kitchen and set them gingerly on the countertop. She leaned against the counter, a finger to her chin as she looked over Paul's flowers. Inspiration struck and she clenched her hands together.

Before long, she held a glass picture frame. She laid it down, removing the inserts. She picked the rose in the best shape and pressed it between the two slides. The petals cracked some, but she replaced the glass into the black frame and assessed her work. It would not be possible to save the whole bouquet, but at least she could preserve the memory.

Not sure where to hang it, she set it on the kitchen island. The rest of the flowers still sat before her. The water inside had dried up long ago, leaving calcium rings all the way down the interior of the vase. Would it ever shine as bright as the day she'd got it?

She slowly removed the flower bunch, careful not to get stuck by one of the remaining thorns. Her foot pressed down on the pedal lifting the lid of the trashcan. She dropped them inside and the cover fell back into place. Laura swallowed hard. Her hand shook slightly, and her eyes began to water. If the emotions came flooding back, there would be no stopping them.

The first few months after Paul had died, she saw him everywhere. She pictured their walks in the park, his smiling face at the ice cream shop as he stole the cherry off her sundae and falling asleep to movie rentals on Friday nights. She recalled the sound of his breathing as she lay against his chest.

They were supposed to be married, have kids and hope to God they would parent them correctly. She wanted to grow old with him, making fun of each other's gray hair and wrinkles. Laura wiped away the tears. The flowers brought back the hard truth of that terrible night. Only now she could finally begin to let go.

Chapter 27

The ringing phone screamed into the early morning waking Laura from a deep sleep. Picking up her cell from the nightstand, the front screen read MOM. She debated setting it back down. She wasn't ready for a conversation this early, but she answered anyway.

"Hey Mom." She worked to rid the sleep sound from her voice.

"Hey honey. Did I wake you?"

"It's okay, I need to get up."

"Were you up late?"

"Yeah, I lost track of time."

"How is the trunk coming along?"

"It's nearly done." Laura sat up, pulling the comforter around her. She took in her last moment of relaxation before she had to start the day.

"That's wonderful, I can't wait to see it."

"You can stop by anytime."

"I'll be in the area later this week."

"You won't believe what I found inside." Laura knew her mother's love of history and couldn't wait to share the story with her. "An old journal was inside from the 1940's."

"That's amazing. How do you suppose that happened?"

"That's where it gets interesting. I found it in a false bottom. No one would have known about it unless they peeled back the fabric on the inside."

"Did you read any of it?"

"I have. Based on what I can tell, I don't think the owner intended to leave it behind."

"Does it say who it belonged to?"

"Her name was Ava Sutton. She began her entries just days before World War II. She continued to write after the attack on Pearl Harbor. It also has the love letters she shared with her sweetheart after he left to fight overseas."

"Wow Laura, that's incredible. What are you going to do with it?"

"I considered trying to find her relatives, if that's possible. I'm going to finish reading it and see if I can't pick up any more clues. Her story is very intriguing and maybe it'll give me an idea where to search."

"I bet the family would love to have their precious mementos returned."

"It's been eighty years, but I suppose there is a possibility I could track her family down, in fact they may live nearby."

"Oh really?"

"A few of the letters have a legible address printed on the front. I think I recognize the street name, but I haven't investigated beyond that. I have to say, the story itself has me intrigued."

"I love a good mystery. I can't wait to come by, so you can fill me in on all the details."

"I'd love to."

"I'll let you go. I wanted to check in on my girl, make sure she is doing okay."

"To be honest, Mom, last night was difficult."

"Another nightmare?"

"Not this time," Laura swallowed hard. "I decided to throw away Paul's flowers."

"Oh honey, do you want me to come over?"

"I'll be okay. The trunk and the journal have been a nice distraction."

"If you change your mind, you're welcome to join your father and me for dinner this evening."

"I appreciate that Mom, I really do, but I'll be okay. Besides, I'm looking forward to doing a bit more reading today. I'm nearly done with the journal and I'm curious to know how it ends."

"Okay sweetie, well I'll leave you to it."

"Mom?"

"Yes?"

"I love you."

"I love you too, honey."

Laura could hear the loving tone in her mom's voice as she responded. She clicked the red button ending the call. Kicking off the covers and avoiding the temptation to hang around in her pajamas all day, she jumped in the shower.

After her shower, Laura opened the journal. Would Dean return home? Could Grayson be sent back overseas? What would life entail for Ava and Tessa? By this point, Laura felt as if she knew them all personally. Reading the journal felt like going back in time and visiting old friends. Times were simpler then. Life may have been more difficult, but people genuinely cared for one another and weren't afraid of the personal sacrifice it took to protect those they loved.

Laura sighed as she looked out the window. If only today's world could be more like the 1940's. Laura found herself in the middle of her daydreaming when she heard meowing from the back room. She rolled her eyes and walked to the workroom. She could see Dusty sitting outside, his Cheshire grin in place.

She sighed as she opened the window to let him in, and he followed her to the kitchen where she took a seat at the table. The cat found a cool spot on the tile floor and Laura opened the journal to where she'd left off the day before. She dove into the next entry and it wasn't long before she was transported back in time.

Chapter 28

February 28, 1943

Dear Diary,

It's almost a year since I said goodbye to Dean at the train station. Each month feels like a decade since we parted and yet it doesn't seem real to have been separated for so long.

It's been a few weeks since Grayson's return, and although he tries to seem upbeat, he's not the same. I didn't expect he would be, but he is unwilling to talk about his time overseas. I fear he will continue to carry the burden of his injuries both physical and emotional on his own. The damage to his eye has made him unfit for duty and he will never fully recover his vision. The glasses should help when he gets them, so he plans to work at the bank but doesn't seem thrilled about it. The guilt of not being able to return seems to be taking a toll. I wonder how much Dean has changed. I don't expect he's the same man either, but I hope the war has not changed him so drastically he is unrecognizable.

Grayson gave me Dean's letters and I've read them all multiple times. From what I know, he sounds okay. Although, I can tell he's leaving details out for my sake. I suppose I am grateful. The less I know, the less my imagination will run wild with terrible assumptions.

Ava pulled at her ponytail hoping to tighten its hold. She gave her gardening outfit a once-over. The dark-blue coveralls were clean, and her checkered red-and-blue shirt was rolled up at the elbows. She adjusted the matching red bow and decided it wasn't perfect, but it'd do. It'd been a year since she or Tessa had bought a new dress. She looked down at her left pant leg and pulled at the denim loop. She had been shocked the day her father told her it was meant to hold a hammer.

"Ava!" Tessa screamed from downstairs.

"Coming!" She ran from her room and took the stairs two-by-two galloping toward the bottom. Tessa stood in a pair of overalls also; her green and white plaid shirt complimenting her olive skin tone and dark locks.

"Girls, how many times do I have to tell you not to yell in the house?" Her mother called out from the kitchen.

They walked over to their mom as she stirred what looked like a muffin mixture and each simultaneously kissed her on the cheek before running toward the front door.

"No running either!" Their mother's voice rose an octave. With all their flaws regarding respectable behavior, their mother had been proud of how she and Tessa were supporting the war effort.

The girls walked up to the community garden where the townsfolk had come to harvest fruits and vegetables. They had been lucky with a warmer year, so they were able to plant a little earlier than usual. They checked in with the woman in charge, took out pairs of garden gloves, and began to fill their wicker baskets with whatever they could find.

Shortly after arriving, the high school boys began flirting with Tessa. Ava could hear them making bold claims they'd soon be eligible to go to war and fight for a girl like her. Tessa played along, though she never committed to any of them. Ava rolled her eyes.

The way the young men fawned over her sister bordered on ridiculous. She knew Tessa took extra care in her appearance specifically to drive them wild and it worked every time.

Ava continued pulling up vegetables but struggled with a carrot that wouldn't budge. She tugged and twisted with no luck. A large hand reached over her shoulder plucking the carrot up, roots and all. Ava jumped at the sudden intrusion to her personal space. Her reaction sent her reeling backward, and she landed on her backside.

"Grayson James!" Grayson moved down on one knee in front of her: a roguish grin crossing his features. He held out the carrot, his deep laughter filling the air. Ava snapped it away, pursing her lips. Her backside now covered in dirt, she attempted to stand. Grayson reached for her elbow, but she pulled her arm out of reach.

"You've helped enough." Her balance shifted once again, landing her right back where she started. Ava flung the carrot in his direction, hitting him square in the chest.

"What was that for?" Grayson attempted to disguise his laughter but to no avail.

"For scaring me half to death." Satisfied to see the carrot left a dirt stain on his denim shirt, she stood wiping away the soil on her pants.

"You didn't have to take it out on the carrot." Grayson attempted to swipe at the mud with no progress. His Superman curl had grown back, and a pair of dark glasses had replaced the pirate patch he'd come home wearing. The cleft in his chin made him a close doppelganger to the comic book hero. He stood with the use of a cane now. His silhouette covered her, but she shielded her eyes as she looked up at him.

"You deserved it."

"Gardening has become a violent hobby since I left."

Ava leaned down and picked up her basket. She walked over to where the rogue carrot lay and dropped it inside along with the rest. Grayson hobbled after her as she made her way towards the main table to turn in the items. Ava picked up two new baskets and turned around. She walked toward him pressing one of the baskets into his stomach, satisfied to hear him grunt in the process. She smiled to herself, calling over her shoulder.

"Well, come on then. The vegetables won't pick themselves."

Ava stood chatting with the ladies at the main entrance when Tessa rushed around the corner of the building, a frantic look on her face. She approached in a flurry, nodding a quick hello to the women in the group.

"We need to talk." She whispered for Ava's ears only.

"Excuse us ladies, but it seems I need to go check on something." Ava hugged them goodbye, thanking them for coming out to help with the community Victory Garden. Tessa pulled on Ava's arm dragging her to the car. When they were safely out of hearing distance, she spoke.

"Ava, I have news." She took a deep breath. "Grayson."

"What about him?" Ava eyed her sister.

"I overheard his mother talking with him today and this is big news." Tessa clasped her hands theatrically.

Ava rolled her eyes. "Everything to you is big news."

"I know, but this is bigger than most of my other news."

"Stop rambling and tell me already."

"I'm not responsible for what I'm about to say." Tessa hesitated, looking around them as if to confirm they were truly alone.

"Tessa," Ava put her hands on her hips and lifted an eyebrow. "Are you going to get to the point? I have things to do other than indulge your dramatic inclinations."

"I was standing behind a large garden trellis in the Victory Garden when who would end up on the other side but Grayson and his mother."

"So?"

"They didn't know I could hear them and Ava, she was talking about *you*."

"Me?" Ava's brow furrowed.

"She asked Grayson if he was ever going to tell you the truth."

"The truth about what?"

"Ava, Grayson has feelings for you. Apparently, he has for quite some time."

"That's ridiculous." Ava turned away, but her stomach dropped. There was no way this was true, it couldn't be.

"I'm serious."

"Tess, that's not possible. You must have heard wrong."

"She said he wasn't being fair to himself or to you by not telling you how he feels."

"We've been friends forever, nothing more."

"If what Mrs. Rockwell said is true, he's had feelings for you since you were kids. He's just been too shy to say anything."

"There is no point in discussing it further, I'm involved with Dean and that's all there is to it." Ava had a strong desire to escape. She needed time to digest. Turning in the opposite direction, her mind reeled, recalling every time they'd been together since he'd been home. Had she given him the wrong impression?

"Now that I think about it, it makes sense." Tessa continued to drone on as she worked to keep up with Ava's pace. "Why he asked you to write to him, why he came to you on Christmas night asking you to watch over his family, the subtle flirting, the reason he never returned my feelings."

"Your feelings?" Ava halted; Tessa nearly bumped into her from behind. "Did you ever tell him how you felt?"

"I did... the night of your birthday party." Tessa grimaced. "He said he was flattered but he had feelings for someone else." Tessa's head dropped. Her next words were barely audible. "He must have been referring to you."

"Oh Tess, it's not true, it can't be." Ava touched her shoulder reassuringly. She'd regretted that her sister had overheard what she did.

"For what it's worth, he told his mom he wasn't going to say anything."

"I wish you'd taken a page from his book."

"I thought you'd want to know." Tessa's excitement faded.

"This only complicates things. How am I supposed to be around him and pretend like I don't know?" Ava briefly felt sorry for her sister. It wasn't her fault.

"Grayson obviously cares for you and has for some time. Doesn't that mean anything to you?"

"I can't talk about this right now." Ava turned away, her face warming under the circumstances.

"I'm sorry, I thought—"

"Tess, you didn't think before you spoke." Ava's words were harsh, even to her own ears. She instantly wished she could take them back, but she couldn't see straight. "We'll talk about this later." She walked home, hoping it would give her time to think.

CHAPTER 29

Ava let her foot drag slowly across the wooden porch as she swayed on the swing. Alone in her thoughts, she'd avoided Tessa all evening. She felt confused, even a little bit guilty. Had she unintentionally led Grayson on? Had it been her fault he might have feelings? She'd cared for him for as long as she could remember. He'd been one of her closest friends, but she'd never considered more than friendship with him. They'd always teased one another and maybe some would say they were flirtatious. Her stomach turned. What if Grayson had misread her? Even worse, had Dean ever felt betrayed by her friendship with Grayson?

Ava couldn't breathe. Her looming headache intensified as she struggled over what to do next. She didn't want to hurt Grayson, but would it be fair to continue spending time with him? Her heart ached at the thought of Grayson not being in her life. If he'd had feelings, why hadn't he mentioned it before? The thought had never crossed her mind that falling in love with Dean would change her friendship with Grayson. Ava scratched the peeling paint on the arm of the swing. The cool air blew across the deck and she rubbed her arms. The sound of footsteps nearby caused her to look up.

"Grayson?" Her voice squeaked. What was he doing here? She wasn't ready to face him. He held a box wrapped in Christmas paper.

He pointed to the swing. "May I?"

Ava didn't respond; but moved over to make room. He sat down jolting the swing backward. Her heart began to race. She didn't know where she stood with him and now, he'd caught her off guard. She shifted awkwardly, forcing a smile. He'd always been able to sense when things were off with her. It took everything within her not to give away her discomfort, but she could feel his eyes on her, so she didn't turn to face him.

"Are you okay?"

Ava lyingly nodded. She swallowed, faking a smile. Needing a diversion, she pointed to the gift. "What's this?" She noted the perfect folds and cuts. Mrs. Rockwell must have wrapped it.

"It's for you."

"My birthday and Christmas are long past, I don't understand."

"I missed the chance to give you your Christmas present." Grayson held out the gift, but she didn't take it. "What's wrong?"

Ava had never been more aware of how she interacted with him. Her subconscious controlling her actions, she didn't wish to encourage him in any way.

"Grayson, I can't accept this." Ava sounded colder than she'd intended.

"I've waited a year to give it to you."

"A year?" Her curiosity overtook her common sense.

"Open it."

Ava eyed him suspiciously. She slowly removed the big red bow and took her time opening the sides, pulling back the paper to reveal a clothing box. She looked to Grayson.

"Go on." He nudged her with his shoulder.

She removed the top. Inside it held a white dress with yellow daisies on it.

"Grayson." Ava only whispered his name, overwhelmed by the thoughtful gesture.

"Do you recognize it?"

"This is the dress I wore to the picnic last year."

"If you recall, I owe you a new dress. I did take part in ruining the first one." He began talking with his hands. "A few days after the picnic, I asked your mom about it and she told me where to get it. Then, before I could follow through on giving you the gift, the war started, and I forgot about it. It's been in my closet ever since."

"I can't believe it." Ava held the dress against her.

"Do you like it?"

"I love it." She touched the yellow waist ribbon. "Only, I feel guilty wearing it when others are using older things."

"It's no different than if you'd kept it aside yourself." Grayson laid his hand on top of hers. He leaned closer. "Do you think it'll fit?"

"That is most certainly none of your business!" Ava jumped off the swing, an excuse to put some separation between. Shocked he'd suggest anything of the kind, she wanted to believe his comment was innocent. He'd never been inappropriate by nature but knowing what she knew now, she wasn't so sure anymore.

"Christmas came late this year, Ava." He stretched his arm out casually along the back of the swing, seemingly unaffected by her reaction.

She took a deep breath, but her hands began to tremble. She had to know how he felt. "Grayson?" She traced the hem of the dress, not able to make eye contact. "I feel silly even asking but do you—"

The front door swung open. Her father poked his head outside. "Ava, it's time to—" His sentence cut off upon seeing them. "Oh, hello Grayson, I didn't know you were here."

"Hello sir." Grayson stood shaking his hand.

"I don't mean to interrupt, but Ava could you come inside? There's something important I need to speak with you about." Ava placed the dress inside the box and scooped up the wrapping paper.

"I'll be on my way then." Grayson turned to leave.

"It was good to see you, son." Her father walked back inside, leaving the two of them alone again. Ava clutched the dress and box to her chest. Grayson made it halfway down the porch steps when she stopped him.

"Grayson? I forgot to thank you. You know, for the dress."

"I'm glad you like it." His eyes twinkled as he turned to leave.

Ava looked down at the new dress, wondering if her father's interruption had been a blessing in disguise. Exhausted from the turn of events, she wondered what her father might have to share that could be so important. Could she handle another emotional conversation?

Ava walked inside setting her new dress on the credenza before heading into the family room. A sullen group awaited her. What had she missed? Her shoulders sank as the weariness of the day caught up with her. Her mother eyed her wearily.

"What happened? Is Dean okay?"

"Oh no, sweetheart, it's not Dean."

Ava let out the breath she'd been holding as she joined her sister on the couch. "For a moment there, I thought the worst." Ava looked from her father to her mother and then to Tessa. "What did you want to tell me?"

Her father shifted in his reading chair; his legs crossed in front of him as he addressed her. Tessa sat next to her with the same confused look on her face.

"Father, what is it?"

"By the end of this week, I'll be on temporary leave at the factory. I'm too old to be handling the machines. They are looking to find me something in the office." Her mother remained dignified as he spoke. "We will need to make some cutbacks until we know for certain."

Ava jumped from her seat on the couch and went to kneel next to her father. She placed her hand on his knee. "Oh Father, we will manage. All we need is each other." She turned to look at her sister.

"Right, Tess?"

"Of course." Everyone saw through Tessa's attempt to remain positive.

"We will find a way to make the most of it." Benjamin placed his hand on hers.

"We will be okay, Father. Please don't worry."

"I appreciate your spirit." He stood, taking out his pocket watch and checking the time. "I'll be in the dining room."

Her family spent the rest of the night lost in their own thoughts. Tessa went to her room early and Ava followed shortly thereafter. She hung her new dress in the closet, touching the skirt one more time. She would need to keep a close eye on it should Tessa decide to borrow it without consent.

Her thoughts shifted to Grayson. If he had given her the dress a few days prior, she would have jumped out of her seat with excitement—maybe even hugged him, but now things were different. She had to be careful with her reactions. Her face warmed as she recalled the way he'd said her name earlier that night. Maybe she'd imagined it, but she sensed a longing there she hadn't noticed before.

"What am I to do?" Ava flopped onto her bed. She couldn't cut Grayson out of her life all together. She bolted upright. What will Dean say when he finds out? Or worse, what will he do? Ava settled back against her pillows holding a stuffed bear against her. She wasn't going to come to a solution tonight. For now, she'd continue as things had been, but she'd eventually have to confront Grayson for the truth. If he did indeed have feelings, her decision would not only be a difficult one, but potentially a painful one... for the both of them.

CHAPTER 30

Ava sat at the breakfast table reading the newspaper and attempting to choke down her Corn Flakes without sugar. Even though it wasn't her favorite, every meal counted. These days, whatever one take, one eats.

Tessa walked in and grabbed one of the last apples from the fruit basket. She stood and stared at Ava as she leaned against the kitchen counter.

"Good morning." Ava's eyes never left the paper.

"So, you're talking to me again?"

"I needed time."

"I saw the gift box from Grayson."

Ava held her tongue.

"Do you believe me now?" Tessa slowly turned the apple stem.

"It wasn't that I didn't believe you, Tess." She set the paper down and focused on her sister. "I couldn't bring myself to admit that what you were saying might be true."

"So, you storm off instead?" Tessa tossed the apple stem in the trash.

Ava pushed back from the kitchen table. Standing abruptly, she took her bowl to the sink. "You're right and I was wrong to act that way."

"I'm sorry, did you just say *you* were wrong?" Tessa bit down on her apple, a smile forming in the process.

"Don't get all high and mighty." Ava rolled her eyes. "You should not have been eavesdropping."

"It's not like I did it on purpose." Tessa held her hands in the air innocently. "Are you going to tell me about the gift, or do I have to go snooping?"

Ava began to wash her dish then placed it on the towel to dry. "If you must know, it was a dress. He meant to give it to me after the picnic last year but then the war started, and it was forgotten."

"I knew it. He does have feelings."

"Maybe." Ava gazed across the room.

"At least he doesn't know."

"Know what?"

"That you know about his feelings for you."

"I should hope not." She pointed a finger at her sister. "You need to keep it that way. Maybe this misunderstanding will go away on its own."

"That doesn't seem fair." Tessa frowned. "How can you ignore what's right in front of you?"

"Love isn't something you throw away because you think something better has come along. I love Dean." Ava lowered her head. "I won't give up on him because he's not here. He asked me to wait for him and I will."

"I'm not asking you to give up on him." Tessa touched her shoulder. "But you need to be honest with yourself."

"Honest with myself?" Ava's voice raised to an octave. "And what, pray tell, am I lying to myself about?"

"We were all a bit surprised the day you started dating Dean." Tessa dropped her apple core into the trash can. "Grayson is a better match for you. The only one who doesn't see it, is you." Tessa wiped her hands on a dishtowel and left the room nonchalantly as if she hadn't dropped such an emotional bombshell.

Ava stood speechless in the kitchen taking in her sister's parting words. Why had her family kept their opinions a secret this whole time? If the war never happened, she might be standing in her own kitchen, one she owned with Dean. Would it have been a mistake? Why hadn't they mentioned how they'd felt about Dean? Or better yet, Grayson?

"What has you so deep in thought?" Her mother walked into the room.

"Nothing." She faked a smile. Why hadn't her mother told her how they'd felt? Tessa did have a wild imagination so she could be exaggerating.

"Whatever you say, sweetheart." Her mother collected a few of the dishes around the kitchen and placed them in the sink. "When you are ready to talk about whatever it is, I'm here." Her mother tossed her a knowing look. She could always tell when Ava wasn't herself. Did she somehow know Tessa had let the cat out of the bag? She would speak to her about it another time. For now, she wanted to figure out what she felt first.

Ava's mother pointed to the hallway. "I brought the mail in. I think there's a letter from Dean."

"Mom!" Ava screeched. "Why didn't you say so?" She ran to the hall credenza and picked up the pile of mail. She tore through the letters in search of the one she wanted to read most. There were two letters. She set the rest of the mail down and ran upstairs. She wanted to make sure nothing interrupted her, and she made herself comfortable in the bay window seat as she opened Dean's first letter.

My Dearest Ava,

I hope this letter finds you well. The ship is different without Grayson here to keep me company. I've made friends with a few of the guys, but I'm homesick beyond belief. I wish my hometown pal were here.

I am assuming he is home by now, so tell him I said hello. He said he would write and let me know how he was faring from his injuries. I hate to say it, but things are only getting worse. We find ourselves going deeper and deeper into enemy territory. The worst part is the *silence when one of the planes doesn't return. I don't wish to burden you with such things, so I'll refrain from sharing the details.*

I have your picture; I take it with me on every mission. It's a bit worse for wear, so if you want to send a new one, I wouldn't complain. I must sound like a broken record, but I count the days until I can come home. I miss you so much, it physically hurts. Please write soon.

Love, Dean

My Dearest Ava,

I can't believe we are mere months away from the holiday season. It's hard to think we've been apart for close to a year. It is your letters that keep me going. The guys are awful homesick; all of us wishing for leave—to go back home, if only for a day. The Admiral says there's no Christmas in the Navy. He keeps a brave face, but I know underneath he feels it like the rest of us.

Tomorrow, I am scheduled for another mission. Each time they send me out, I pray to make it back safely. I'll admit I've had a bullet or two graze me, keeping me ship-based now and then, but I've been lucky all things considered. I love you Ava and can't wait to find myself back in your arms.

Love, Dean

The last letter fluttered to the floor. Dean had been shot. It had been months and she was only now getting the news. Imagining the worst, and knowing he'd avoid worrying her, the missions were becoming increasingly dangerous. She jumped off the bed and went straight to her writing desk. She'd do the only thing she could, write him a letter and send the picture he'd requested. As she finished the letter, she pursed her lips together promising herself she would be here when he returned.

CHAPTER 31

ARIL 18, 1943

Dear Diary,

Spring is here and a welcome sight. Even with The Victory Gardens in full bloom, we've had to be very careful managing the food. Tessa and I have been babysitting for the wives of soldiers who've been working in the factories. It doesn't pay much and it's long hours, but they need the help. Mother has also found ways to help bring in money here and there.

Grayson's father is still dealing with his heart condition and has given Grayson full control of the bank. He's been working with people finding ways to adjust their finances, so they can adapt to a new way of living. Women are taking jobs in factories on the outskirts of town and building some of the planes to be shipped overseas. This winter made us stir-crazy, and I am happy to see spring is here.

Ava finished drying the last of the dishes and put them away in the cupboard. The days were warmer now, but the nights were still chilly. She looked outside wishing she had something better to do than sit around listening to the radio while her parents devoured the newspaper.

She'd played cards with Tessa the night before but tonight she didn't have plans and she wanted to go out. Tessa had been asked to attend a movie with friends, so she had made her way downtown already. Ava tossed aside the dish towel and decided to take a walk.

She grabbed the second pair of shoes she owned. She could tell the bottoms were beginning to wear badly, but they were the most comfortable pair of the two. She'd eventually end up stuffing them with cardboard. It wasn't a permanent solution, but it kept her feet dry. The government shoe ration only allowed for one pair of shoes a year. Since she walked everywhere, she'd end up wearing holes through the bottom by the time it came to get new ones.

She slipped on her shoes and told her parents she'd be going out for a bit. She flew down the porch steps making it to the sidewalk in record time. She slowed her pace, not sure why she found herself in such a hurry.

By the time Ava made it to the edge of town, things seemed quiet. During the middle of the week most people were at home. The lights from the theater bounced off the street and Ava wondered if Tessa and her friends were enjoying the movie.

She continued her walk approaching the diner. While other stores struggled, the town diner managed to stay in business because, war or not, people still had to eat. Ava got closer and noticed a familiar figure inside. Grayson sat there, eating alone, most likely another late night at work. She stood frozen. In the past she would have strolled in and joined him without a second thought but now she wasn't sure.

Nothing felt different for him, but she was concerned because he had an uncanny ability to see straight through her. It didn't help that she'd never been skilled at hiding her emotions. Before she could change direction, he'd seen her and motioned her inside.

To leave now would be blatantly rude. Rather than explain an out of character response, Ava took her time getting inside the diner. Once inside, she collapsed on the bench seat across from him, and Charlotte approached to take her order.

"What can I get you darlin'?" Charlotte stood in front of her with a notepad, chewing her gum openly.

"A cup of decaf would be nice."

Moments later, Charlotte returned with the coffee and began clearing Grayson's plate. Not knowing what to say, Ava waited for him to start the conversation.

"Are you out for a nightly stroll?" Grayson shifted his notebook to one side as he focused on her.

"I had to get out of the house. I was beginning to feel stir crazy."

"I can relate." Grayson removed his glasses and rubbed the bridge of his nose.

"Rough day at work?"

"You could say that."

"How's your father?"

"He's managing to help here and there but he really should be resting. The doctor says it's his heart." Grayson sipped his coffee.

"I'm sorry to hear that." Ava had been determined not to allow herself to get caught up in the idea that Grayson had feelings for her. He'd never let on, so she pretended things were as they used to be. Eventually, after seeing one another a few times, her comfort level would return. She sipped her coffee enjoying the warmth spreading through her hands. It had been chilly by the time she'd arrived and a part of her started to dread the walk home.

"Where's that crazy sister of yours?"

"She's at a movie."

"Well, at least one of us is having fun." Grayson attempted a smile, the lines around his eyes crinkled.

The bell over the entry door chimed and some high school boys walked in. Ava recognized one or two of them because they'd been a few grades behind her. They had matching letterman jackets, so she figured they were part of the football team. They came in loud—the quiet conversation she and Grayson had been having was now over. Grayson nodded toward the group. "You want to get out of here?"

Ava nodded downing the last of her coffee. Grayson tossed

enough change on the table to cover them both and escorted Ava to the front door. One of the boys stood up from the counter blocking their exit. "Well look who it is, Grayson Rockwell, the war hero." His voice oozed with sarcasm.

"Eddie." Grayson towered over him, but the other boys stood as well outnumbering him. Ava tried to pass but Eddie placed a hand on her shoulder.

"What's your hurry Sweetheart?" Eddie sneered. "The boys and I were talking about the war and thought your boyfriend here might want to give us a firsthand story."

"He's not my boyfriend." Ava's stern response garnered a laugh from the group.

"Maybe another time." Grayson stepped between her and Eddie.

"Too bad, we were looking forward to it." Eddie pretended to be hurt over Grayson's reply.

"Not tonight."

"When we get over there, we'll do what you couldn't, end the war." The boys started hooting and hollering.

"You'll only finish what we started." Grayson protectively took Ava's arm. "If you even last that long."

"Is that so?" Eddie motioned to Ava. "At least I ain't putting the moves on Dean's girl while he's off fighting the war." The guys behind him snickered. "I'd like to see how long you last when he gets back."

"I'm escorting her home, nothing more."

"Would Dean see it that way?"

"You don't know what you're talking about."

"Dean's a good guy. It doesn't feel right, you stabbing him in the back like this."

Grayson ignored him as they passed, and Eddie pushed him from behind. Ava moved out of the way. She swallowed her growing concern. The boys were clearly looking to pick a fight.

"If you boys have an issue, you take it outside!" Charlotte yelled down the counter. Grayson took the moment to help Ava with her coat and open the front door.

Once outside, Eddie followed them pushing the front door so hard it flew open banging against the exterior wall. Ava froze, unsure what to do next. This time, he directed his comments at her.

"You're no better you know." Eddie pointed at her as he stepped closer.

"What's your problem?" Grayson stepped up, meeting Eddie at eye level. Soon all Eddie's buddies crowded behind him, but Grayson's didn't waiver.

"What if it's you tough guy?" Eddie narrowed his gaze.

Grayson unclenched his fist and instead turned back toward Ava. Eddie stood behind him fuming, his buddies prodding him by making comments under their breath.

"Hey Grayson, one more thing..." Eddie's eyes flashed. He grabbed Grayson's shoulder, yanking him around. His fist flew landing squarely on Grayson's jaw forcing him to stumble backwards. The boys behind him cheered.

Ava debated running to Grayson, who began to favor his jawline. Deciding it wise to stay put, she cringed over his bloodied upper lip glistening under the diner's neon sign. In less than a second, Grayson turned into someone she didn't recognize.

He charged toward Eddie, his six-foot frame giving him a clear advantage. Before anyone could react, he had Eddie pressed up against the wall, his arm against his throat. Eddie began to panic, gasping for air. The boys with him charged but Grayson used his free hand to shove the first one to the ground and the rest took note. Ava covered her mouth. She looked toward the diner, but no one had seemed to witness the commotion outside.

"You want a story? Let's start with basic fighting techniques." His tone was guttural, his stare unwavering. He pressed his forearm into Eddie's vocal cords causing him to yelp. "You owe Ava an apology."

Eddie looked over his shoulder making eye contact with her, his eyes begging her to call Grayson off.

"Now!" He pushed against his throat and Eddie squealed.

"I'm sorry." His voice came out sounding like a child.

"If you ever disrespect her again, or take a cheap shot at me, I'll wallop you so hard, you won't be fit for duty." Grayson removed his arm and Eddie doubled over, grabbing his throat and coughing. Grayson backed up in Ava's direction, his arms still at full length as if he was preparing for another surprise attack. When it seemed they were at a safe distance, he turned toward her. His eyes held a faraway look, his stance rigid. He looked down at her. "Are you okay?"

Ava looked over his shoulder towards Eddie then to the man in front of her. Without a word she took Grayson's arm and held tight as he walked her home.

Grayson's lip had begun to swell on the way home, but the bleeding had slowed. Neither of them mentioned the fight. Once they arrived, Ava insisted he stay and ice his mouth. Leaving him on the front porch, she went inside to gather the items she needed.

She held tightly to a dish towel as the chill of the ice inside began to seep through to her fingertips. As she approached the screen door, she noticed Grayson had made his way to the wrought-iron recliner and her father had joined him. As she got closer, her father's words gave her pause.

"Not every man would take a punch for my girl."

"With all due respect, your daughter can fend for herself. She used to beat me up as a kid and could still put up a good fight."

"That's probably true." Her father chuckled as he pulled out a cigar. "You don't mind, do you?"

"That depends. You got another one tucked away?" Grayson's voice held a hint of teasing.

Was he serious? Ava took a deep breath. When did Grayson start smoking? He'd always been against the idea. Her father had smoked all her life, but her heart sank with disappointment that Grayson had picked up such a bad habit during his time overseas.

"I've been saving them for a special occasion, and I'd say this is as good as any." Her father leaned forward offering to light the cigar for him. "It's not every day I share a cigar with a hero."

"I'm no hero."

"You put your life on the line for this country and suffered the consequences. You took on multiple guys to protect my daughter's honor." Her father paused. "That's true bravery."

"If anything, you're the hero. This war is bad enough, I can't imagine what it was like to fight in The First War."

"War is a terrible thing no matter how you look at it." Benjamin sat back in his chair. "You can live through it, but you'll never get over it."

Ava leaned back against the wall, letting it support her weight. She'd never heard her father speak of his time during the war, not even to her mother.

"There is no way to prepare yourself to take the life of another. The constant smell of death and disease. The filthy surroundings and rotten food." Her father slowly rocked back and forth as the creaking of the old chair filled the silence. "I kept my distance, didn't make many friends. I never knew if they would be around the next day." Her father sat forward. "Have you slept since you've been home?"

"Every time I close my eyes, I'm back on the ship. I can still hear the bullets from the warships below. They pierced the sides of our planes like paper and hammered the metal footing beneath us as we'd fly over." Grayson inhaled a large puff of the cigar and slowly released the smoke into the cool of the night. "Planes would return, but some of the men did not. They would send more guys right back out in their place." Grayson cleared his throat. "I suppose that would've been my fate too, but my injuries got me a one-way ticket home. So why would I do anything to go back? How am I supposed to enjoy life here, when there's still a fight to be had there?"

Ava swallowed anxiously. Would Grayson leave again? Worse yet, if they called on him, he'd go. She edged closer to the door. Her father had to speak some sense into him.

"It's not the severity of war that gets to a man, but the duration. Ironically, the longer you're there, the stronger the desire is to stay. But the fact is, your time there is done now." Her father taped his cigar on the ashtray. "External injuries heal, it's the internal ones that haunt you a lifetime. That is the real struggle."

"I could still make a difference; help win the war." Grayson ran his hand through his hair, the frustration in his voice evident.

"When it comes to war, there are no winner's son, just hundreds of broken men left trying to pick up the pieces." Silence filled the air. "It's not easy, but you need to figure out how to adjust to civilian life again. Don't let your guilt suffocate what's left of you."

Ava stood still. She knew neither of them would ever speak so boldly in front of her. Her insides turned; she'd heard enough. Wooden steps creaked behind her and Ava spun around. Tessa sat on the last step of the staircase, her arms crossed over her knees and her face wet with tears. She'd heard everything. Ava reached out to her, but Tessa stood, tearfully taking the stairs towards her room.

Ava looked down at the towel she held which now contained very little ice and had soaked her fingers frozen. She wasn't sure if she should go check on Tessa or attend to Grayson?

A split second later, her father entered their home. Looking past him, she could see Grayson in the wicker chair, his head back, his eyes closed. Benjamin eyed his daughter, saying nothing to announce her presence. Instead, he touched her shoulder and nodded toward the porch. She slowly opened the screen door and it creaked loudly.

Grayson opened his eyes attempting a smile. "You get lost?"

She ignored his teasing and instead placed the towel against his lip. He firmly stilled her hand, turning his head to the side. "Ow!"

"Sorry." Ava cringed, not wishing to cause him anymore pain.

"I told you I could do this at home." He frowned, grabbing the cloth from her.

"We both know you won't." She placed her hands on her hips. "Are you afraid of a little ice?"

"Just the person applying it." He warily placed the towel against his mouth, wincing. "Had I known you had such a rough bedside manner, I'd have let *you* punch Eddie."

"I see you haven't lost your sense of humor." Ava felt a little guilty knowing Grayson's pain came from defending her. "I can't believe he picked a fight."

"He is young and stupid."

"It seems like more than that. You want to tell me what's really going on?"

He sat up, setting his long legs on either side of the recliner. He sighed as he set the cloth on the table next to him. "A couple weeks ago, they wanted to talk about the war. I told them it's not something to be glorified; people are dying every day. They got cocky and started asking why I haven't gone back yet... said I was gutless to hide behind my injuries."

"That's a terrible thing to say."

"I didn't get mad till they brought you into it."

"Me? What do I have to do with it?"

"It's not important."

"Grayson..." Ava waited as he worked to find the words.

"Dean is a hero to them. They know you two are going together and naturally see our friendship as a betrayal to him."

Ava tread carefully, recalling the discussion between Grayson and her father. He already suffered from guilt over not returning. She touched his hand gently. "Grayson, you nearly lost your life. You earned a purple heart for your service."

"Dean is still there. They all are." He avoided eye contact, focusing on something in the distance.

"That doesn't devalue your time there or your sacrifice." Ava leaned toward him.

Grayson swung his leg over the recliner and stood. Ava stood too and in doing so she reached up, turning his face toward the porch light and inspecting his lip.

"You're lucky you don't need stitches." She lightly tapped his chin. "You'll have to forgo the lipstick for a while."

Grayson started to smile and flinched. "Do me a favor and forego the jokes for a few weeks."

"Ah, I see." She pointed to the cigar buds in the ashtray. "Your lip doesn't hurt too much to support your new habit, but my jokes are the problem?"

"I think it best I head home." He lowered his head making his way toward the steps.

Ava's smile faded. She'd clearly overstepped. "Grayson, wait." She walked towards him. "I didn't mean to—"

"I know." He touched her arm reassuringly.

Ava quickly changed the subject. "Have you heard anything from Dean recently?"

Grayson avoided eye contact; his face registered an emotion she couldn't pin down. "I got a letter but I'm not sure it's a good idea that you read it."

"Why not?"

"A guy can be far more candid with his comrade than his girl."

"Grayson?" Ava's breath quickened with concern. What hadn't Dean been telling her? "Please, let me read it. I'll worry more not knowing."

"It's against my better judgment," Grayson sighed as he pulled out a billfold from his jacket and removed what looked like a note. "but since you won't let this go..." He reluctantly handed her the V-Mail envelope, and she took it eagerly.

"I'll return it when I'm done."

"Take your time." Before he got to the sidewalk, he turned and gave a polite wave.

Ava watched him disappear into the darkness. The envelope in her hand captured her attention. She'd been so desperate for news she tightly clutched the small letter in anticipation.

The chill of the night air surrounded her. She would read Dean's letter in her room. She squeezed out the dripping towel on the sidewalk and head inside. As she passed through the living room, she gave her parents an update on Grayson's lip. When her father had initially heard what happened, he had been tempted to go down to the diner and teach the boys a lesson himself.

She dropped the towel in the kitchen sink and grimaced when she saw bloodstains. One would never expect a street fight in her small town, but the war was taking a toll on folks. Letting the cloth soak, she made her way upstairs.

Ava paused at the cracked door a few feet away from her own bedroom. She peered inside to see Tessa laying on her side facing away from the door. Hearing what their father had said to Grayson had affected them both. Ava gingerly stepped inside, the door creaking as she made her way to the bedside. Tessa didn't move a muscle and Ava wondered if she was asleep.

Stepping around the bedside, she saw her sister's tear streamed face. She squeezed the pillow she'd been holding, and Ava took a seat on the bed next to her.

"Do you want to talk about it?"

"It's not fair. Why must our country, our friends, have to fight a war we never asked to join? First father and now Dean and Grayson. I don't understand."

"I wish I had a good answer Tess. All I know is if we don't stand up for what is right, there will be nothing left to fight for."

"Father is the strongest man I know. He's still suffering and there is nothing we can do." Tessa sat up and laid her head on Ava's shoulder. "Dean and Grayson will endure the same fate."

"We must try our best to support them. That may take some understanding on our part."

"It doesn't feel like enough."

"No, I suppose it doesn't."

"I can't bear to think of the horrific situations they've survived, and here I've been selfish and spoiled reveling in the attention of soldiers as if this were some sort of game." Tessa looked to her sister. "I need to do more."

"What more is there to be done?"

Tessa got off the bed and picked up a newspaper laying on her desk. "This." She pointed at the front page. The photo showed a hospital room with empty beds, the article mentioned men would be returning from the fight in the Pacific and arriving within a few months. "They need volunteers, and I plan to be one of them."

"But that's hours from here. How will you manage it?"

"I'll figure it out." Tessa stood in front of Ava, her hands on her hips. "I can't sit around and do nothing; I need to help men like Grayson and father. Men who have no one to care for them because their family is still far away."

"Tessa, I'm not sure you've thought this through."

"Ava, who do you think cared for Grayson before he got home?" Tessa's face softened. "There are men out there who need medical assistance, they need someone to help them heal so they can return to their families."

"But you have no medical training."

"I'll learn. Besides, you said we need to sacrifice when necessary."

Ava stood and hugged her sister tight. "I didn't mean go do the first thing that crosses your mind." She held her sister by the shoulders. "Father will most definitely have something to say about this."

"I'm of age and perfectly capable of making decisions on my own."

"We will see." Ava shook her head when Tessa left to go speak with their parents.

After changing clothes, Ava brushed her hair and slipped into bed to read the latest news from Dean. She grabbed the V-Mail envelope sitting on her nightstand and pulled back the flap. A smaller piece of paper fell into her lap. It looked like a scribbled note, not a letter. Curious, she opened it and began to read. Halfway through, she gasped, covering her mouth. She finished the worn note, then slowly set it on the nightstand.

The words on the paper were ones she'd never forget. After all, she had a similar note tucked inside her journal, only that note had been written in Dean's handwriting. The worn paper sitting beside her was written by Grayson. The note listed the nineteen things Dean loved about her, the same ones he told her the night of her birthday. Why on earth did Grayson have a note with the exact things Dean had said? She had never spoken to Grayson about that night. It's possible he'd heard about it from Dean, but why would he have a written copy?

Ava's hands shook as she read the small paper again in disbelief. She gently folded the worn paper along the same lines. It had clearly been read many times over. Why would Grayson have the note in his billfold? That night had been something only she and Dean had shared. It had to be a mistake.

CHAPTER 32

A few days later, Ava walked towards Grayson's house. She strolled along and her mind went to words she'd read in the letter from Dean to Grayson.

Grayson,

Christmas has come and gone now. I wonder how many more holidays' I'll be away from home. The guys are optimistic we will have the war in hand soon, but I have my doubts. It feels like we've been gone forever and yet barely made a dent.

I know you wish you were here fighting alongside us, but the Japanese only get more brutal each day. The conditions are horrific. If I don't die in a plane, I can't say the disease or infections won't kill me. You know how it is, another day, another mission. I had a few steak dinners, but I couldn't enjoy them. You know the type of missions that follow.

For now, I'm okay but I can't say the same for our comrades. Every man down has only strengthened the resolve of those that are left. One day this war will be over, and we'll look back knowing we did what was necessary to protect the country we love.

Take care, Dean

Grayson had been right. Dean would never have sent her such

an honest letter. She'd never admit it, but her heart broke as she began to understand his situation with more clarity. Her prayers went out to all the men bravely fighting for the country.

She found herself standing in front of Grayson's house wringing her hands. Inside her purse she carried the letter from Dean along with the small note. She'd planned to return the letter but hadn't been ready to confront Grayson about the handwritten note she'd found along with it. He must not have realized it had gone missing. She'd considered ignoring the whole thing but after what Tessa had shared with her, she couldn't go on allowing Grayson to think there could be anything between them. That would be unfair to both of them. As difficult as it'd be, she had to know the truth.

Tentatively placing one foot in front of the other, she knew this conversation would change everything between them. She said a silent prayer that he'd be home. She didn't know if she could work up the courage to confront him on another day. She softly knocked, hearing the sound of her own heartbeat as she waited. The side curtain moved and then the door opened. Grayson stood there; surprise written across his face. He wore a white dress shirt with the sleeves rolled up and a pair of loose suspenders hung around his waist.

"Ava?" Grayson walked out, shutting the door behind him.

"Is this a bad time?"

"No, not at all."

"Can we sit?"

"Of course." Grayson held out his hand toward a table and chairs a few feet away. She sat down, then reached into her purse and pulled out the letter from Dean. She set it on the table between them.

"I wanted to return this."

"You didn't have to come all the way for that. I could have gotten it back the next time we saw each other."

"That's not the only reason I came." Ava lowered her head. She couldn't look him in the eye. She took a deep breath wishing she could be anywhere else.

"What is it?"

"Open it." She nodded to the letter. A puzzled look crossed his face, but he followed her instruction. As he unfolded the large letter, the smaller note fell onto the table. The stillness that followed felt unbearable. The atmosphere between them shifted. He didn't need to read the note, his audible sigh told her he knew. Slowly raising her head, she finally made eye contact. Without warning, his face told her the feelings he'd tried so desperately to hide were real. She sensed a mixture of pain and regret and at the same time he silently begged her to understand.

"I'm sorry." He folded the note and shoved it into his pocket. "You were never supposed to see this."

"Why do you have a copy of that?" Ava desperately wanted to understand. Anger stirred inside her the longer he stayed quiet. How dare he control what information she knew when it was about her?

"It's not how it looks." Grayson ran his hand through his hair and stood. He walked over to the porch railing. It creaked under his weight as he looked toward the street.

"Those are the exact words Dean spoke to me the night of my birthday—and they are in your handwriting. What am I supposed to think Grayson?"

"I wrote it."

"Excuse me?" Her eyes widened.

"He didn't know what to get you. He wanted something special so—I helped him come up with the words."

"Helped or wrote it all? Dean couldn't figure out what to say on his own?" Ava felt her temperature rising, the warm day intensifying her discomfort. Had everything she believed been a lie? Ava could feel tears surface but pushed them down.

"Dean has never been a sentimental guy." He turned, leaning against the rail.

"Don't make excuses for him." Her chair screeched across the wooden deck as she swiftly rose and marched over to Grayson.

"Did Dean say those things to win me over?"

"Ava, please."

"I don't know what to believe anymore."

"Please, don't blame Dean."

"And who else is to blame... you?"

"His heart was in the right place."

"By having you write the words he couldn't?" She felt her stomach lurch, so she grasped the railing to steady herself. Grayson instinctively reached out to her. Ava pulled away, slapping him firmly across the face. "Don't, touch me." Her voice shook. She clasped her purse tightly. "You lied to me. You both did." She strode past Grayson and darted toward the street.

"Ava, wait!"

She could hear the distress in his tone, but she prayed he didn't run after her. She couldn't bring herself to face him. Unable to stop the onslaught of tears, she ran. She ran until she couldn't run anymore.

CHAPTER 33

L aura closed the journal. She'd had enough for the day. She empathized with Ava. Having to let the man she loved go to war and then questioning if he loved her the same way she loved him. To make matters more confusing, his best friend had feelings for her. Laura couldn't imagine how hard it'd been finding out and having to confront him for the truth. Now that it had surfaced, what could she do about it?

She didn't blame Ava for being angry with Grayson but part of her felt bad he'd been on the receiving end of her insecurity and confusion. Grayson had valiantly stepped aside, sacrificing his own feelings for his best friend. He'd been her protector and loyal confidant when Dean hadn't been able to. It wasn't fair to either of them. Laura found herself wondering if Dean truly loved her or if it was the idea of her that he'd been in love with. It seemed from his letters that his love had been genuine but to what degree?

Laura counted herself lucky to have only loved one man. Paul had been the clear choice from the moment they bumped into each other. Anyone else would have been a replacement. Although it had been a year since he died, she knew the grief of losing him would haunt her the rest of her life. It wouldn't be fair to make someone else carry her baggage, it would be better to stay on her own.

Plenty of people had given her advice. She'd dealt with comments about why she had not yet moved on, but no one seemed to understand. To suddenly lose the person you'd planned to spend the rest of your life with, is not something one just gets over.

She couldn't imagine being in Ava's shoes. Two men she cared about went to war, one came back injured and the other may not return. The strength she displayed inspired Laura. She found herself wishing she had the same resolve, but it was easier to live in fear than risk falling in love. If she remained alone, she could control her environment and prevent herself from ever feeling such pain again. April had called it a prison of her own making and maybe she was right.

She didn't imagine that'd be the advice Ava would have given her, but the story wasn't over, and Laura found herself eager to see how Ava solved her predicament. For now, she had to step away from the emotions and collect her thoughts. She touched the letters on the journal softly. "My dear girl, I don't know how you managed it."

Chapter 34

May 28, 1943

Dear Diary,

Tessa informed the family she'll be volunteering at the hospital for wounded veterans. Overhearing Grayson's conversation with father really impacted her and now she wants to assist the injured men returning home.

It's been nearly a month since I've spoken to Grayson about the note I found. I do regret slapping him. I don't know what came over me. I've been carrying the guilt of it ever since, but I haven't had the courage to face him. Tessa said not only was it within my rights to slap him, but she'd slap Dean on my behalf if he weren't at war. I told her bluntly that no one should be slapping anyone, it wasn't Christianly.

I do wish Dean were home so we could sort this out. It's eating me up inside, to think, I've been living a lie. I need him to explain. The situation is so confusing, it's absolutely awful. I want to forgive them both, but I don't know if I feel guilty because Dean is still fighting while we are all home safe. Can I find it within myself to forgive such a lie of omission?

A va stood outside the grocery store twisting the wire ring around her finger. It had become a subconscious habit. She found herself waiting on Tessa as usual. Looking down at the ring she questioned her relationship with Dean. The subject had plagued her since she'd discovered the note. Had Grayson been feeding Dean lines from the beginning? Why hadn't he asked her out if he'd felt the way he did? In all the years she'd known him, he certainly had time. In all fairness, the day she'd confronted him, she hadn't exactly given him time to explain his side of the story.

"You ready?" Tessa approached her balancing a bag full of groceries.

"Can you fit all that in one basket?"

"We may need to split it up." Tessa began to separate the groceries into their bike baskets. They were giggling when she pulled out the butter substitute she'd purchased. It tasted nothing like the real thing, in fact it tasted like nothing at all. Ava's laughter subsided upon seeing Grayson walk around the corner. He came to a halt as soon as he made eye contact.

"I would not want to be in his shoes right now." Tessa leaned towards Ava, clicking her tongue.

"Tess, hush." Ava continued organizing the items in her bike basket.

"The man got himself into troubled waters if you ask me."

"No one asked you." Ava nudged her as Grayson closed in.

"Good morning Ava." Grayson nodded. "Tess."

"Grayson." Ava's voice was cold.

Silence hung in the air when Tessa spoke up. "I'd stay at arm's length pal; she's still upset with you."

"Tessa!" Ava's mouth hung open. Her sister didn't mince words, but she could have worked on her delivery.

"Well, you are." Tessa whispered back.

Grayson stood with his hands in his pockets. "You ladies have a nice day." He walked toward the storefront as if he were any other stranger that had greeted them.

"That went well." Tessa dropped the last of the items in her basket.

"No thanks to you." Ava rolled her eyes and slipped her leg over the bike frame. She began to pedal toward home, leaving Tessa in her wake.

"Hey, wait up." Tessa caught up and they pedaled in silence for a few blocks. She huffed when Ava remained silent. "Are you ever going to forgive him?"

"One day."

"He's kind of pathetic-looking."

"I didn't notice."

"See? You *are* still cranky."

"I'm hurt. To be honest Tess, I'm upset with Dean too. Only I can't yell at him right now." The girls continued to keep a steady pace.

"No, I suppose you can't, but it's no reason to hold your anger with him against Grayson."

"Is that what I'm doing?"

"It sure comes across that way."

Ava looked at her sister. She'd never truly been in love, what right did she have to give her a speech about relationships?

"In my opinion, the first step is forgiving Grayson."

"But he lied to me."

"Dean lied to you," Tessa turned toward her. "Grayson lied to himself."

"What do you mean?" The girls approached their home and ped-aled down the driveway to the garage behind the house. They put their kickstands down and removed the groceries from their bas-kets.

"Grayson lied to himself because he thought he could keep his feelings for you to himself while his best friend courted you." Tessa sounded so matter of fact, Ava could only listen in silent disbelief. "Besides, if Dean truly loved you, wouldn't he show you how he felt?"

"Men aren't the best at conveying their feelings."

"Be that as it may, Grayson's in love with you and has been for some time. He kept that secret, and now it's costing him your friendship. What if he figured it was too late for him—so he kept it to himself hoping he would get over you?" The girls began walking toward the back door. "I bet Dean is clueless about Grayson's feelings."

"When did you become so intuitive?"

"I was born brilliant." Tessa dramatically flipped her hair with her free hand. They walked into the kitchen giggling.

Their mother stood at the counter and eyed them suspiciously. "Do I even want to know?" She wiped her hands on the edge of her bright yellow apron.

"Oh Mother, I'm giving Ava advice on men."

"Oh heavens," She shook her head. "Tessa what am I to do with you?"

"Nothing Mother." Tessa pranced around on her tippy toes. "I'm perfect."

"Far from it." Ava nudged her playfully, throwing her off balance. Before she could push back, her mother interrupted.

"You girls help me unpack these things before they spoil, then I want you to help prepare dinner." They both grudgingly obliged as they grabbed matching aprons hanging on a nearby hook.

Ava turned on the radio and "Harbor Lights" floated across the airwaves, a crackling sound filling the living room. The song began to float out to the front porch, so Ava grabbed her shawl and went outside to enjoy the evening.

She sat in the recliner and closed her eyes recalling the night she and Dean danced to the song at her birthday party. The weather, the music, everything had been perfect. Pulling her shawl tighter, she imagined him holding her close. She'd been anxious, unsure if he would kiss her. Then as if he'd read her mind, he did. He'd been waiting for the perfect moment. She never could have predicted a year and half later she'd be alone.

As the song changed on the radio inside, her mind drifted to their farewell at the train station. He stood there—eyes for only her—the taste of her tears as he kissed her goodbye, the vanishing touch of his fingertips as she watched his figure move slowly out of sight. She twisted the wire ring around her finger, the metal now tarnished and worn. Her finger did have a green hue as he'd predicted, but she couldn't bring herself to take it off. It symbolized a promise: a guarantee he would come back to her.

A man cleared his throat, breaking the silence. She opened her eyes. Grayson stood a few feet away shuffling his hat in his hands.

"Grayson?" Ava sat up surprised. He found his way to a chair across from her and took a seat.

"I was out walking. I've been thinking and after seeing you earlier, I had to try and set things right."

"I'm not sure—"

"Please hear me out?" The concern on his face looked so pitiful she allowed him to continue. "Everything Dean feels for you is real. From the moment he met you he was smitten."

"If his feelings were real, why come to you for his words?" Ava adjusted her shawl around her shoulders.

"He was clueless. I wanted to help."

"Only for my birthday or have you been *helping* all along?" Ava exhaled slowly, working to keep her emotions at bay.

"He asked for advice." Grayson's tone sounded regretful. "I should never have given him the words he used for your birthday gift. I should have let him figure it out."

"And the words you wrote," she looked up, her eyes meeting his. "Were those real?"

"Yes." He barely breathed the word as he studied her.

"Why didn't you say anything?"

"By the time I got the courage, Dean had already made his intentions known." In the glow of the porch light, his face held a mixture of pain and sadness. "I had to respect that."

Ava's anger dissipated. She tried to put herself in his shoes. He'd felt so strongly and had kept it hidden for years and to have it come to light this way had to be difficult.

"How long have you felt this way?"

"As long as I can remember." Grayson leaned towards her lightly touching her cheek.

"Are you still—" she bit her lip. She was treading into deep waters. Would it be right to ask him to confess his love for her knowing it would not be returned? His eyes never wavered and without a word, she knew his answer.

"Dean will be home soon. You'll get married, have kids and grow old. Nothing has to change."

"Knowing how you feel changes everything." Ava stood hastily, walking to the edge of the porch; she stared into the shadows, her hands gripped the railing.

"I don't understand."

"I fell in love." She turned back to face him. "With two different men."

"Ava—"

"Would I be in love with Dean if he'd pursued me with his own words?" A single tear slipped down her cheek.

Grayson joined her. Pulling out his handkerchief, he offered it to her. "I spent every day with Dean and all he ever talked about was coming home to you. I assure you; his love is real."

"What about you?" She looked up at him. He'd always been a childhood friend but now she stood in front of a man and she was breaking his heart.

"If you love someone," he tucked a stray curl behind her ear. "That may mean letting them go."

"Grayson, you don't have to—"

"Ava please," his tone begged her not to try and console him.

"I owe you an apology." Ava touched his cheek. "I shouldn't have slapped you. My anger got the best of me."

"I'll make you a deal." Grayson smiled mischievously. "I'll forgive you, if you promise to slap Dean for his part in all this."

Ava's mouth hung open. "I wouldn't dare!" She snapped it shut again defiantly. The radio inside began playing a romantic song.

"I should go." Grayson cleared his throat.

"Grayson?" Ava wrapped her arms around his midsection. She didn't care if it would be deemed inappropriate. Their friendship might never be the same and part of her already missed what they shared. She closed her eyes as he held her close. She could feel the rhythmic rise and fall of his chest.

The breeze picked up and she released her hold. Grayson touched the front of his shirt, now damp with her tears. He reached out to her, but she dashed past him and into the house; the screen door slamming shut behind her.

CHAPTER 35

JUNE 10, 1943

Dear Diary,

There is still no word from Dean. I know well enough the mail can be slow and not to worry. However, this time it's taking longer than usual. It's difficult being so far away from him. Especially when we need to talk. I need to know his side of the story. I can't ask him in a letter, because he doesn't need the distraction.

Grayson has remained distant since our night on the porch. I can only imagine things are more difficult for him now that I know the truth. Honestly, I'm not sure I know how to act around him. I don't wish to lose his friendship, but I can't rightly lead him on either. Have my feelings been misplaced from the beginning? I feel guilty regardless. Is it possible to be in love with two men at the same time?

Ava wiped her forehead with the back of her hand. She'd worked up a sweat pulling weeds. The Victory Garden had become a chore with all the rain. Her mother sat on a stool a few feet away picking over the tomato vines for the ripe ones.

"The rain has created a bit of extra work today, but we will have plenty to eat." Her mother wiped her hands as she stood overlooking their progress. "Where is your sister? I sent her to the shed to get more seeds and she never came back."

"Tessa is distracted so easily who knows what's keeping her." Ava frowned as she struggled with a weed. "She gets lost within a few hundred feet." Ava continued to fight the weed in front of her. As if on cue, Tessa came toward them, but she wasn't alone.

"Ava." Her mother's serious tone caused her to look up.

Walking solemnly next to Tessa was Sheldon Wheeler, Dean's father. Ava stood slowly as they approached. Everything around her moved in slow motion. Her mind raced. No letters. His father must have gotten news about Dean. If he'd come in person, it could only be bad news.

"What is it Sheldon?" Her mother dared to ask.

"Our boy—" he struggled to get the words out. Ava covered her mouth and Tessa wrapped an arm around her. "Dean is missing in action."

Ava sunk to the ground covering her face with her hands. Tessa held her as she sobbed. Their mother hugged Sheldon, who seemed to barely be holding his emotions in check. Tessa spoke softly, but Ava didn't comprehend a word. She worked to catch her breath, but the tears kept coming. She felt her stomach lurch. Tessa helped her stand but didn't release her.

"When?" Ava tried to focus on Mr. Wheeler.

He wiped away a few tears and placed a hand on her shoulder. "The details are unknown. The plane and everyone inside are unaccounted for."

"But he could still be alive?"

"We are praying so."

"Sheldon, are you able to stay for a cup of tea?" Her mother asked.

"I have to get back to my wife, but I appreciate the offer."

"If there is anything we can do, please let us know. Our prayers are with you both."

"Thank you." Sheldon nodded his goodbye; his shoulders slumped as he walked away. The emotional burden he carried had been all too familiar to their small town.

Ava and Tessa wrapped their mother in a hug. Ava could hear Tessa weeping softly. The three of them stood in the middle of the yard, each one leaning on the other for support. Ava let out a silent prayer that Dean would be safe, and eventually return home.

CHAPTER 36

A week had passed since Ava had received the news about Dean. She lay in bed as a single stream of sunlight broke through the curtains. Emotionally exhausted but too awake to fall asleep, a majority of her time had been spent in bed. When she did go downstairs, she couldn't bring herself to eat. Her parents tried to lift her spirits by reminding her Dean had only been assigned as *missing* so there was still hope.

She tried not to think of what could be happening to him. Captured? Lost? Scared? The Wheelers weren't given much information in the telegram. They could only wonder and pray for his safety.

Ava refused to believe the worst, but her imagination ran wild. She pulled back the bed sheet and sat up slowly, not ready to face the day. The family planned to attend church that morning and if she were going to do anything, going to church to pray for Dean should be at the top of her list. If she went on living the way she had been, she would lose her mind.

After she finished getting ready for church, she went downstairs and sat on the couch. She found it unusual to be waiting on her family. Normally, her mother had threatened her they'd be leaving without her by now. Ava's family had been supportive, but it wouldn't be long before they'd expect her to pull her weight around the house. However, tending to the family's Victory Garden and sewing clothes for the neighbors left her too much time to think.

She looked at the coffee table stacked full of magazines. Sorting through them, *The Saturday Evening Post* cover intrigued her. A woman in a blue jumpsuit and red bandana appeared to be flexing. She browsed the inside for the cover article. The editorial referred to the woman on the front as "Rosie" and pushed for more women to enter the workforce as machine operators—building planes, tanks, and other vehicles for war.

"What do you have there?" Ava's father walked in, interrupting her thoughts.

"It's an article encouraging women to begin working in the factories and shipyards."

"The longer we are at war, the more we will need to rely on everyone here at home for support." Her father stood in the hallway adjusting his tie in the mirror.

"Maybe I should look into it." Ava closed the magazine and set it back on the coffee table.

"That kind of work is not for the faint of heart, my dear."

"I'm sure it won't be easy, but I could use the distraction, and it's not like the family couldn't use the extra money." Her father paused, his smile falling away. "Oh Daddy, I'm sorry. I didn't mean—"

"Ava," he raised his hand. "I know what you meant and you're right."

"It's time we get going." Her mother came into the living room to collect them for church before Ava could reply, but she decided she'd refrain from making additional comments about the family finances. It had not been her intent to suggest her father had not been a suitable provider for the family as they were better off than most.

Once the church service ended, Ava stood on the front steps waiting for her parents. Tessa had gone off with some friends deciding to come home later that afternoon. Ava became impatient and quietly told her mother she would walk home.

She looked down at the soles of her shoes. Another hole had begun to wear near the front. It appeared she would have to cut some additional cardboard inserts to prevent her feet from being attacked by the elements. Her brow furrowed as she dropped her foot back to the ground.

"Those shoes have seen better days." Grayson stood closely behind her, looking over her shoulder.

"I doubt I'll make it home with them in one piece."

"I should walk you home, just to be safe." His eyes twinkled over his own joke.

"Grayson, I don't know if—"

"I insist."

"Suit yourself." She moved onward leaving him behind.

He sprinted to catch up, walking in step with her pace. "How are you?" His voice held a hint of concern.

"I'll be fine." She hadn't planned to discuss Dean's disappearance so soon.

"Can we talk about Dean?" He pulled at his tie.

"What do you want me to say Grayson? That I think he's still alive? That I'm still in love with him? That every night I pray he comes back but know there is a good chance he may not?" Ava stepped up her pace as her frustration grew.

He reached out, placing a hand on her shoulder stopping her.

She avoided eye contact, gazing down instead. "Do you want me to say... that every moment I'm with you, I feel guilty?"

"You shouldn't—"

"I do," she looked up at him. "Don't you?"

"I don't feel guilty for spending time with you." Grayson sighed. "But when I heard the news about Dean, I was devastated. I carry the guilt of letting down my best friend. Why wasn't I there to keep him out of trouble? I promised to have his back. If I'd have been there, it would have been different."

"If you'd have been there, you would have ended up in the same situation."

"Truth is, we'll never know."

"It's not your fault." Ava studied him.

"If anything happens to him—" His expression was sober.

"I haven't slept since I heard the news."

Grayson lightly touched her chin. Before she knew it, he enveloped her in his arms, resting his cheek against her forehead.

She let him hold her, longing to feel safe and protected. Dean's image came to mind and she slowly pushed back from him, her hand on his chest. She could feel his heart beating beneath her fingertips. "We are both upset and in any other circumstance, I'd want to talk this out with you. I know you understand, but until we know for certain if Dean is dead or alive, I feel like I'm betraying him by spending time alone with you." She stepped away from him.

"I won't apologize for caring about what you must be going through."

"I never asked you to—"

"I want to be here for you." Sadness clouded his features. "But I'd never put you in a difficult position."

"You are a good man, Grayson." Ava gently touched his arm. She could see being near him was doing more harm than good. She couldn't give him what he wanted, and it was hurting him deeply. "Thank you."

"For what?"

"For loving me enough to let me go." She stepped up on tiptoe kissing him softly on the cheek. Grayson's eyes held the pain of a broken heart. She squeezed his fingers reassuringly as she turned to go. This time, he didn't follow her.

Chapter 37

Her mother looked up from her magazine when Ava walked through the front door. Setting it down, Hannah walked toward her, pulling her close. After her discussion with Grayson, Ava had not been able to make it home as quickly as she usually did. Ava returned her mother's hug and they stood there in silence before taking a seat on the couch.

"When you weren't home when we arrived, I became anxious." Her mother always sensed when she needed comfort.

"I ran into Grayson." Ava leaned into her mother's side just as she'd done as a child.

"Oh?" Her mother put an arm around her.

"He asked how I was doing."

"That's sweet of him."

"The conversation became a bit emotional." Ava played with the couch pillow nearby. She wasn't sure how to broach the subject.

"I can imagine. It's the first time you've seen him since you both found out about Dean." Her mother prodded softly. "You want to tell me what's going on?"

"How did you know father was the one?"

"We were lucky, I guess." Her mother stroked her daughter's arm soothingly. "I can't say it was love at first sight, but we knew we had something special."

"Did anyone else ever court you?"

"When I met your father, we knew from the beginning we were meant to be with one another."

"But how?"

"Your father balanced me. Where I was weak, he was strong. He saw every little flaw and loved me anyway. He cherished me."

"Do you suppose it's possible to be in love with two men at the same time?"

"I think you can love more than one man in a lifetime, but when it comes to love, I think we are only truly in love with one person at a time."

"I'm so confused."

"Sweetheart," Hannah pulled back. "Are you in love with Grayson?"

"Maybe." Ava threw her hands in the air slumping back against the couch in frustration. "I don't know." Ava buried her face in her hands. "Can you tell me what I must do?"

"What does your heart tell you?"

"I thought I was in love with Dean, but now, I'm not sure. Grayson wrote the words Dean spoke to me. If he has been helping him all along, then did I truly fall in love with Dean? If I don't have feelings for Grayson, why do I feel guilty being alone with him?"

"Can you be sure Dean never said what was in his heart?"

"I'm not sure."

"Love is more than words and feelings, it's actions." Her mother squeezed her hand and Ava looked up at her. "Even so, if the words being used aren't one's own, your heart may have been fooled by the idea of love."

"Have I been falling for Grayson this whole time?" Ava sat up. She swallowed hard awaiting her mother's reply.

"Search your heart. If you are honest with yourself, the answers will present themselves in time."

"I have been honest Mother," Ava sighed. "I only end up more confused."

Her mother pulled her into a hug and Ava leaned on her for support. The day's emotions had caught up with her. "We are living in difficult times. Life will never be easy; in fact, it only seems to become more challenging. All we can do is the best we know how."

"What if I make the wrong choice?"

"Let's not make any decisions today. There's no rush to make a choice—right or wrong." She adjusted Ava's hair back into place. "I suggest we grab a cup of tea. We can revisit this after you've had some time to think." Hannah draped her arm around Ava's shoulders. "I love you sweetheart."

"I love you more." She wrapped her arms around her mother's midsection and held her close.

CHAPTER 38

Dear Diary,

I started a job at the factory on the outskirts of town. The hours are long, and the work is backbreaking. I have yet to work a night shift, but from what I hear, it's tougher to adjust and no one looks forward to it.

My hands have become dry and calloused. I don't even bother painting my nails anymore. However, it has provided the distraction from my thoughts that I'd been hoping for. The factory is so loud, I can't hear myself think. There are times I feel crazy for even taking a job like this, but then I tell myself one of the planes I'm building could be the one that brings Dean home.

Tessa signed up for the hospital volunteer program after weeks of convincing our parents she could handle the responsibility. The hospital is far enough from our home, she's been staying in a dorm nearby with some of the other volunteers and nurses. In her last letter, she said it felt good to be making a difference. She signed up for six months, so she won't be home till the holidays. I'd never admit this to her, but it's been rather lonesome since she left.

When it comes to Grayson, I still find myself conflicted. I don't trust where I left things with Dean and now it seems there may be no way to confirm or deny it. I can't bring myself to embrace the idea that he is not coming home. I still love him, and a part of me always will.

A va sat in the bay window of her room when her father walked in, a solemn look on his face. He approached her without a word and reached into his vest pocket, removing a letter.

"Your mother and I weren't sure how to—" Ava grabbed it, tearing it open, everything else forgotten. Her eyes quickly scanned the letter. It was from Dean. She didn't notice her father quietly making his exit.

My Dearest Ava,

Your letters from home have been a godsend. I appreciate you checking on my mother. She worries about me. Every letter she sends, she asks when I'll be on leave. I'm glad to hear Grayson has fully recovered and has been able to be there for his parents.

I can't believe it's been another year and we are still fighting this blasted war. More planes go missing the deeper we go into enemy territory. I am hesitant to connect with the new fellas. When planes go missing, I pray for their safety. I wonder if my luck is running low and someday it will be me. I apologize for the honest thoughts, but without anyone here to speak to, I feel my only option is to share these thoughts with you.

I want to come back to you so desperately. One of the guys had a record shipped to him with a message from his wife and kids back home. The whole crew heard it. We all listened to the message as if it had been our own family who'd sent it. The guys are awful homesick, me especially.

One fella put on "Harbor Lights" and it brought me back to the dance we shared at your birthday party. I'll never forget seeing you walk down those stairs in your pastel-pink dress, holding you in my arms, or the moment I kissed you for the first time. I hold on to those memories when things get tough. I pray this letter finds you well. I miss you more each day.

Love, Dean

Ava folded his letter. She held two more letters. Her heartbeat rapidly. Would his next two letters give her more information? As she placed the top letter to the side, her heart sank. She recognized her own cursive scroll across the front. A big red stamp shown across the address: RETURN TO SENDER. The second letter had the same stamp. They were the letters she'd sent Dean a few months prior. He must have gone missing in action by the time they'd arrived.

She picked up Dean's last letter and held it close. A tear slipped down her cheek as she looked out the window to the street below. The afternoon sun pushed its way through the trees, as their shadows danced upon the sidewalk. She shuddered over the thought that she could be holding the last words he ever wrote. She shook the thought from her mind. Until the military confirmed it, Dean was still alive.

CHAPTER 39

Laura wasn't sure exactly when she'd fallen asleep but the kink in her neck made her rethink her current reading spot. The journal lay in her lap, still open to the last page she'd read. Dean had gone missing in action. A chill swept over her. Had he survived? Not sure what ending she'd expected, she didn't wish to learn of his death. Knowing how it felt to lose Paul, she wouldn't wish that on anyone, but the reality of the war was that loved ones didn't always come home.

The journal didn't have many pages remaining. Laura wasn't confident she'd find a resolution. She found herself with more questions than answers. Dean was missing in action; Grayson had feelings for Ava, and Ava questioned her feelings for each man. What a complicated mess this had turned out to be.

Laura had decided not to jump ahead, spoiling the ending. She'd hope for the best outcome whatever it may be. She'd followed along with Ava's ups and downs, sympathizing with her as if she knew her on a personal level.

It may have been a coincidence their stories mirrored one another but finding the journal had given her a new perspective on her own life. Ava lived during a time where struggle and sacrifice were part of daily life. They had loved and lost, and each of them had to learn how to live through grief. Laura felt torn, eager to know the end of the story but afraid the ending would not be what she'd hoped for.

Her curiosity kicked in. She turned the page. The last journal entry stared back at her, the script on the page now just a haunting memory. She took a deep breath. Hoping for the best, she started reading.

CHAPTER 40

Dear Diary,

I promised myself I'd never wait this long between entries, but my factory job has me so busy I haven't had much time for anything else. Six months later and we find ourselves another year into the war. Father says the war is still very much a part of our lives. The allies have made headway, but no one expected it to last this long.

Tessa has been home the last couple weeks for the holidays. It's been good to have her around, I've missed her. Even though her crazy personality drives me nuts sometimes, it's been good to have someone to talk with again. She's told me some of the stories of the men she's been assisting, and it sounds like she has her hands full. I'm not sure I could handle the sight of all those wounded men. I'd only think of Dean. I'm thankful she can help where I cannot.

It's been months since I received the last unopened letter, I mailed Dean. A few additional letters have come back since that day. I don't expect there's many others that will be returned, but every one that comes back, breaks my heart a little more. The situation is becoming more of a reality each passing day.

It would be a miracle if he were alive, and yet I can't bring myself to admit he would be anything else. They say time heals a broken heart, but I have yet to confirm if that's true. I'm stuck between grieving what I've been told is the reality and holding on to the hope Dean will walk through my door one day.

Everyone has moved forward as if he is not coming home. Grayson purchased war bonds in his name to honor his sacrifice. My family speaks of him in the past tense. His parents refuse to admit he's dead and I feel the same. I still hold onto hope he's alive but if all I'm left with when the war ends is the memories we made, then I'll cherish them forever.

One thing has changed with time. I no longer struggle with the guilt of spending time with Grayson. Our time together has become therapeutic as we share memories of the past. When I think of Dean, I can't help but smile. Grayson has respected my wishes and has kept his feelings to himself. I have kept my distance and the space has given me time to sort out my own feelings. All this time I've been trying to do what is right for Dean and Grayson. I never considered what might be best for me. I cannot live my life trying to make sure everyone else is happy, I have to follow my heart wherever it may lead.

As for today, I'll not lose faith in love. If I remain hopeful, I will always have something to live for no matter how challenging life becomes.

A va finished up the journal entry noticing she'd nearly run out of pages. She made a note to stop by the store to pick up a new one. She scowled at her chipped nails. Would there ever be a day they didn't have grease underneath them? It would be a lost cause until other suitable work could be found but she looked forward to the day she could paint them once again.

Pausing, she touched the wire ring still in place on her finger. Slowly pulling it off, she placed it inside the journal, closed the book and set it aside. She looked down at the spot the ring had been. The green hue would fade and along with it the emotions brought on by memories of the past. Placing her journal in the trunk, she locked it and put the key in its special hiding place.

Ava heard the doorbell. She'd finished getting ready early and chose to write in her diary while she had a few extra minutes. After one last look in the mirror, she flew downstairs; her white dress flowing around her legs as she reached the bottom. The yellow ribbon in her hair matched the daisies on the dress just as it had the day of the picnic so many years before.

A few weeks prior, she had accepted Grayson's invitation to the New Year's military dance. It would be good to get out and forget life's difficulties for one evening. She'd saved the dress for a special occasion and the dance felt like the perfect place to wear it for the first time.

She opened the front door. Grayson filled the doorframe. He wore a double-breasted suit she'd never seen before. The navy-blue tones brought out the color of his eyes and the tailored fit accentuated his shoulders. The corner of his eyes crinkled when he smiled. He handed her a bouquet of flowers but kept hold of a second bouquet. Ava eyed the extra flowers, slightly confused.

"For Tess." He said as if reading her mind.

"You mean I'm not getting two bouquets?" Ava enjoyed the flush that crept up his face. She stepped to one side, so he could come in. Before he could reply, Tessa joined them at the door.

"For me?" She placed her hand over her heart dramatically. "Grayson, you shouldn't have. All my boyfriends at the hospital will be jealous."

"Oh, but of course." He handed her the flowers laughing.

Ava rolled her eyes, handing her flowers to Tessa as well. "Would you mind putting these in water, and make haste, we're already running behind."

"Ava, it's in style to be fashionably late." Tessa pranced by them waving the bouquet in the air.

Ava playfully nudged her sister toward the kitchen. "Hurry along, or we're leaving without you."

Grayson smiled observing the good-humored interaction.

"Don't laugh, you'll just encourage her." She playfully slapped him on the arm.

"I saw you crack a smile, so you have no room to talk."

"I'm not sure whether she amuses me or exasperates me."

"I'll wager it's a little of both." Grayson smiled as he helped her put on her coat. "Admit it, you're glad to have her home for a visit."

"I am but I still pity the poor man she ends up marrying."

"He will discover he's married to a rather charming woman." Grayson's eyes sparkled in amusement.

"Charming? You give her far too much credit." Ava couldn't help but smile as she buttoned her coat down the front. At times she'd been hard on Tessa, but considering all they'd been through, her sister had never lost her sense of humor. Ava grabbed her purse off the hall table and observed Grayson as he adjusted his tie. He seemed happier than he had been in a long time.

"Are you both ready?" Tessa rounded the corner, her purse and coat over one arm and her free hand motioning them toward the front door.

"We were waiting on you." Ava looked heavenward.

"My dear sister, let's not focus on trivial details, shall we?" Tessa sauntered by Ava whose mouth hung open. "What?" Tessa asked innocently as she put on her own jacket. She draped her purse over her shoulder and headed toward the car.

"It's your turn to keep an eye on her." Ava directed her comment at Grayson as she followed her sister outside.

Grayson threw his head back in laughter as he closed the front door behind them. He caught up to Ava leaning in close for only her to hear. "I already have my hands full keeping an eye on you."

"The temperature must have dropped twenty degrees." Ava held on to Grayson's arm as they left the dance hall. The sounds of laughter floated outside as the folks inside made the most of the last song. Considering the state of the country, most people were in good spirits. The sense of patriotism had been evident, and it made Ava proud to see it.

"If you are right; we may get snow this year."

Grayson's reply brought her back to the conversation. "I can't wait to take off my shoes." The dance had been full of military men. All eager to dance with the young ladies in attendance.

"I don't think you sat out one dance. I can't blame them. What guy wouldn't want to dance with the prettiest girl in the room?" She hoped he couldn't see the flush she felt creeping into her cheeks but then again, maybe he hadn't been referring to her.

"I don't know where Tessa gets her energy." Ava replied hoping her comment would bring some clarity to his meaning.

"I wasn't talking about Tess." Grayson opened the car door for her. "But like she said, she's doing her part to support the war effort."

"And if you believe that, one might say my little sister has you wrapped around her baby finger." She paused, sizing him up. He hadn't hinted at flirting for months and tonight he'd already made two comments that would insinuate otherwise. She lifted an eyebrow in challenge as she slid into the front seat.

"Now why would you ever assume that?" Grayson raised his voice two octaves and clutched his chest attempting his best Tessa impersonation.

Ava burst out laughing. He shut her door making his way to the driver's side. She had tears in her eyes by the time he got behind the wheel. He looked over, a smile spreading across his face. "It's been a long time since I've heard you laugh."

"There hasn't been much to laugh about lately." Ava wiped at the corner of her eyes trying to avoid smudging her makeup.

"Are you sure Tess has a ride home?"

"She mentioned heading home later with a friend."

"Lord help her friend; that girl is a handful." Grayson put the car into gear. They laughed all the way home as each one took turns sharing their favorite Tessa quotes.

Grayson tapped his fingers on the steering wheel in rhythm to the song on the radio as they found themselves arriving in front of Ava's home. Her feet were throbbing, and she found herself relieved they were partially frozen. Grayson turned off the engine and as he walked in front of the vehicle, Ava saw him tighten his coat to fend off the chill from the night air. He opened her door and held out a gloved hand to assist her.

The frigid night brought an eerie but calming stillness to the neighborhood. The streetlights glistened as they reflected in the dew forming on the sidewalk. With not a soul in sight, the neighborhood almost felt abandoned. Grayson offered his arm as he escorted her up the pathway. He shifted self-consciously once they stood at the stairs of the front porch.

"What is it?" She nudged him playfully.

"Nothing." He casually dismissed the question and instead stuffed his hands in his pockets.

"Are you sure?" Ava curiously tried to read his facial expression in the dim light.

"I'm positive." He avoided eye contact, instantly fidgeting with his tie. His gloves made loosening it difficult.

He wasn't acting like himself, but she decided not to pry. "Here, allow me." Ava stood on the first step of the porch bringing herself up to his height. She pulled him closer to get a better look. The scent of his cologne caught on the breeze briefly causing her to lose focus. Her fingers slipped and he flinched.

"If I didn't know any better, I would say you were trying to choke me."

"Oh, don't be such a baby." She chewed on her lower lip engrossed with the task at hand. "I've seen father do it many times, but you really got yourself a knot here." She scrunched her face in concentration. "One... last... knot." Her thin fingers found a way into the binds of the tie, loosening it for him. She could feel

Grayson's gaze on her. Her hands stilled but she didn't relinquish her hold. Her focus shifted upward. His piercing blue eyes stared straight through her, penetrating her resolve. She could no longer deny the electricity between them. A heightened level of emotion soared through her as he tenderly tucked a strand of hair behind her ear.

"I never intended to fall in love with you—" His tone held an unapologetic desire she could not ignore.

"I know," her voice barely a whisper.

"Then again, maybe I always have been."

Her free hand rested on his chest and she felt his heartbeat quicken beneath her touch. She couldn't bring herself to look away. If she didn't stop him, he would kiss her. His focus shifted to her mouth and he wrapped his arms around her waist pulling her close. The sound of the front door creaked. Ava pulled back and he released her. She attempted to catch her breath. Her heart raced. When no one walked outside, she knew it had been the breeze.

"Goodnight, Ava." Grayson dropped his head in defeat. The moment gone. He turned away but Ava still held his tie. She pulled on it softly, drawing him back toward her. His face mere inches from hers, she gently pulled him forward till his lips met hers. His hand lightly touched her face as he kissed her softly. Any fear she'd been harboring fell away and she found herself responding to his kiss. Ava felt the cool smoothness of his lips and the warmth beneath them. Grayson wrapped his arms around her, indicating no hurry to release her. When a snowflake landed on her cheek, she laid her head against his chest responding to the warmth and safety he provided.

She had overlooked the depth of the relationship that had developed between them. A part of her heart would always belong to Dean, but her feelings for Grayson went deeper than surface level. He knew her better than she knew herself and loved her anyway. He had selflessly committed to being there for her and when she'd asked him to, and he'd been prepared to let her go, allowing her the time she'd needed.

She shivered from the cold and her thoughts found their way back to reality. Grayson responded by holding her close; his confidence proving he'd had more time to get used to the idea of a developing romance between them. The gravity of her feelings, however, were as new as the snow falling around them. Somewhere along the way, the love she'd felt for him had grown beyond friendship.

"Let's get you inside." Grayson's deep baritone resonated between them as he tenderly wiped the snow flurries from her cheek. He tucked her freezing hand into the warmth of his own and escorted her to the door. She felt her face warm as he leaned towards her. Had he planned to kiss her again? His mischievous smile told her he could read her mind, but always the gentleman, he reached around her opening the front door instead. "Goodnight Ava."

"Goodnight." She released his hand and stepped inside. She watched him adjust his collar closer to his neck before heading out into the night. He turned back for one last glance before getting into his car. She waved and then he was gone.

Dear Diary,

I can't sleep tonight. My thoughts have been racing since Grayson brought me home from the dance. Is Dean alive? Am I dishonoring his memory if I move on? No one will ever take his place, but is it time to make room for another?

I love Dean and I've grieved deeply as if I've lost him. If it's true and he's really gone, is it worth the cost to love again? Can my heart manage any more heartbreak?

Grayson's kiss tonight took me by surprise. I'd never imagined being with anyone other than Dean, but Grayson and I share an undeniable connection. In any other circumstance, I'd have said it was the perfect ending to a lovely evening but there are still so many unknowns, and the biggest of all, what my heart truly wants.

CHAPTER 41

Laura shuffled through the last pages of the journal. That was it? She looked through every letter sitting on the table—checking to make sure she'd read each one—double-checking all the journal entries to see if they were two-sided and she'd missed something. She sighed causing her bangs to lift slightly. The story couldn't end this way; which man did Ava choose?

Laura got up so quickly the chair screeched against the kitchen floor; she flew down the hall to her workroom. Walking over to where the trunk sat, she knelt beside it carefully, reaching inside. She moved her hand around the bottom hoping she missed something inside. Feeling nothing more than the splintered wood, she gave up.

Removing her hand, her fingers were coated in dust. She leaned against the trunk, defeated. Her arm hung over the side and she laid her forehead against it. She looked down at the empty inside.

She'd been taken on a journey only to discover she had no resolution. Laura wiped her hands against her jeans. She looked down on the vintage chest with new eyes. She imagined Ava and Dean sitting on it as they said goodbye, the playful interactions she'd had with Tessa as she tucked her journal into its secret hiding place.

Had Ava known the journal had gone missing? How could she not? Tracking the most formative years of her life, the journal had been forgotten. Maybe Ava wanted to keep her thoughts secret.

The previous owner covered the false bottom with fabric so they hadn't even taken the time to properly restore it, or it would have been found by now.

Questions raced through Laura's mind as she sat looking at the piece. She may never find the answers, but it wasn't going to stop her from bringing the old trunk back to its original state. She'd planned to sell it but now she couldn't see herself letting it go.

Laura grabbed her restoration tools, fully determined to finish the work she'd started. She pulled up the stool and began carefully bringing the piece to life one section at a time. She worked late, finally calling it a night around two o'clock in the morning. It didn't take long before she found her way to her room, collapsing on the bed in exhaustion.

The next morning, a groggy Laura wiped the sleep from her eyes as she walked downstairs. She clicked on the coffee pot, hoping the aroma would wake her from her dazed state. The steam sounded, and she could hear the drops hitting the glass pot. She popped a bagel in the toaster and grabbed the cream cheese from the fridge.

She poured herself a cup of coffee, added some creamer, and delighted in the first sip. She held the mug with both hands, letting the warmth seep through her fingers as she walked down the hall, her blue fuzzy slippers scuffing the floor as she went. She sat next to the trunk she'd worked on most of the night. She'd made decent headway but would need a few more things before she could complete it. She touched the freshly sanded wood and appreciated the natural color. Once stained, it would look nearly as close as it once did.

Laura heard the toaster click and made her way back to the kitchen. Setting her cup down on the table, she noticed all the letters spread out in front of her just as she'd left them. She picked up the V-Mail noting the return street address. There wasn't a zip code, but it would be worth a shot to research it online.

Laura ate the bagel faster than was ladylike. Maybe a little investigation would help turn up some answers. Determined to find out what happened to Ava, she couldn't give up on her story altogether. Had she ever married? Did Dean come home? Had she been in love with Grayson after all? The questions drove her mad.

She shuffled across the room to her laptop and opened the search engine. Placing the letter with the address next to it she typed it into the map's search bar. She held her breath as it pulled up the nearest locations with that address. The first one wasn't too far from her. Laura leaned back in her computer chair. Could the address be the same as the one on the envelope? Based on the descriptions in the journal, a few of the landmarks nearby could be the same.

Zooming in on the satellite view, she searched some of the immediate areas, noting there was a church close by and what looked like a small shopping plaza. She touched her chin, wondering if it could be the same place. She couldn't live with herself if she didn't at least look into it. Public records showed a woman by the name of Samantha Spencer currently owned the home. The last name didn't match any in the journal, but she didn't exactly have any other leads. Laura decided to drive to the house and see if she could connect with Samantha. Maybe she knew something about the Suttons. If it was within her power, she'd track down Ava's family and return the journal and the trunk.

CHAPTER 42

A few days later, Laura found herself standing in front of 2121 Hillcrest Drive. From the white picket fence to the wrap-around porch, Laura couldn't help but wonder if this had been the house she'd been reading about. The exterior seemed to fit what she'd imagined.

The wind stirred the leaves of the big oak tree above her, bringing her attention to the second-story bay window peering out over the street. Its design set the house apart from the others, having a large middle windowpane on the front and two smaller ones on the sides. Below the window a custom wood design looked like it had been handcrafted.

She took a deep breath, anxiously clutching the journal against her, wondering if Ava had felt the same way the day she stood in front of Grayson's house. She'd taken the time to wipe the dust off the old book and sort the letters back where she'd found them. She nearly turned back toward her car when she heard commotion coming from the backyard. The sound of a handsaw and hammering led her to assume there was a construction project going on nearby. If she didn't walk up the porch steps, she'd lose her nerve completely.

As she approached, she found herself outside a gorgeous solid wood door. She knocked hesitantly. Standing on the porch, her nerves got the best of her as she waited for someone to answer.

Had anyone been standing next to her, they would have heard her heart pounding. She'd considered what she planned to say over the last few days, but if Samantha Spencer had no connection to the people she'd read about, it could all be for nothing.

She'd been standing there long enough for someone to answer, but decided to knock again, this time a little harder. Her hands began to sweat against the leather as she held the journal close. She switched hands, wiping her free hand down the front of her jeans. She saw movement on the other side of the door and held her breath.

A woman with dark shoulder-length hair opened the door. She wore a T-shirt, jeans and a pair of light-blue running shoes. She had steel-blue eyes and a dimple in her chin that gave her heart-shaped face a sense of innocence. Laura judged her to be in her early sixties, but the woman had clearly taken care of herself.

"Can I help you?" Her tone depicted a sense of curiosity.

"Hello. My name is Laura Turner and…" Laura paused, her rehearsed speech dissipating, leaving her in a fog. "Well, you see, I have something I'm trying to return to its rightful owner, but all I have is this address." Laura shuffled awkwardly. "Are you the owner of the home?"

"I'm sorry, but this home hasn't been lived-in for a couple years. I'm not sure how much help I can be."

"Actually, I was hoping to track down a prior owner."

"Now that information, I can help with." The woman smiled. "The house may not have been lived-in recently, but it's been in my family for generations."

Laura felt hopeful for the first time since she arrived. "Do you perhaps know an Ava Sutton?"

"Sutton?" The woman's eyes widened. "Yes, of course."

"So, you know her?" Laura worked to contain her excitement. One wrong move and this woman would think she was a crazy person. She took a deep breath, working to calm her nerves.

"She was my mother." The woman's expression softened as she

looked to be reminiscing. "Unfortunately, she has since passed away."

"I'm so sorry to hear that." Laura's heart dropped. She knew there had been a slim chance Ava would still be alive, but she'd secretly hoped it would be so. "In that case would you know the owner Samantha Spencer?"

"I've always gone by Sam, but yes Samantha is my given name." She reached out to shake Laura's hand.

"Sam, it seems I have something that belongs to you." Laura held up the journal. Relief flooded in, knowing she'd be returning it to Ava's daughter. "Do you have a moment to chat?"

"Of course, of course. Do come in." Sam held her hand out, stepping to one side as Laura walked into the foyer of the home. It looked just as she imagined. The living room on the left side, with a small half table sitting in the hallway underneath a mirror—only the piece had a more modern design. The dining room looked to be right off the kitchen with a pair of French doors leading to the backyard. The staircase in the main entry took her breath away with its engrained sketching in the wood. She turned a circle, taking it all in. It felt like she'd walked into the real-life version of the journal she'd come to cherish. Laura stood in awe before whispering. "It's exactly as I imagined."

"Have you been here before?" Sam gave her a skeptical look.

"No," Laura laughed. She realized how she must be coming across. "I promise once I explain, it should make more sense."

"Sounds like this story requires a cup of tea. Would you like one?"

"Yes, thank you."

"Well then, make yourself comfortable on the couch and I'll be right back."

Laura walked into the living room picturing the conversations Ava had with her parents. From the time she announced wanting to get married, to the day she sat with her mother asking for her advice on what choice to make. The day they'd listened to the President's speech on the radio and the night they sat quietly observing the Christmas tree. The sound of a pendulum clock ticked back and forth from a Regulator clock that hung on the wall near the entry. Her eye went to the staircase, envisioning Dean at the bottom as he saw Ava for the first time the night of her nineteenth birthday. She smiled thinking of the girls taking the stairs two at a time as Hannah reprimanded them for running in the house.

Laura scanned the living room devoid of the blackout curtains that had kept the family safe. It seemed surreal to be standing in the room where the family gathered during the air raids. The fireplace in the corner of the living room had a few framed pictures on the mantle. Laura's interest piqued when she saw they were all black and white. She set the journal down on the coffee table and walked over to the mantle.

Laura gasped, covering her mouth. The picture in the center revealed a beautiful blonde woman wearing a white dress. Next to her stood a stunning woman with dark hair and a hint of mischief in her smile. Laura touched the side of the picture frame. Both reminded her of the 1940's movie stars, their hair falling in waves about their shoulders. They seemed older in the photo and she wondered if it'd been taken after the war.

"That's my mother." Sam set down the two cups of tea and joined Laura. "And that's my aunt Theresa next to her."

"I thought she preferred to be called Tessa?" Laura chuckled, recalling the moments Tessa had threatened anyone who used her given name.

"How did you know that?" Sam tilted her head.

"May I?" She motioned to the couch nearby. She better get to the point before she got herself kicked out for knowing too much without an explanation.

"Please." Both women took a seat on the couch and Laura handed Sam the journal. She watched in silence as recognition dawned on her face.

Unwrapping the leather cord holding it together, she carefully opened it. She sat there methodically sifting through the pages, careful not to let the letters spill out. "Where did you get this?" She whispered, looking up, her eyes glistened.

"I restore antique furniture and I found it inside an old steamer trunk I purchased from a shop downtown."

"As long as I can remember, my mother had a journal. She said she lost one right after the war, one that held many precious memories." Sam wiped at the tear that slipped down her cheek.

"I can't tell you how relieved I am to return such a family treasure."

"You say you found it in an old trunk?"

"That's right." Laura couldn't sit still. "I have so many questions I don't know where to begin."

"I think it best to start at the beginning." Sam picked up her cup of tea and took a sip.

"First, let me apologize for reading her personal journal."

"Oh nonsense." Sam waved her off.

"As you can imagine, it was rather tempting." Laura averted her eyes. "I'd so hoped to meet her, but even though that's not the case, I feel like I know her based on her stories. Her journal discussed everything from her nineteenth birthday party and into the war years, ending with Grayson returning from war and Dean missing in action. It ended rather abruptly, so I found myself wondering—"

"You want to know who she ended up with?" Sam smiled behind her teacup.

"I've been dying to find out." Laura leaned forward eagerly. By that point, containing her excitement any longer was not an option.

"My mother would tell me stories of how she and my father fell in love. She didn't know it at the time, but she always counted herself lucky to fall in love with two men during her lifetime." Sam sat there seemingly engrossed in her memories. "After she found out Dean went missing in action, I'm sure you can imagine, she found herself torn between her devotion to him, and the long-lasting love my father had shown for her. It wasn't until the war ended, they discovered what had happened to Dean. Sadly, they found his remains on an island in the Pacific."

"That's awful," Laura covered her mouth.

"The details are a bit vague, but they were told he washed ashore after being forced to bail out of his plane. While he was there, he helped a lot of people escape the island. Eventually they found their way to safer locations. He'd secretly gone back and forth between the villages as often as he could, but when one of the villages was bombed, he didn't survive the attack."

Sam walked over to the mantle, pulling down a picture of a blond man in a Navy uniform. She handed it to Laura. "He died a hero. His parents were sent the awards he'd earned for bravery and when they sent his remains home, the military gave him a proper burial."

"Your mother must have been devastated." The picture became blurry. Laura wiped a tear away with the back of her hand.

"She'd always claimed she knew he had been alive. She told me she never felt he was gone until closer to the day he died. She never gave up on him. I don't think she could truly move on until she had tangible proof of his whereabouts."

"What happened after that?" Laura handed her the picture and she put it back in its place.

"Nearly a year after his death, she married my father." Sam removed another picture from the mantle and handed it to Laura. Ava stood in her white dress with yellow daisies, a tall man in a gray vest next to her. His clean-cut dark hair showed one piece falling stubbornly against his forehead.

"Grayson." Laura let out the breath she'd been holding as she looked at the couple in the photo.

"My father worshiped the ground she walked on." Sam smiled proudly.

"When did your mother know she was in love with him?"

"She always had been, but she didn't realize it at the time. Dean was her first love, but they were young, and the war made their situation confusing. She waited for him because she didn't want to betray him. She told me when I got older; her love for Dean felt akin to puppy love, where her love for my father ran deeper. It wasn't until they confirmed Dean was gone, that she felt she could marry my father without carrying guilt into their marriage."

"Did he ever feel like he was second place?"

"My mother had to deal with emotions beyond either of their control, and he never saw himself with anyone other than her." Sam resumed her seat on the couch next to Laura. "Mother said he was the most patient man she'd ever met. Which, I suppose, came in handy when I arrived." She chuckled. "She loved my father but couldn't allow the sense of betrayal to cloud their relationship."

"I have to admit her journal captivated me from page one."

"My parents always spoke fondly of the years they spent together. My father told me when I was born, they wanted to honor Dean, so they named me after him."

"But your name is Samantha." Laura set the photo down on the coffee table.

"Dean's middle name was Samuel so; Samantha was their next best option."

"What a beautiful tribute."

"My mother spent a great deal of time documenting our family history, which is why it means the world to me that you found this and returned it."

"That reminds me," Laura's eyes widened. "Do you know how the journal got left in the trunk?"

"As it turns out, my grandfather ended up selling the trunk, not knowing my mother still had one of her journals inside." Sam set the book down. "He felt terrible but the couple that had bought it said they were passing through. We thought it was lost forever. I count myself lucky that someone like you found it and brought it back to us." Sam reached out, covering Laura's hand with her own. "Not a moment too soon either."

"It was pure coincidence I ran across it. Someone had covered the interior of the trunk with fabric." She smiled knowing the joy she'd brought Sam by returning the long-lost treasure.

"Call it coincidence if you like, but I call it fate." Sam looked around the room with a nostalgic look on her face. "A few weeks later, we may not have been here. We're selling the place once we finish the remodel."

"Selling it?"

"My husband and I live on the other side of town. Unfortunately, we don't have the time or the energy to keep up both homes."

"It's a shame you aren't able to keep it in the family. I wish I'd found the journal a few years sooner. I would've loved to meet your mother."

"She would have loved meeting you too. You both would have gotten along well."

"More than you know." Laura lowered her head, her mind shifting to her own loss. She too had experienced losing the man she loved—the guilt that came with the idea of moving on and the question of whether she could love again.

"I sense there is a story behind that solemn expression."

"I relate to your mother. I lost someone I loved deeply." Laura covered her mouth. "Your mother's story parallels my own in many ways, I'm afraid."

"I'm so sorry for your loss." Sam touched her shoulder.

Laura didn't want to break down in front of the woman, so she just nodded.

"I may have something you'd like to see." She left the room, and Laura wondered what this woman must think. A few moments later, she returned with a letter in hand. She gave it to Laura who recognized the handwriting immediately.

"Mother gave me this the day I graduated and left home. If she were here today, and speaking to you herself, she would have said something similar." Sam picked up her teacup and walked into the kitchen, giving Laura a moment alone.

Dearest Samantha,

It's your graduation day, and it seems to have come overnight. To-morrow, we lose our baby girl to college. You came into my life like a wind that took my breath away. As I am only now catching my breath, you are preparing to grow into your own life. It's hard to let you go, but I know the most exciting years are still ahead of you. One day, you will get married and have children of your own.

Life will not always be easy and may require sacrifice and selfless-ness when you don't think you have enough of either. You are stronger than you realize. If the world brings suffering to your doorstep, never lose hope. When you triumph, enjoy the moment to its fullest. Love without condition and always be kind to the less fortunate. It is in the most trying times we discover who we truly are and whom we are meant to be.

If you remember anything, always know I am here for you. I am so proud of the woman you are and look forward to the woman you will become.

All my love, Momma

Laura folded the note holding it in her lap. Somehow it seemed fitting that the last words she would read; were the ones she was meant to hear the most. In losing Paul she'd also lost herself. She had to admit that since finding the journal, her outlook on life had shifted. She followed along as Ava went through some of the most difficult trials a person could endure. She cried with her when she let Dean go at the train station, felt the burden of the self-sacrifice she made to get through trying times and experienced the depth of betrayal when she learned the love wasn't what she thought. Most of all, she related to the pain of losing someone she deeply cared about. Now she needed to find herself again.

The words from a woman she'd never met, had given her new perspective on her own life. Ava's story gave her hope she didn't have; something to believe in. She could love again, but the choice would be up to her. She only had to open her heart up to the pos-sibility.

"I believe my mother would have been happy to know you found her journal." Sam returned, taking a seat on the couch next to her. "She went through her fair share of trials, but she found joy in the end and I believe you will too."

"Thank you." Laura held out the note to her. "I think being here today has given me the closure I needed," Laura sighed. "To be honest, I think my outlook started to shift the minute I began following your mother's journey."

"I can't tell you how much it means to me to have her journal back." Sam smiled. "I truly thought it'd been lost forever."

"There's one more thing," Laura's eyes widened. "The trunk."

"The trunk?" Sam looked curious.

"I finished the restoration. I'd like to return it to your family."

"Oh Laura, I don't know what to say." Sam reached into her purse. "At least let me pay you for it."

"Absolutely not." Laura reached over and touched her hand. "It was your mother's, and based on what she told you, she never wished to part with it. It rightfully belongs with your family."

"I can't believe your generosity." Sam became misty-eyed and took a Kleenex from the box nearby. "I'd be happy to stop by sometime this week and pick it up."

"That would be perfect." Laura smiled and grabbed her purse. "I'll leave you my card and you can call and schedule a time."

"This is unbelievable. I can't wait to tell my husband." Sam stood and hugged her. For the first time in a long time, Laura felt genuinely happy. She'd used her talent to give back to someone else instead of a distraction from her own pain.

"Speaking of your husband, I think it would be a good idea to bring him along. The trunk isn't exactly light, and it may take the two of you to load it."

"I will make sure I do that." Sam smiled as she walked Laura to the front door. "Thank you again, Laura, for everything." She reached out, pulling the young woman into another brief hug.

As she reached her car, Laura realized she'd been with Sam for

most of the afternoon. Spending time with her seemed to be therapeutic. As she drove home, her heart filled with a joy that had been
missing since the night she'd lost Paul.

CHAPTER 43

Laura paced the hall of her suburban home. She had made plans with Sam to pick up the trunk and found herself anxiously excited to show it to her. She'd stayed up late the night before making all the finishing touches, and it looked as close to the original condition as she could manage. She had done it justice and had no reason to be nervous. However, after everything she'd learned about the Sutton family, she wanted it to be special. She checked her watch. Sam would be arriving soon.

She stared into the hall mirror for what seemed like the tenth time since she got downstairs. She applied a bit of lipstick and ran her fingers through her hair. Her white shirt and casual, blue-fitted blazer gave her a relaxed but sophisticated look. She'd paired it with blue jeans and a pair of tan wedge heels. The rose-gold jewelry seemed the perfect complement to the outfit.

She heard a car pull up into the driveway. The chest would finally be going to its forever home. It gave her such joy to return it. She walked to the door and opened it. She stopped short. It wasn't Sam standing in the doorway, but another woman—one she'd never met before. The short older woman stood there tapping her foot with her hands on her hips, her gray curls bouncing with every tap.

"Can I help you?"

"I'm looking for a cat."

"A cat?"

"Orange tabby, kind of a tubby around the center. Darn thing keeps escaping."

Laura looked at her watch. Sam would be arriving any minute. "Is he your cat?"

"Nah, he hangs around my place. He's been MIA the last few weeks, so I thought I'd ask around."

"Oh." Laura had a hard time following the conversation knowing she had company coming any minute. "I've seen him around but not recently."

The woman held her hand over her eyes, as she looked up into the tree in Laura's front yard. She reached into her blouse and handed Laura a card. "If you see him again, would you give me a call?"

Laura held the card between two fingers not exactly fond of knowing where it had just been. "I'll be sure to do that."

"Thanks for your time." The woman waddled down the path and got into her car. She slowly drove the street, poking her head out the window occasionally. Laura didn't have time to dwell on the random visit, because she heard the phone ring inside. She arrived in time to snatch it off the table before it went to voicemail.

"Hello?"

"Laura?"

"This is she."

"This is Samantha."

"Oh, hi."

"My apologies for not being there to pick up the trunk when I said I would. The contractor held me up on a project here at the house, so I had to stay behind and handle the details."

"I'm sorry to hear that. Do you want to reschedule?" Laura tried to hide her disappointment. She'd been looking forward to visiting with Sam again and seeing her reaction to the newly refinished trunk.

"I'm hoping you don't mind, but I sent my son to pick it up in my place. I wish I'd been able to come myself, but I'm stuck here at the house. Although I'm dying to see it."

"Of course."

"I hate that I'm going to miss you and was hoping to thank you in person. Would you be able to join us for dinner sometime?"

"I'd love to." Laura heard a vehicle pull up. "Sam, I think your son just arrived."

"Perfect. Thanks again for everything, Laura. I'll call you in a week or so to set up a time for dinner."

"Sounds good." Laura hung up the phone as the doorbell rang. She quickly made her way to the door. When she opened it, she halted; her phone nearly slipped through her fingers.

"Caleb?" Her heart skipped a beat as she stared at the man in front of her.

"Laura?" Caleb's face seemed to mirror the surprise she felt.

"What are you doing here?"

"I'm here to pick up a trunk— my mom sent me?" His voice faded as he held out a small piece of paper with her address on it.

"Samantha? Is your mom?" Laura's eyes broadened in surprise.

"Last time I checked." He leaned against the doorframe smiling.

"So that would make you—" Laura paused as all the pieces started to fall into place.

"Make me what?" He stood there watching her intently.

"Ava's grandson?" Laura slowly walked past him onto the porch. She sat in one of the white patio chairs, hoping to get her bearings.

"Well, I just called her grandma." He sat in the chair across from her, his face turning to concern. "Are you okay?"

"How much did your mother tell you?"

"Not much, she asked me to come over and pick up a trunk. She said it belonged to my grandmother and it'd been restored." He paused; his eyes widening. "Is this the same trunk you've been working on? The one I originally carried in the day we met?"

Laura nodded.

"That's a funny coincidence."

"I think your mom referred to it as fate." Laura smiled, remembering their first meeting. "It makes sense why I've never seen you around town until recently." Laura stood, and Caleb followed suit. As she started to head inside; he followed her. "You must be here to help remodel your grandmother's place."

"I am." Caleb continued to follow her down the hallway. "Mom can't wait to see it. She felt terrible not being able to come along."

"That's okay, she's got a lot on her plate with the remodel." Laura escorted Caleb back to the workroom where the trunk sat. He looked around her room as Laura walked over to the trunk and took off the blanket.

"It looks amazing." Caleb made his way over, kneeling before the trunk. He touched the sides carefully like it was made of glass. "She's going to love it."

"You really think so?" Laura smiled behind him. She'd impressed him with her work.

"Absolutely!" He opened the trunk revealing the gorgeous natural wood. What once had been dusty and cracked, now stained to perfection. He ran his hand along the inside admiring the framework when he stopped, noticing the small panel near the bottom. "What's this?"

"It has a false bottom." Laura leaned down next to him pulling up the wooden piece to reveal the space below. "This secret hiding place... is the whole reason I found your family at all." Laura replaced the small piece of wood back to its well-fitted space.

"I'm going to need an explanation." Caleb had a comical look on his face.

"I found it when I began restoring it. Inside was a journal your grandmother had written in 1941."

"You're kidding."

"According to your mom, when your great-grandfather sold the trunk, he didn't know it was inside." She shrugged, lifting her hands up. "I couldn't help myself; I read it."

Caleb let out a hearty laugh over her childlike explanation. "I'm glad you did. If you hadn't, we may never have gotten it back. It means the world to my mom to have both items returned." They both stood admiring the trunk.

"So, how much do we owe you?" He pulled out his wallet and she placed her hand on his arm.

"It's on the house." She sighed; she felt sad that the story had come to an end. Once the trunk and journal were gone, so was her connection to Ava.

"What you've done is invaluable. Can we not repay you somehow?" He looked down at her hand still on his arm; she quickly moved it back to her side.

"Caleb, reading your grandmother's story, realizing what she sacrificed—she gave me hope. Something I haven't had in a long time." Laura began to fold a piece of tack cloth sitting in front of her. "I'll spare you the details, but let's just say your grandmother's story helped me to overcome some things I've been dealing with."

"I'd still like to repay you." He placed a hand on her shoulder. "Would you at least let me buy you a coffee?"

Laura's heart began to beat rapidly. His deep-set eyes searched her face. She couldn't deny the way he asked made it hard to resist. She placed a hand over her stomach trying to control the butterflies. "I don't know if that would be a—"

"It's only coffee," he spoke softly, challenging her. "I understand, you want to think about it."

"Think about it?" She suddenly felt defensive. Putting her hands on her hips she watched as Caleb wandered around the workshop checking things out.

"You told me you're a planner. Your workspace is clean enough to eat off and every one of your tools is organized by size. Your work on the trunk is perfect, and each time I've asked you a question, it takes you more than a few seconds to answer." He stood in front of her.

"I'm not sure it would be a good idea."

"What could go wrong?" He leaned towards her. His grin turned mischievous, and he whispered. "I bet you've already asked yourself if I'm asking you out as a date or to repay you for your kindness."

"I most certainly have not." Laura lied. She avoided eye contact hoping to cover her reaction but based on his grin, it seemed he could see right through the charade. She narrowed a look in his direction. "All right, I'll go." She regretted the words as they came out of her mouth.

"I'll pick you up at seven." He walked over to the trunk and closed the lid.

"Seven?" Laura's voice registered a higher pitch than intended.

"Yes, seven."

"Tonight?" She scanned his face. Surely, he couldn't be serious.

"Yes, tonight. Why? Do you have a date already?" He winked at her as he lifted the chest off the floor.

"No, but...that's a little presumptuous don't you think?"

"Then it's a date." He began making his way down the hall, carefully maneuvering the trunk, trying not to knock over anything on the way to the door.

"A date? Oh no, it's not a—" She grabbed the blanket he'd left behind and ran after him.

"Would you mind getting the door, this is kind of heavy." He winced under the weight of the trunk and Laura grabbed the door for him. He walked outside making his way toward the truck. She followed behind him. Setting down the trunk, he opened the tailgate.

"Here, this will help protect it." She handed him the blanket and his fingers brushed hers. Her heart raced. What she'd just agreed to? Nerves clashed with excitement, and she wasn't sure which feeling was in control.

Caleb lifted the chest into the back of his truck, wrapping the blanket around it and carefully securing it with the cords he'd brought. He closed the back of the tailgate and turned his attention to Laura.

"See you at seven." He smiled as he jumped into the truck and drove off.

Laura slowly walked toward her home. The last hour had been

a whirlwind. She looked down at her watch. She had an hour. She grabbed her phone from her back pocket.

"I'll text him and say I need a raincheck." She paused. "Ugh! I don't have his number." She put her hand to her forehead trudging back to the house. She'd considered calling Sam, but how would that sound? *Hi Sam, your charming son asked me out and I need his phone number so I can call and cancel.* She didn't have a choice; she was going on a date.

CHAPTER 44

Laura stood in line at the coffee shop with Caleb waiting to order. They'd spent the drive over talking about the remodel his parents were doing on his grandmother's home. They got their drinks, and he found a quiet little corner in the café for them to sit uninterrupted. Laura decided to keep the conversation on the remodel, as she had a natural interest in bringing old things back to life.

"How is it that you can take this time off work to do a remodel with your parents?"

"I'm an independent contractor. I flip houses; so, this is another job for me." He smiled leaning back in his chair. "Family discount, of course."

"I thought your mom said she was having trouble with her contractor?" Laura had the distinct impression she'd been set up.

"I have a bit of a confession." Caleb shifted in his seat.

"I'm listening." The slight sarcasm in her tone posed a challenge. She leaned back, crossing her arms.

"I saw you leaving my grandmother's house the other day. I was surprised so I asked my mom about you. When she told me how you found us and that she planned to get the trunk, I asked her if I could go instead." Caleb tugged at his shirt collar. "I wanted an excuse to see you again."

Laura cleared her throat, attempting to cover her surprise over his direct honesty. She took a deep breath, not sure what to say. She recalled the times they'd run into each other in the last few weeks and couldn't think of a time when she'd made a good impression. She sat for a minute, and he broke the silence.

"Are you mad?" The way he asked sounded so genuine.

"Under the circumstances, I suppose it's rather flattering."

"And yet you don't seem happy about it."

"No, it's not that."

"Then what has you so deep in thought?"

"Was it the time you caught me talking to myself or when I ran into you at the hardware store that made you decide to ask me out?" Laura's serious expression faded when Caleb chuckled.

"Maybe I found both endearing." He leaned toward her with a teasing expression.

"I didn't make the best impression." She leaned in, matching his gaze.

"Oh, you made an impression all right."

"See? I knew it!" Laura frowned.

"I saw a cute girl who needed help, so I offered." He smiled across from her. "And don't think I didn't see you coming my way in the hardware aisle... all distracted with your pen and paper."

"What! You mean you *let* me run into you?" Laura's eyes widened.

"I thought you were going to look up when you got closer, but you didn't." He laughed. "If it helps, I did feel bad when you fell. I wasn't expecting that."

"I can't believe it." She crossed her arms. "You let me think I was a total klutz."

"You were a total klutz."

"You should feel a little guilty." She narrowed a look in his direction. "I hit my head."

"Did I look more handsome after you came to?"

"Now you're fishing for compliments." She raised her chin defiantly.

"I have no shame. I'll take anything a pretty girl is willing to give me."

Laura felt her cheeks warm. It had been a while since a man openly complimented her. She, in turn, had not been attracted to anyone since Paul. She hadn't exactly put herself out there. Caleb made her question all that. He had an annoying way of getting under her skin, but she couldn't find it within herself to truly be mad at him knowing his heart was in the right place.

"Well?"

"Well, what?" Laura laughed, not willing to fall for his pretenses.

"Was I more good-looking after you hit your head?" He lifted his head, posing like a statue.

"I don't hand out compliments on the first date."

"A second date then." He waggled his eyebrows.

"Only time will tell." Laura gave him a sly look while swirling her coffee cup. "I have a busy schedule."

"I guess I better ask you out soon, so you can pencil me in."

"We'll see."

"I'll find a way to convince you."

After an hour of swapping stories from their childhood, Caleb recalled the relationship he'd had with his grandparents. Laura enjoyed those in particular. She felt like she personally knew Grayson and Ava and could imagine the scenes as he described them. When he told her a few stories Grayson had shared with him about the war, she found herself a bit emotional. There had been so much Ava hadn't known by only reading their letters. Laura empathized with what it might have been like to fly above an enemy carrier ship as they were hit from below with bullets and how terrifying that must have been. It truly had been a different time. Everyone was not only willing but eager to sacrifice for the country.

Caleb had an early morning so the two called it a night and he drove her home. He walked her to the door and paused. "I had a really nice time." He casually leaned against the doorframe; his arms crossed.

"I did too." She reached inside her purse and fumbled to find her keys in the dim light. Once they made their way to the surface of her purse, she opened the door.

"Would you join me for dinner sometime?" He moved closer, placing a hand on the doorframe above her. He gazed down at her and she felt her breath quicken. She couldn't form a reply. He leaned toward her. She fought the urge to move away even though everything inside her told her to.

"Whoa!" Caleb jumped back looking down at his feet. Laura's eyes flashed to the ground. Dusty purred as he rubbed up against Caleb's leg. "Friend of yours?"

"No, but he sure seems to like you." Amused, she watched Dusty flick his tail back and forth, sitting between the couple. He seemed happy with himself and if Laura were honest, she found herself relieved by the interruption.

"Where did you come from?" Caleb knelt, scratching the cat behind the ears.

"He's been hanging around my place lately." Laura knelt as well. "I may have met his owner earlier today, although I'm not clear if he actually belongs to her."

"You mean she never came looking for him before today?"

"I'm not sure she knew where to look. She said she was stuck with him and that seemed a strange way to refer to it." Laura pat Dusty on the head and he seemed to enjoy the attention.

"How long has he been coming around?"

"A few weeks, I think."

"Why don't you adopt him?"

Laura covered Dusty's ears with her hands and whispered. "I'm not a cat person."

"Oh, I see." Caleb whispered back.

Dusty began to meow at her like he did when he wanted inside. "Not tonight, Dusty." She stood and closed the door to keep him from getting inside.

"You named him?"

"Well," she shrugged. "I couldn't keep calling him *cat*."

"Good point." Caleb stood. "I guess that's my cue to leave.

Goodnight, Laura." He kissed her lightly on the cheek and turned to leave.

"Goodnight," she whispered under her breath as she watched him head toward his truck.

She looked down at Dusty who stared up at her hoping she'd change her mind about letting him in. "I'm not sure whether to reprimand you or thank you." She watched as Caleb backed out of the driveway and drove away. Dusty meowed. "Listen pal, it's been a day and I need some serious R&R. Be a good cat and run along." She watched him wander off and closed the door behind her.

Chapter 45

Laura removed her hoop earrings, tossing them in the candy dish on the hall table. She walked into her kitchen and pulled a bottle of water from the fridge. For a day that she'd planned to be relaxing, she found herself emotionally drained. She hadn't eaten much with all the nerves and her stomach growled. Junk food always helped her sort through her feelings, if not eat them.

Before she could grab a bag of chips from the pantry, she felt her phone vibrating in her pocket. She debated answering, wanting the time to herself. She decided to answer after seeing April's name flash on the screen. She would end up telling her best friend about the evening anyway, so she clicked the green button, a smile in her voice. "Hey stranger."

"Hey bestie! Whatcha doin'?"

"I'm about to dive into some junk food. Why do you ask?" Laura plucked the bag of chips from the shelf and made her way to the table putting April on speaker.

"Really? Are you sure that's all?"

Laura heard suspicion in her voice. "April, why don't you tell me what you think you know, and we can go from there?" She heard her friend let out a sigh.

"Laura, why am I always the last to know about that handsome man in your life?"

"What are you talking about?"

"Caleb?" April sounded put out.

"First, he's not the man in my life, and second, what do you mean last to know?"

"Well I heard from Vanessa, who heard from Desiree, that she saw you having coffee with a good-looking guy earlier tonight."

"Oh, good grief! Is nothing secret in this town?"

"So, you *did* have coffee with him!" April's voice squeaked in excitement. "This is the first time I hoped the rumors were true. Oh, this is so exciting. Tell me everything and don't leave out the details, better yet, I'll come over and you can tell me in person."

"Okay, hold on a second." Laura knew she had to interrupt, or April would not only continue to ramble, but would be knocking on her door if she didn't stop her. She imagined April grabbing her purse as they spoke. She loved her friend, but the day had already been a whirlwind of emotion. "I'll tell you over the phone, you don't have to drive all the—" Laura's doorbell rang.

"Too late!" April squealed, and Laura sighed. "I'm outside, so come let me in." Laura walked toward the front door as April continued. "Did you know that cat is out here again? He's giving me a weird look."

"I doubt that."

"No, seriously, he's looking at me with his little beady eyes all suspicious and what not."

"Come on in." Laura had no sooner opened the door than April, breezed by turning her phone off as she passed.

She spun around, her face bright. "I want junk food and details but not necessarily in that order." She grabbed Laura's hand dragging her back to the kitchen and the untouched bag of chips sitting on the table. She sat down, her chin in her hands waiting for Laura to join her.

"It's kind of a long story."

"I don't have anything better to do." April nonchalantly grabbed a chip and popped it in her mouth. April's smile was ear-to-ear excited to catch up on her friend's romantic ventures.

An hour after April arrived, Laura concluded her story. She'd filled April in on everything from meeting Samantha, learning the rest of Ava's story, and how the journal and trunk were connected to Caleb. The surprise on April's face had mirrored her own when she'd put it all together. She told her how Caleb had not only smuggled a date out of her, but later confessed he'd connected the dots days before her.

"He definitely has a thing for you." April had nearly finished off the bag of Doritos as she licked the cheese off her fingers. "The fact that he withheld information to get you on a date—"

"I know, red flag, right?"

"Actually, it's kind of romantic." April clasped her hands together. "Some of the best relationships start off with a little dishonesty."

"You've been watching too many romantic films. That's not how it should be at all."

"What? Not every romance is a Hallmark movie." April smiled slyly.

Laura frowned, snagging the chip bag away from her. Reaching inside, she discovered it empty. She neglected to hide her disapproval as she turned it upside down watching a few cheesy crumbs fall to the table.

"What's the point anyways? He's only here to help his parents with their remodel and then he's going to leave." Laura walked to the pantry pulling out a box of cookies. She bit into one, moping.

"He might change his mind. He seems like a nice guy who is genuinely interested."

"Maybe you're right." Laura dropped the cookies on the table and slumped into the chair across from April.

"Of course, I'm right." April grabbed a cookie for herself. "It's a good thing you called me."

"But I didn't call you."

April dismissed her with a wave of her hand. "I've been helpful, that's what matters here."

"The only thing you've helped with, is eating *all* my food."

"That *is* helpful. You'll want to keep that figure if you hope to keep Caleb interested."

"Oh, you've got to be joking." Laura threw the cookie she'd been munching in her direction.

April dodged it, holding her hands up. "Okay, I surrender."

The shocked look on April's face caused Laura to break into laughter and the girls spent the rest of the night acting like they were in high school again. April made her spill all the details of the evening. When Laura told her how Dusty had ruined a potential kiss, April sulked, vowing vengeance on the cat when she saw him again.

Laura neglected to share her relief over the interruption. She wasn't ready to delve into how she was feeling yet. She paused, thinking maybe April had been right after all. Some of the best relationships do have a bit of dishonesty to them. She smiled to herself. She could sort out where she stood with Caleb later when she had a better idea how she felt about dating again.

Laura lay in bed that night thinking about Caleb. Had he been thinking about her too? She pushed the thought aside. He would be leaving once the remodel was complete. His family would sell the house and he'd go back home. She hadn't thought to ask him where he lived. She made a note to check with him the next time she saw him.

She let out a long sigh as she lay in the dark staring up toward the ceiling. She never thought she'd find herself in this place—having loved and lost and now having to decide if she wanted to start over again. Even if it wasn't Caleb, she didn't want to be single the rest of her life. She missed sharing experiences with Paul and wished she had someone she could spend time with.

Would Paul have liked Caleb? She smiled to herself because she knew he would. He liked everyone he met. The two men couldn't be more different. Paul was a serious business investor for a large corporation. Caleb had a more light-hearted attitude and ran his own company. Paul had been direct in asking her out, where Caleb had taken a craftier approach. They were both kind and genuine but different personalities all together.

Shaking her head, she still couldn't believe she'd fallen for Caleb's little scheme. She gave him credit though. If she had time to think about it, she would not have gone. She ended up having a wonderful time after she'd gotten over her nerves. April told her she was glad to see her moving forward, but Laura felt a small stab of guilt when she thought about it.

Her life had been centered on Paul for so long. Even after he died, her grief went so deep he'd never been far from her thoughts. She poured herself into project after project, hoping the escape would take away the pain. It did for a time, but like anything, it eventually ended, and she didn't find herself any further along than where she started.

Laura turned on her side. She would do anything to fall asleep. Instead, her mind raced with thoughts of what to do next. The following day her mom would be over first thing in the morning to drop off her cabinet. She wasn't looking forward to waking early, especially since she found herself awake as she lay in the darkness. Instead, she prayed sleep would overtake her and eventually it did.

CHAPTER 46

"L aura, I love it!" Sam squeezed Laura so tightly she nearly knocked her off her feet. Laura had clearly misjudged the power of a petite brunette on an adrenaline rush. Sam released her, pulling her into the house before she could get her bearings. "Would you like to see where I put it?"

Laura nodded excitedly following her up the stairs. She secretly hoped she'd put the trunk in Ava's old room. She wanted an excuse to see it. Sam slowed outside a closed door, a huge smile on her face.

"Is this her room?" Laura felt her face betray her excitement. Sam didn't say a word, instead she opened the door. Awestruck, the first thing she saw was the steamer trunk against the rear wall under the window. The last of the afternoon sun shone through the bay window adorned with the white-lace curtains and a small desk sat in the corner. As Laura approached the piece, she knew it was nearly an antique.

"Is this?" She turned to Sam.

"Yes," Sam nodded enthusiastically.

"It's lovely." Laura touched the desk visualizing Ava writing down her thoughts with perfect penmanship. She moved to another part of the room looking into the mirror that sat atop the dresser. She could see Ava getting ready for her outings, discussing outfits with Tessa and saying goodbye to Dean the night he came to tell her he'd enlisted. The bed had a modern bedspread and sat in the exact spot she imagined it would be.

Laura walked over to the trunk that had sat in her workroom for weeks. She lifted the lid slowly. Inside were a few blankets and a small decorative pillow. A tear slipped down her cheek. Unsure what had caused the emotions, she closed the lid, turning to see a smiling Sam behind her.

Sam's smile faded upon seeing Laura's tears. "What's wrong?" She walked over to her, placing a comforting hand on her arm.

"I don't know." Laura laughed at how ridiculous she felt.

"Oh honey." Sam pulled her into a brief hug.

"You probably think I'm a wreck."

"Not at all. I can't even imagine what this must be like for you. You got to know my mother through her stories and now you get to see what you'd been imaging the last few weeks." Sam led her to the edge of the bed, and they sat down.

"It means a lot to me to have restored one of her most personal artifacts and returned it to you." Laura wiped at a stray tear. "I wasn't prepared for the emotions though."

Sam seemed to consider her next statement cautiously. "The last time you were here, you mentioned you lost someone you loved. Would you mind telling me about it?"

"A little over a year ago my fiancé Paul died." Laura played with the tassel hanging off her purse. "The night he asked me to marry him...he was in a car accident." Laura looked straight forward, unable to look at Sam.

"Oh sweetie, that's terrible."

"It went from being the best night of my life, to the worst. I'd come home after the proposal, went to bed, and got the call from his mother in the middle of the night saying he'd been taken to the hospital." Laura swallowed, realizing she'd never spoken about the details of that night aloud. "I rushed down there, of course... but by the time I arrived, he was in surgery. They did their best, but his injuries were too severe."

"Please tell me you weren't alone." Sam took Laura's hand in her own.

"Not that night, but I spent a lot of time alone after it happened. I purposely shut people out and buried myself in my work. I couldn't face the fact he was gone, and I'd been left behind. I became tired of everyone feeling sorry for me, not that I gave them much choice."

Sam waited patiently for Laura to collect her thoughts. The calm feeling the room emanated filled the silence. She believed many difficult conversations had once been had in that same room.

"I started coming to terms with his death but stayed close to home. I worked on various restorations hoping to distract myself. It worked for a while, but I'd find myself grieving again when things slowed down."

"It's difficult to run from the truth, especially when it's the painful loss of someone you love."

"It wasn't until I became swept up in Ava's story that I started to see that hope and sacrifice go hand in hand—and that sometimes loving someone means letting them go." Laura finally looked at Sam. "That's why I had to find you."

"How so?"

"I had to see firsthand that someone who had suffered so greatly, could prevail in the end." The corner of Laura's mouth turned up in a subtle smile.

"I couldn't be more grateful to you." Sam wrapped her in a maternal hug. "As sad as I am to hear about what you've gone through, I'm glad my mother's stories were an encouragement to you."

"Your mother was right; she *was* lucky to have loved two men in her lifetime. In a weird way, her story gave me hope that one day I can love again." Laura looked around the room. She could see why Ava had spent so much time there. "I still can't believe I'm sitting in her bedroom." Laura grinned. "What it must have been like growing up in this house."

"It's surreal for me as well and I did grow up here." Sam walked over to the window. "I'm so glad the trunk is home where it belongs and where it will stay."

"Stay?" Laura stood immediately. "I thought you were remodeling the house to sell it?"

"We are selling it." Sam gave her a puzzled look.

"Won't you take the trunk with you?"

"Oh honey, we are selling the house to Caleb. He decided to buy the house from us."

"Oh, I see." Laura breathed a sigh of relief.

"I didn't mean to panic you." Sam crushed her concerns with her matter-of-fact tone. "I thought Caleb had told you he was buying the house."

"He neglected to share that detail." Laura placed her hand over her chest regaining her composure.

"Yes, I told him we'd give him the family discount." Sam smiled. "I figure he's done most of the repairs after all. Besides, from what I've been told, there's a certain young lady he'd like to see more of."

Laura's head shot up. "Well, I... uh," Laura felt the heat creep up her neck as she stumbled over her words. She avoided eye contact hoping Sam would let her off the hook.

"You know. I think the lasagna is about done." She held her hand out to Laura. "Why don't you come down and help me finish the salad?"

"I'd love to." Grateful for the change of subject, Laura followed Sam downstairs to finish preparations for dinner.

As she descended the stairs, she swallowed the anxious feeling inside her. Caleb would be joining them for dinner. She hadn't seen him since their coffee date and found it surprising he'd not only mentioned her to Sam but had requested her help to schedule time to see her. Now fully aware she'd be outnumbered; she'd discovered this family had an odd way of making her uneasy while welcoming her at the same time. They were easy-going, but always had something up their sleeve that seemed to catch her off guard.

The introvert in her wanted to run toward the front door, but there was no going back now.

CHAPTER 47

Relieved to get through dinner without too many personal questions from the Spencer family, Laura had avoided most of the attention directed her way. Sam must have picked up on the fact Laura wasn't ready to talk about her personal life and seemed to shift the discussion to Caleb instead. Sam spent most of the meal telling stories about Caleb growing up. Her husband, Matthew, joined in the fun as well. Laura found herself laughing harder than she had in a long time. From what she could tell, Caleb got his great-aunt Tessa's knack for finding trouble by saying anything that came to his mind.

From the sounds of it, he still found himself in troublesome situations. She looked across the table. Caleb waved his hands around dramatically as he defended himself over a story where he'd gotten a piece of cereal stuck up his nose. Each time he held out his hands to make a point, the muscles in his arms flexed and his T-shirt pulled tight against his chest. His eyes lit up as he laughed at his own jokes.

How had she found herself here? It felt familiar and yet lonely at the same time? Memories of spending evenings with Paul and his family began to surface. They'd had nights with his parents or her parents that felt so much like this moment.

She had formed a deep connection to Ava and Grayson through their story, and they'd instilled a strong sense of family in Sam, but right now she felt like an observer. Could it be possible to feel close with complete strangers?

Caleb made eye contact. Laura averted her eyes but not before catching the subtle wink he sent her way. She focused on the coffee cup she held. Sam had passed out dessert, and Laura made note to tell her how delicious everything had been. Being on her own, she didn't feel the need to make many homemade meals, so eating a home-cooked dinner was a treat.

"Laura what do you think?" Matthew had asked her a question and she'd completely missed it.

"I'm sorry?"

"What do you think of the area? I assume you've lived here for a while."

"Oh, it's wonderful. I adore living in a small town."

"Sam and I considered a place in this neighborhood, but she decided we need large retail stores nearby."

"What he's trying to say is I like to shop too much to live in a small town." Sam smirked in Matthews's direction before turning her attention back to Laura. "I'm sure Laura can understand a woman's need to shop."

Laura smiled, not wishing to take sides. She could tell Sam and Matthew were perfect for one another. They flirted and teased one another, but she could see they loved each other deeply. Her concerns from earlier slowly vanished as she saw the family interacting together. The evening started to wind down and Matthew stood from his spot directing his next comment to Caleb.

"You know the deal, son." He dropped his napkin on his plate. "The person who cooks doesn't do the dishes."

"Are you offering to do the dishes, Dad?"

"Absolutely not. Your mother made the meal and she and I count as the same person."

"Funny how that's never the case when it's *our* turn to do dishes." Sam rolled her eyes. She turned to Laura. "He's always trying to get out of work."

"Honey, you know that's not true." Matthew pretended to be hurt.

"You do too, Dad, and you're rather good at it." Caleb begrudgingly stood and started collecting their plates, so he could take them to the kitchen. Sam picked up a few of the food dishes and followed her son.

"Laura, it was nice to meet you, but I think it's time I took my wife home." Matthew smiled at her then whispered. "I need to leave now, or they'll put me to work."

"Well, we don't need that." Laura whispered back giggling.

"You may want to consider an escape plan as well before my son tries to convince you to help him." His expression was serious. "He is a professional influencer."

Laura burst out laughing. She'd been on the other side of Caleb's charm and had fallen for it.

"Dad, what are you telling her?" Caleb and Sam returned, curious over the inside joke they had missed.

"Nothing." He lifted his hands innocently. "You ready to go my dear?" He looked at his wife and she nodded. After they said their goodbyes, the older couple left, leaving Laura and Caleb standing on the porch, waving goodbye. Caleb turned and noticed she held her purse. He gave her the saddest face he could muster.

"Oh, no you don't. Your dad warned me about this." She lifted an eyebrow as she draped the purse over her shoulder.

Caleb exhaled slowly, pretending to be put out. "Could I convince you to join me on the porch for a bit?"

"I don't know—"

"No dishes, I promise." He held up both hands in surrender, giving her puppy-dog eyes. "I'm using you as an excuse to procrastinate."

She forfeited her resolve. "A few minutes but that's all."

Caleb held out a hand gesturing for her to sit down on the wooden swing. He sat next to her and it creaked beneath his weight. "I'm going to have to lay off the lasagna." He looked down, tapping his stomach.

Laura couldn't help but laugh. "From what I can tell, you'll be fine."

"You think so?" Caleb turned toward her, placing his arm along the back of the swing. It occasionally brushed against her shoulders as the swing swayed back and forth. Laura found herself acutely aware things were shifting beyond her comfort level.

"Your mom told me you're going to buy the house."

"After working on it the past few weeks, it seems a shame not to keep it in the family."

"I'm sure your grandmother would appreciate that if she were still here."

"She would have loved you."

"I would have loved to meet her."

"I guess you'll have to settle for the rest of us."

"I don't know about that; your family seems pretty great." Laura toyed with her purse as the swing swayed back and forth.

"I agree with you."

Laura winced when the cool breeze crossed her arms, sending a chill through her. Caleb responsively dropped his arm around her shoulders moving closer. The quiet evening and the dim porch light automatically set the mood for romance. Laura began to feel uneasy, but the warmth of his closeness reminded her what it had been like when someone had cared for her. Still, she needed more time, no matter how she felt about him. She stood suddenly, the swing pushing backward.

"I should get going."

"Are you sure?"

"It's getting late."

"Last time I checked; you could stay out as long as you want." He stood, gazing down at her. In the dim light she couldn't read his face, but the hushed baritone in his voice was implicitly clear. Laura didn't want to hurt him, but she wasn't ready for the feelings welling up inside her.

"Caleb, I'm not ready for a romantic relationship." She looked down. "At least, not yet." She swallowed her nerves hoping she hadn't hurt him with her honesty.

He touched her chin, lifting her eyes to meet his. "I'm not going anywhere; take whatever time you need."

Laura hadn't expected his reply. In a few words, he'd lifted a burden that had weighed heavy on her heart since he'd made his interest clear. She released the breath she'd been holding. Caleb wrapped his arms around her, placing his chin on the top of her head. She let herself be held and closed her eyes; it'd been a long time since she'd felt safe enough to be vulnerable. When he finally released her, she whispered her goodnight and left.

CHAPTER 48

I t had been six months since Laura stood on the porch that night
with Caleb. Now she found him leaning against the workbench
in her back room. He spun a gimlet between his fingers as he
watched her work on a broken drawer of a large bombe chest. He'd
come over to pick her up for dinner, but she'd been so focused
she'd barely heard him come in. The owners were coming to pick
up the chest in a week and it wasn't even close to being finished.

Since they began dating, he'd quickly learned when he found her
focused on a task, everything else disappeared. During their time
together, he'd been patient, waiting for her to come to terms with
her grief and decide when she was ready to date again. He told her
he had to wait, because Sam told him if he didn't get her off the
market, someone else would.

He'd listened the night she'd told him about Paul and held her as
she cried over the pain of the past. He'd promised to be there for
her, and he had been. Laura hadn't been surprised their personalities fit so well together.

She bit her lower lip in concentration, working on a stubborn
screw that prevented the drawer from closing. Her chestnut hair
had been pulled back in a ponytail and she wore a pair of reading
glasses. She'd picked them up a week ago hoping it would help
when she worked on the smaller items. Her white-cotton shirt held
a few smudges of dust, so she still planned to change before dinner.

She could feel Caleb's gaze on her as she struggled to release the drawer.

"Can you hand me a different sized screwdriver?" Laura held out her hand but kept her focus on the task in front of her. Caleb sorted through a toolbox looking for one he thought might fit but didn't seem to be having much luck. Laura finally turned her focus toward him when he neglected to place the tool in her palm.

"With as organized as you are, one should be easier to find." Caleb's brow furrowed as he kept looking for a smaller version of the tool. Laura stood joining him near the workbench and took a turn sifting through the tools. She found herself so focused on the task, she didn't see Caleb pull the small screwdriver from his back pocket. "Oh, here it is."

"I knew it had to be here somewhere." Laura reached for it, but Caleb held it just out of her reach. She tried again, dodging his movements, but he held it above his head. She scrunched up her face, pulling on his arm, but it was pointless. "Caleb! Come on, I need to make a little more progress before we leave."

"I have a better idea." He grinned and moved toward her, his arm still above his head.

"I can only imagine." She said playfully, tapping his chin with her finger. She couldn't bring herself to be upset. He'd been tolerant with her work up to that point.

"I could help you finish after we get back from dinner."

"You'd only distract me." Laura pushed against his chest playfully and he accepted the challenge. He set down the screwdriver and began to walk slowly toward her. "Caleb, don't you dare." She backed into the bombe chest realizing she had nowhere to go. He placed an arm on either side of her, preventing her from escaping, but she wasn't planning to run either. He slid his index finger over the rim of her glasses pulling them down the bridge of her nose and set them to one side. Wrapping his hands around her waist, he hoisted her on top of the bombe chest, so she sat eye to eye with him. "If you scratch this chest, I'm—"

Caleb kissed her soundly, not waiting for her to finish. He'd kissed her plenty of times, but each time felt like the first. Laura grasped onto his shirtfront to keep from losing her balance. When he pulled back, she looked into his amber eyes wondering how she had been so lucky. She touched the stubble along his jawline, enjoying the feel beneath her fingertips.

Out of nowhere, Dusty sprinted across the room, running in-between them and throwing Laura off balance. Caleb reached to steady her as Rufus ran into the room barking at the cat who now taunted him from the top of the workbench.

"That cat has the worst timing." Caleb shook his head, holding tight to Laura who had managed to stay upright.

"You're the one who told me to adopt him." She smiled, enjoying the fact Dusty managed to get under Caleb's skin.

"Since when do you ever do what I say?" He leaned towards her seductively.

"Never," she laughed, pushing him away from her. "We better get going or we're going to be late. April gets irritated if anyone holds up her eating schedule."

"Do we have to go on a double date?" Caleb whined dramatically.

"Oh, stop." Laura poked him in the chest. "You'll be fine."

"Maybe I want you all to myself tonight."

"You want me all to yourself every night." She laughed as his frown grew. Looking above his gaze, she focused on his hairline. She touched the stubborn piece of hair lying against his forehead. He'd needed a haircut but had been too lazy to set an appointment. She tried to set it back in place. He had the same tenacious curl Grayson did and she'd never noticed it before.

"What?" Caleb asked curiously.

"Nothing." Laura smiled, keeping the secret to herself regarding the family resemblance. She'd tell him one day that he had his grandfather's Superman curl but not today. She didn't have long to sit with her thoughts as Caleb set her back on solid ground. He wrapped his arms around her, and she held him back. Things had turned out differently than she thought they would. Just when she thought she'd never love again, he came into her life—her second chance at love.

ACKNOWLEDGEMENTS

Hearts Under Fire was a labor of love reinforced by a team of behind-the-scenes supporters. Writing a story may be the solitary part of an author's journey but editing, publishing and marketing a book requires a team. I'd like to thank some of those individuals for their help.

Both sides of my family offered first-hand accounts from World War II. My grandfather, Stanley Orlowski whose time in the United States Pacific Fleet Air Force provided the specifics used for Dean and Grayson's time overseas. My great aunt Arleen Stenger whose first-hand account of time spent on the Homefront, became an invaluable part of Ava and Tessa's storyline. Although you are no longer with us, your stories of self-sacrifice will live on and I only hope I've done them justice.

To all US Veterans, regardless of when or where you served. Freedom is never free and your selflessness to serve and protect this country should never be overlooked or forgotten.

A huge thanks to my brother Greg, you are a Master of Design. Thank you for the amazing book cover; not to mention the beautiful website. You inspire me each day to elevate my creativity to new levels. Thank you for always having my back and your willingness to work for a six-pack of beer.

Thank you to April Chapman, for challenging me to write against the grain of my original plotline. The story turned out better because you pushed me to take the high road and trusted in my ability to pull it off as an author.

Thanks to all my beta readers for your honest feedback during the writing process. New readers are enjoying a better version of the novel because of you. Thank you to Shellie, Laura, Ardriel, Camryn, Desiree, Charlotte, Vanessa, Pat, and Sue.

To all my cheerleaders:

My Family Fanatics: The Holder's & The Orlowski's (We did it!)

The Quad Squad: Lindsay, Blake, Brandon, Will (For the 1 AM phone calls.)

On-Call Author's: Marci, Sarah, Marcy (Thanks for helping a rookie.)

Thanks to my mom, for finding the balance between encouraging me and challenging me. You will always be your kid's biggest promoter. Thanks to my dad for always believing in me and setting the example of how a man should care for his family. Thanks to both of you, it wasn't a challenge to write The Sutton Family into existence.

Last but not least, Bentley the Puppy for keeping me company all those late and lonely nights. Little buddy, if you were human, I'd make you my agent.

Learn more about the Lady Crew apparel worn by your favorite *Hearts Under Fire* characters!

Lady Crew is a 501 (c) (3) non-profit organization dedicated to raising funds and awareness to fight human trafficking and 100% of their proceeds are donated to survivors. The Lady Crew donor partners and volunteers back the creation, printing, administration and fulfillment of the shirts which allows them to do a full donation from every purchase they receive.

Each time you wear a Lady Crew shirt, it helps raise awareness and provides financial assistance to a survivor in need.

If you'd like to support this awesome organization, you can purchase apparel and other merchandise on their website at www.wearladycrew.com or follow them on Instagram at @wearladycrew where you can stay up to date with what they are doing to help change the world.

About the Author

Cori Lynn is a novelist and screenwriter based in Phoenix, Arizona. In addition to her latest novel, *Hearts Under Fire*, she has written multiple screenplays including two feature-length films. Cori graduated with a Global Business degree from Arizona State University and works full time in Marketing. She spends her free time playing with her puppy, redecorating her home and crafting her next story.

You can follow Cori online at:
www.thewritersjournal.net

Join the Facebook Group at:
facebook.com/groups/heartsunderfirefanpage

twitter.com/lynncorey
instagram.com/corilynn.author

Made in United States
North Haven, CT
04 April 2022

17909735R00169